"Tell me your dream, my sweet," he whispered.

Katherine shook her head and sobbed, clutching his shoulders.

"Do you have this often?"

She began to quiet in his arms, and sighed. "No," she whispered.

He resigned himself to her silences. He resolved to himself that he would discover her secrets—all of them.

Suddenly, she seemed to realize where she was and how he held her. Instead of bolting from his arms, she studied him, her blue eyes dark as the stormy skies outside. "Why do you care about me?" she asked. "I tell you nothing, as if you were untrustworthy."

He hesitated a moment, feeling the weight of her body across his thighs. "You are frightened, but you will tell me why eventually."

"You are so sure of yourself, then?" She arched one eyebrow, showing more spirit.

"Sure of my power over women."

Other **AVON ROMANCES**

GAYLE CALLEN

THE DARKEST KNIGHT

AVON BOOKS ◆ NEW YORK

This is a work of fiction. Names, characters, places, and incidents either are the product of the author's imagination or are used fictitiously. Any resemblance to actual events, locales, organizations, or persons, living or dead, is entirely coincidental and beyond the intent of either the author or the publisher.

AVON BOOKS, INC.
1350 Avenue of the Americas
New York, New York 10019

Copyright © 1999 by Gayle Kloecker Callen
Inside cover author photo by Tarolli Studio
Published by arrangement with the author
Visit our website at http://www.AvonBooks.com
Library of Congress Catalog Card Number: 98-93305
ISBN: 0-380-80493-X

First Avon Books Printing: January 1999

AVON TRADEMARK REG. U.S. PAT. OFF. AND IN OTHER COUNTRIES, MARCA REGISTRADA, HECHO EN U.S.A.

Printed in the U.S.A.

WCD 10 9 8 7 6 5 4 3 2 1

To my husband, Jim,
who always believed in me, and never doubted
that I could make my dreams come true.

Chapter 1

England
August 1485

He stood with his back against the crumbling brick wall, fists clenched, his cowl falling against his perspiring cheeks. Once again, he heard the sound, a woman's low moan, quickly muffled. He took a deep breath and slowly leaned towards the corner of the wall, allowing himself to peer once and then pull back. In that moment, he saw the scene quite clearly under the eerie light of a full moon. A man, not one of the brethren, gripped a struggling woman.

For a moment, Brother Reynold Welles hesitated in disbelief. When he looked again, a second man had joined them, wearing the black mantle of the Benedictine brotherhood and carrying a flickering candle. This man gestured, and they moved off towards the cloister court, the heart of the monastery.

What brother would need to have a woman

1

brought to him? In the past, Reynold had known a monk or two who'd left one night, and come back with more satisfaction than they felt the peace of the church could give them. Though Reynold well understood the lure of women, he could not so easily break his vows. But bringing an unwilling woman to St. Anthony's Priory was sheer folly—or desperation.

The promises he had sworn to God and his family warred within him until his head ached. His sins still burned him, playing out over and over in endless nightmares. He should only care about his own redemption, not a stranger's. But he could picture the woman, bound and alone, forced here against her will. How would he live with himself if she died, adding another death to his conscience?

Lady Katherine Berkeley yanked her good arm free and tugged at the filthy gag covering her mouth. For her trouble she received a quick blow to the head, a tap truly, but one that set her ears ringing and almost knocked the blindfold askew.

A hot mouth pressed itself against her ear. "I don't want ta hurt ye, liedy. They tol' me not to, but I will if ye make me."

The offending mouth remained a moment too long, and Katherine cringed with fear. He had not hurt her so far, this brutal man who'd taken her as she rode near her father's hunting lodge just two days before. But two days seemed like a lifetime of humiliation and terror. She had ridden blindfolded on a horse with more bones than flesh, perched on the thighs of a man twice her size. Gagged into silence, she had to repeatedly clutch the man's arm for a moment's privacy behind a bush. And even then, she could not know if he watched.

She shivered in revulsion at the memory, as her silent captor dragged her forward. She was beyond exhaustion, beyond caring where she was. She only knew it was earth beneath her, not a galloping horse. They suddenly stopped, and her head bounced forward until her chin hit her chest. She heard a door open in front of her. A damp, sour smell assaulted her nose, and her eyes stung inside the wet blindfold.

"Here," an unfamiliar voice whispered.

"Ye're sure 'tis safe?"

"This place is falling into ruins. No one uses the undercroft for storage anymore. She'll keep safe enough long as she's gagged."

As Katherine was prodded forward, she felt the ground squish beneath her leather slippers. A whimper escaped the gag. The room seemed to stifle all noise except the skittering of tiny feet. When she was released, Katherine panicked, not caring that this was the same man who had so brutally abducted her. She sobbed in a hoarse, muffled voice, clutching at his sleeves.

"Bind her!" the new voice said.

Katherine frantically shook her head, falling to her knees to silently plead with them. Everything was dark and cold and foreign, except the man who had tried not to harm her. Yet now they yanked her arms behind her back, and though she feebly struggled for a moment, her will seemed spent. It was all too much for her. She wished she didn't know their secrets. She would have been safe at home, awaiting her betrothed. She had been so naive. Would they now kill her for her knowledge?

Katherine realized she was alone when the door latched shut. Lurching to her feet, she waited a moment, listening. The air was still and oppressive with silence. She shuffled forward, then stopped, hearing the echoes far above her head. Where was she?

She edged sideways, trying to feel the door with her arm instead of her face. She banged her elbow and barely noticed the pain as she turned her back to run her bound hands over the door. Solid old wood, set firmly into a stone wall. She kicked once with her foot but made little sound. She did it again, harder. Did they intend to leave her here indefinitely—bound and gagged until she died?

Katherine tugged hard at the ropes biting into her wrists, hating her weak arm. Sobbing, she pulled and pulled until the pain became unbearable and the blood trickled down her fingers. She staggered and fell, crying, until the world retreated for a while and she drifted into an exhausted sleep.

Katherine came awake with a jerk, then winced at the shooting pain in her shoulders. Her hands seemed numb and unresponsive. Frantically she sat up and began to wiggle her fingers, then sighed as sharp little prickles tormented her skin from inside.

With her head bowed, Katherine forced herself to think through the last few weeks. She tried to tell herself she would have done something differently, but it wasn't true. Her life meant nothing when King Richard's life was at stake. She had learned of a plot against the king from a woman too terrified to publicly come forward. If Katherine did not escape soon, it would be too late. The king's enemies, whom he thought of as loyal friends, would turn on him. If only her chambermaid hadn't overheard her plans and told the kidnapper, betraying Katherine for a few coins.

But she couldn't give up as they all expected her to do. For the first time in her life she faced a real challenge, with no one to help her. Whoever was behind the plot to kidnap her obviously wanted her kept alive. Why? Was it because he had something more sinister in mind for her—or maybe because he didn't want her seriously hurt. She couldn't possibly know the person—could she? Dread quivered through her stomach. She had to escape.

As quickly as her bound hands allowed, Katherine explored her prison, tripping over toppled barrels and ripped sacks of grain. By the time she returned to the first and only door, she knew she was in some sort of storage room, unused and containing no windows. She had tried to cut her ropes on a broken crate, and instead set her wrists to bleeding again. When the hours began to stretch out behind her, she felt the seedlings of true panic. Had her captor been decent enough on the journey, only to allow her to die forgotten? When the door finally opened, she allowed herself a moment of relief that they remembered her.

When hands touched her she began to kick wildly. She prayed that the door was still open and she could escape. Arms gripped her, lifting her easily into an unfamiliar embrace as she struggled. This was a different man than her captor, harder, taller. In sheer terror Katherine fought him, until she felt fingers at her head, loosening her blindfold. She stilled immediately and waited to see what he had planned. A candle blinded her for a moment, then the man turned her to face him. She gasped in shock and revulsion.

A monk held her in a painful grip, a monk garbed in black with a cowl hiding his face. She shrank away in terror as he lifted one hand, but he only motioned for quiet and reached for her gag. He peeled it off and her cracked lips stung unmercifully.

"My hands," she croaked.

He turned her around by the shoulders and she staggered at his strength. Katherine suffered his rough touch until her hands were free, then whirled away from him. She rubbed her raw wrists and watched him suspiciously, waiting for his next move. After all, men who chose this life usually had some dark, hidden reason. But this one merely watched her, his head cocked to one side, a black hole for a face. Why didn't he remove the hood?

Katherine lifted her chin with what she hoped was a show of strength. "Are you releasing me?"

As he nodded, the cowl dropped forward and swayed.

She shivered with deep-rooted unease. "Then move aside and I will leave."

He pointed to himself, and then the door.

Katherine walked along the wall, never turning her back on the monk. "Nay, I will go alone. Is he gone yet?"

As his head dropped to one side, she almost leaned over to see his face, then thought better of it.

"The man who brought me here," she said.

He shrugged broad shoulders in answer.

"Do you not speak? Is your tongue damaged?"

He shook his head, then pointed to the door with more urgency, taking a step towards her.

Katherine shrank away from his menacing height and breadth, then crept around him, hoping he would leave her alone to escape. But she felt his breath on the back of her neck and shuddered as a chill swept up her spine.

The open door revealed a shadowy world of sagging stone walls and covered walkways, all lit by a cloudy moon. Across the courtyard stood an ancient church. The sound of deep voices chanting their prayers drifted on the breeze. A monastery. Who would think of looking for a noblewoman here?

Katherine took a step forward and almost fell when a strong hand yanked her back behind the building. She fought the monk, terrorized by the thought of what those big hands might do to her. He merely shook her once like a child, then put a finger to his lips. He did have lips; she could see the faintest shadow of them. He pointed to himself, then her, then behind him, opposite the way she had meant to go. As Katherine began to walk, she silently debated her childhood fears. She would follow this monk as long as he proved himself trustworthy. But only until she was free of the monastery.

From what Katherine could see by moonlight, everything around her was in a state of neglect. Walkways were pitted with holes where cobblestones used to be. Off to her right, dead branches hung from trees in the orchard.

She was so intent on not tripping, she only vaguely noticed that the chanting had stopped. But the monk in front of her went rigid, then put out a hand behind him to stop her. When his fingers almost grazed her chest, Katherine swallowed back the sour taste of nausea. Surely it had been an accident. He hadn't even looked back at her. But her hands started shaking. She held her weak arm with the other one, a habit she wished she could conquer. With her attention diverted from the ground, she began to stumble, falling farther behind him. The dark cowl swung back towards her and she almost ran in blind fear.

Katherine gasped when the monk veered towards the orchard at a sudden run. The practical side of her wanted to warn him that she didn't run well. She tended to twist ankles and bruise knees— not always her own.

When he motioned towards her frantically, she took off at a fast run, hoping nothing lay in her path. Her skirts had a life of their own as they threatened to trip her or snag on overgrown plants. She pushed through the last weeds on the far side of the orchard, only to skitter to a sudden halt on the banks of a creek. She naturally lost her balance and swayed forward, flapping her arms to stay upright. The monk caught her against him, his arm beneath her breasts, his head bent well above hers. Before Katherine could collect her frag- mented thoughts, he pushed her forward along the bank. She walked as fast as she could, if only to escape the warmth of his breath from behind. She tried not to think of her parched throat. The cool water continued to lure her gaze but she would not get down on her knees before him to drink.

One of her slippers was captured by the mud. Katherine bent over to reach it, and the monk bumped into her backside. She almost shrieked, but instead gasped in outrage and straightened so suddenly that the top of her head slammed into his cowled face. He grunted.

"Be quiet—they'll hear you!" she hissed. "I lost my slipper!"

The monk raised his wool-covered head to the sky for a moment, then bent to search the mud. She grimaced when he handed the dripping shoe to her and motioned to her feet. Hopping on one foot, she put her useless slipper back on and continued alongside the creek. A wall loomed up out of the darkness. Her rescuer waded knee-deep into the water, and reached out to her.

"Is there a gate on the other side?" Katherine whispered.

He gestured for her hand once more.

"I can cross unassisted," she said, setting one foot into the water. She slid down a moss-covered rock and landed hard against the monk's side, her face striking his shoulder. Before she arched her head away, she smelled the clean scent of the wool and for a wild moment wondered what kind of monk he was. She came to her senses and pushed at the muscled wall of his chest, his obvious strength bringing back her fright. He turned her about like a doll until her backside was pressed into his hip and his arm encircled her chest. As her breasts were flattened in his embrace, and the water tugged at her skirts, Katherine began to feel faint. Her tongue was swollen and dry, and the water dripped its sweet temptation.

The monk's other arm snaked out before her, pointing downstream. She peered ahead, squinting.

"Does not the water go below ground?" she whispered.

She felt the slither of wool across her tangled hair as he shook his head. With his large hands at her waist he urged her forward, holding her up against the lure of slippery rocks and deep mud, until the monastery wall loomed above them in the shadows. Katherine braced both palms against the gritty stone.

"I can go no farther," she said softly. "Where is the gate?"

The monk dropped to his knees at her side, and pointed to where the water rushed beneath the lip of the wall.

Katherine swayed with disbelief but the monk held her up. "Under there?" she squeaked, watching in a daze as the water current caught his black robe at the waist.

He pulled and the flaccid muscles of her arm gave way beneath his strength until she fell to her knees on the bed of the creek. As the cold water chilled her, she gave in to temptation and scooped some into her mouth. He watched in silence, a darkly robed man in the shadowy moonlight of an ancient monastery. She ceased drinking and gaped at the black hole that was his face, repelled yet fascinated by what must lie beyond. He suddenly sank beneath the surface. Katherine stared at the circular waves made by his departure until she felt a tug on her skirts.

"Oh no." She gasped a lungful of air and was pulled below.

Chapter 2

⟨decorative scroll⟩

The water was so very cold. Katherine thrashed in the dark, frigid creek for a wild moment, sand swirling into her eyes. The current dragged her downriver, and with her weak arm she could not swim effectively. Panicking, bursting with her need for air, she kicked herself upward and smacked her head on the thick stone wall of the monastery. She drifted motionless, dazed, forgetting to swim, forgetting everything. She was so tired.

Something yanked hard on Katherine's hair, pulling her forward. The last air bubbled out of her mouth as she broke the surface, gasping and gagging. Two strong arms lifted her out of the water. The monk held her like an orphaned kitten, dripping and bedraggled as she coughed weakly. Then he did the last thing Katherine expected.

"Will you survive?" he inquired politely.

Katherine gasped as she hung over his arm, her ribs compressed, her legs dangling. She managed to push wet strands of hair from her face, and look over her shoulder.

"Did—did you say something?"

"I did," he said, in a voice deep and cultured, though muffled by his cowl. "I thought you had finally succeeded in killing yourself."

Katherine kicked and squirmed until the monk released her. She pushed away from his chest and strove to appear unaffected, to be brave, although the dark wilderness and this strange monk frightened her.

"Kill myself?" Her voice lowered to a whisper. "You tried to drown me! Surely going over the wall would have been preferable."

"For me, perhaps. But I could not carry you, and you do not have the strength in your toes and fingers to climb. Now we must leave."

After picking up a dark bundle from the base of the wall, the monk moved to catch her arm. Katherine backed away.

"Leave? With you?"

The dark cowl remained still as he spoke from its depths. " 'Tis only a matter of time before we are discovered."

Katherine felt almost as trapped as she had in the undercroft. She had no idea where she was, what she should do. The monastery walls rose behind her, stooped with menace. The monk stood between her and the forest.

"Where are we?"

"Western Yorkshire."

Katherine sighed. She knew nothing of this part

of England. But she did know that Nottingham—
and the king—were farther south. But how to get
there?

"We must leave," the monk repeated. When he
would have touched her, Katherine stepped aside
and began to walk into the forest. The trees closed
in around her, shutting out the last of the moonlight. She felt her way from tree trunk to tree
trunk, scratching her hands on rough bark, tripping over roots. She refused to ask for help, although the monk continued to follow her silently.

Soon enough Katherine's knees grew weak with
hunger and exhaustion. She was about to admit
defeat, when the forest began to thin, and she
could see glimpses of the moon between the
branches. Stumbling to a halt at the edge of the
woods, she looked out in dismay as the moon
hung in the sky over a broad flat plain that sloped
down away from her and seemed to stretch on forever.

"You are tired," his deep voice said behind her.
"I know a place where you can sleep, where no
one can find us."

He'd said "us." Katherine shivered. But she was
too exhausted to protest. She even allowed his arm
to settle around her waist and steady her over the
uneven ground. He led her to the left, skirting the
edge of the tree line, until the sheer wall of a cliff
rose up before her in the darkness. They walked
beside the wall for less than an hour, both silent.
An opening appeared in the cliff face, like a jagged
crack straight down from the top of the moor. The

monk disappeared into it, pulling her along behind.

Katherine staggered, disoriented. The earth seemed to press in all around her.

"We can rest here," he said. " 'Tis dry, protected from the wind."

He stood in the shadows. She couldn't see his eyes or his face to read his intentions.

Katherine clasped her arm absently, and turned away from him. "Why do you speak now and not before?"

"I observe the Greater Silence while within the monastery."

"The Greater Silence?"

"The brethren do not speak at night except to pray and sing."

Katherine peered over her shoulder at him. He stood solid and dark as a mountain, blending into the night and the rock. She shivered as cold water dripped down her body beneath her ragged clothes. No sounds disturbed the peace. She was alone with him. She took another step away, wincing as her ankle turned on a stone.

"Why did you help me?"

There was a long moment of silence before he spoke. "You seemed in need of help."

His voice was suddenly deeper, and rumbled over buried emotions she could only guess at.

"How did you know I was there?" she asked.

"I saw them bring you into the monastery. I—I couldn't sleep."

Did Katherine imagine that hesitation? What

wasn't this monk saying? Her doubts grew larger, heavier, until she felt overburdened by cares a young woman shouldn't have.

"I could not leave you to whatever they planned," he said softly. "I heard you crying."

His rough voice shook something deep within her. A new and dangerous sensation curled like heat through her stomach, and she convinced herself it was fear. "Thank you for your kindness. You can go back now."

He remained silent, still.

"Go on," she insisted. "I will be fine." She stared out from the crack in the cliff, squinting, looking for a road or path by moonlight.

"I cannot return at the moment," he said. "Your captor will know soon that I have aided you, and the prior might already have discovered my absence."

Katherine felt the weight of guilt, which she immediately put aside. It was not her fault that this monk had helped her, risking his own position.

"Where will you go then?" she demanded.

There was no mistaking the long, tension-filled pause before he spoke, his words suddenly cold. "With you. You cannot possibly travel alone."

Katherine turned towards him, her skin cool and clammy with fright, as she swayed on the edge of defeat. She did not know this monk, nor did she want to. She'd never traveled farther south than York. And now she'd been dragged off to a ruinous monastery, bound, gagged, treated like an animal, rescued by a monk who almost drowned her.

She wanted to laugh hysterically, and she wanted to weep at the same time. But most of all, in some deep hidden place in her heart, she wanted to prove to herself that she could accomplish one important deed before becoming wife to the Earl of Bolton.

But she was standing soaking wet inside a cliff at midnight, with no food, no horse, and no sense of direction. How would she ever get to the king?

"You cannot travel with me," Katherine finally said. " 'Tis not—proper."

The monk set his sack down. "My lady, you are not thinking clearly. You must be hungry and cold. I have brought food and even a change of clothing. It would not do to look like a noblewoman."

Katherine choked on a laugh and spread out her wet, dirty skirts. "How can you tell what I am?"

"Your voice, my lady."

She shivered. The moon overhead was about to slide behind clouds, leaving her in total darkness with a stranger twice her size. True panic began to creep back up her throat.

Cold and wet and miserable, Katherine looked up at the monk. "Please, can you not just give me the food and leave me be? I don't want your help."

"In all honor, I cannot leave a woman alone in the countryside."

"What do you know of honor?" she asked bitterly, remembering that other monk so many years before.

The head of her rescuer tilted to one side, but he did not answer. Instead he lifted his hands to the

cowl and began to pull it back. Katherine felt a
deep thread of fear wind its way slowly up her
throat, making it hard to breathe. She did not want
to see his face, did not want to think of him as a
man. He was a monk like the others, not to be
trusted, having hidden reasons for everything he
did. Yet she did not turn away as the hood fell in
wet folds to his shoulders.

In the shadows of the night his face looked
carved of rock, with a square jaw and a cleft beneath his thin lips. His brows hung heavily over
the sockets of his eyes, turning them to blackness.
When his lips turned up in the faintest semblance
of a smile, she felt a strange chill.

"I cannot travel with you! Just give me the
clothes and I'll leave."

"I come with the clothes," he said in a voice
made more menacing by its softness.

"Then I will do without." Katherine turned
away and promptly tripped over her wet skirts.
She landed on her hands and knees in the dirt. She
longed to cry in despair, but the monk picked her
up under the arms as if she were a child's toy and
set her on her feet.

"You need me," he said flatly. "Unless you can
outrun me, I will follow."

"But why?"

He hesitated, and this time Katherine could see
anguish flicker across his face for but a moment.
Could she have imagined it?

"I cannot leave you to whatever dangers are out
there," he said. "You are helpless against the ele-

ments, helpless against these men should they choose to pursue you. I still do not understand why they kidnapped a noblewoman, when for a few pennies, a peasant girl would have—" His voice broke off.

"Would have what?" Katherine demanded. Her face flushed with heat. "You think they took me for—themselves?"

"Perhaps a ransom?" he said quickly.

Refusing to answer, she shivered and remembered the two humiliating days at the hands of her captor. Again, it nagged at her, how careful her kidnapper was not to harm her. The monk was right—they would try again. She knew their treasonous secret. And now that she'd escaped once, would they be so anxious to keep her unharmed?

"Why do you distrust me?" he asked, his head hovering above hers, his voice deep and harsh. "What have I done short of rescuing you from an unknown fate at the hands of men who kidnapped you? I have offered my help at the loss of everything I have strived for at St. Anthony's."

"I can't trust you!" she cried. "I know you not. Yet you help me."

Katherine covered her eyes with one hand. It hurt to remember that other monk, that "religious saint" her mother had trusted. No one had protected Katherine from him. If a man like that could claim a calling from God, anyone could. The next priest who cast a spell over her mother was little better, though he left Katherine alone.

She was alone now, with no choice but to turn

her life over to a man whose calling she despised, one who professed a need to help her but could give no true reason. She was too far away from King Richard's Nottingham castle, with no idea how to get there. The bleakness of her situation settled about her soul like a shroud.

"I shall spread a blanket for you while you change out of those wet clothes," the monk said, his voice only a sound in the darkness, but not unkind.

Katherine hugged her arms over her chest, feeling the warm dampness of her gown. Change?

"The moon has left us, my lady."

"After I've slept," she said, wondering if she would fall over in sheer exhaustion. What did it matter if she changed now or in the morning?

Rough cloth was placed into her hands out of the blackness.

"You must change tonight, before you catch a sickness. This is an undergarment to protect your skin from the woolen gown. You can sleep in it tonight. Please obey me in this. I don't wish to watch you die."

"There's no privacy," she whispered, hugging the smock to her.

"I cannot see you."

Katherine heard compassion roughen his voice, and her resolve to be strong crumbled beneath the onslaught. She began to cry softly as she loosened the laces at her back. She shrugged the bodice forward and pulled off the wet, tight sleeves. With her embroidered girdle gone for many days, the gown fell from her hips into a pile at her feet. Katherine sniffed, not even bothering to wipe the tears from her grimy cheeks. If only her own smock were not soaked, she could sleep in it. Instead she peeled it from her body and stood there naked in front of a strange man, a monk, who she only hoped could not see her.

A sob caught in her throat. The linen scratched her skin as she pulled it over her head and down her body.

"Here is a blanket," he whispered, bumping her hand with his and finally grasping it. "Come down, lady."

Fresh tears streaked her cheeks as she fell to her knees. As if she could be called "lady" after undressing in front of a monk and sleeping beside him wearing naught but a smock. She lay against the scratchy wool of the blanket, only vaguely feeling the weight of another blanket laid atop her. She told herself she was too tired to care that he lay close beside her. All that mattered was sleep, a sleep with no dreams. Yet the rise and fall of his chest stirred the blanket, and his even breathing kept time with the rhythm of her heart. He gave off heat that kept her as warm as any fire. She wondered if sleep would come.

Brother Reynold Welles came awake with a start, then remained still, listening. The slit of sky above his head was pale gray, heralding the coming dawn, illuminating the rough, gritstone chasm where they slept. For a brief moment, he wondered if it had all been a bad dream, but when he looked, she was there, stretched out on her back with her face turned towards him in sleep.

Reynold inhaled sharply, smelling once again the scent of woman. He closed his eyes and tried to suppress the groan of sheer pleasure that threatened to escape. He could not remember the last time he had seen a woman, let alone been close enough to smell one. Sensations he had struggled for months to suppress now rose in chorus to distract him. He remembered a serving girl at his parents' castle, the white flesh of her thighs, the scent that lingered on her breasts. She was not afraid of him, like so many others. He had buried himself in her, and the heat and warmth of her even now seemed so real. Just when he was resigned to the life of a monk, to serving God for his sins, this woman appeared, in need of rescue.

Reynold propped himself up on one arm and looked at her. He regretted it almost instantly, as the serving girl disappeared from his mind and a new woman took her place. She glowed with a quiet beauty, this dirt-streaked girl, with her honey-blond curls draped over half of her face. Without thinking, Reynold allowed his trembling fingers to touch her hair, to lift it away from her mouth. His hand looked so large and brutish beside the delicate bones of her face that he snatched it back as if burned. He told himself he was a monk now, that there was no turning back. A sly second voice whispered that he was only a novice, that his final vows had not been spoken.

But that was the path to the sins he had once committed. He had to help this woman because honor demanded it, because a good Christian brother always helped those less fortunate. Yet Reynold's gaze did not look for her soul. He saw long, golden-brown lashes resting on cheeks blushed red from the sun. Her face was saucy, heart-shaped, with lips soft and full for kisses.

Reynold broke into a sweat, but still he could not stop looking at her, could not move away even if the prior himself had come upon them. She was all soft and round and feminine, so small to his bulky body with its awkward height.

He suddenly saw the way his mind was moving, and he was horrified. His lust was unforgivable—only her safety mattered. For just one moment, her white, still face reminded him sharply of Edmund's face.

My God, Edmund. It was still almost too painful to think of his brother, who had labored so long over books that his skin rarely saw the sun. That was what had brought Reynold to Katherine, her weakness, her need. He had tried to crush these things in his brother, as if such people weren't worthy of the great knight, Sir Reynold Welles. He had paid for that pathetic arrogance, paid over and over with his brother's blood. He had vowed to take his brother's place as best he could, to atone for his sins, to help any poor soul who needed him, no matter the task. And yet—

And yet he was a man who appreciated spirit and courage, of which he suspected this girl had

aplenty. He would help her, though resisting her
appeal might prove harder than any penance he
had suffered.

Stretching out one arm, he rested his head upon
it and continued to gaze at her. Her eyes suddenly
opened and looked straight into his.

Chapter 3

K atherine choked back the scream that threatened to erupt from her throat. She lay face to face with the monk, body beside body, the heat of him overpowering the cold of the earth below. He stared at her from under dark brows, with eyes whose color she could scarce comprehend. They were a brilliant, clear purple, shining out of the prominent bones of his face, searing her with strength and a terrible intensity. What could he possibly want from her? He could so easily take everything by force.

Katherine scrambled up and away from him, her back against the moor cliff, the chasm closing in on her.

The monk slowly raised himself up on one elbow. "A good morning to you, my lady," he said.

Clad in only a smock, Katherine crossed her arms over her chest and sank down against the uneven wall. The gritstone scraped her back, but she would do anything necessary to stay far from the monk. Yet he did not look like one of the brethren anymore.

"Where is your habit?" she asked.

He sat up and glanced down at the peasant's short wool tunic he wore belted at the waist. "I borrowed these clothes from the almoner's supply. Surely you and I are people in need."

She didn't answer, but remained staring at his hairy legs.

The monk shrugged. "I have stockings here somewhere."

Katherine looked away from those intense eyes. "You don't look like a monk anymore."

"Is that bad? We do not wish to be noticed, after all."

"We" again, she thought, and shivered. She had once wished her life were not so boring; now she sat before a monk while wearing nothing but a smock. Her dirty feet were bare, and her long hair unbound and snarled.

"My lady, what is your name?"

She hesitated. Could he be her enemy, part of the plot to lull her into security? She could not risk her information for the king. "Katherine."

"Lady Katherine . . ."

He drew out her name, waiting, but she remained silent.

"Do you remember more, my lady?"

She nodded.

"Yet you will not tell me."

"I can't," she said, hugging her knees to her chest.

"Why? Have I done something to lose your trust?"

She bit her lip, trying to suppress a hysterical laugh. Her trust? No one had her trust anymore, least of all this dark monk who'd secreted her inside the earth. "Brother, please, understand that I can trust no one. A man kidnapped me."

"Someone might resort to kidnapping if he desired to wed you for your dowry, but why imprison you at St. Anthony's?"

"Since I am already betrothed, perhaps they feared a confrontation?"

The monk watched her from beneath his low brows. There was nothing soft about his face; it was all hard angles and strong bones. She could not help but study him, fascinated despite her wariness. From the pale training scars etched across his hands, she guessed he had not always been a man of God. And when his unusual eyes pierced her, saw through her, she couldn't look away.

"You do not believe that," he said. "You know exactly why they took you. But you will not tell me."

She blinked her eyes against the entrancement of his gaze, and turned her head away. "I can tell no one," she whispered, rubbing her arms. "I trusted someone once, and was stolen from my home. I will not risk that again."

"Do you plan to return home?"

"I can't. They will be waiting for me."

"Where will you go?" he demanded, firing each question at her until her head spun.

"Nottingham."

"Do you have relatives there?"

"Yes!" she said, smiling weakly to give credence to her lie. Was this a search for information? Now that he was outside the monastery, could he indulge his own plans for her? Katherine sighed. She hated feeling that everyone was an enemy, but she had no choice.

The monk stared at her in cold silence, obviously seeing through her deception. "Do you still plan to travel alone?"

Katherine nodded. "I do not wish to endanger you."

"You will be vulnerable to any man who comes upon you," he said quietly.

She recognized the truth of those words. Her face burned and she refused to meet his gaze.

"I could protect you."

Katherine looked up at him. His voice was hard and unyielding, his body massive. No gentle words of God's love had yet passed his lips. "Then I would be vulnerable to you," she finally said.

He nodded, then fixed her with the brilliance of his gaze. "I give you my word of honor I will not harm you."

A familiar pain twisted her heart. "A monk's word does not mean much."

He stiffened and slowly got to his feet. Looking down on her from his great height, he said, "Mine does."

Katherine felt suddenly small against this monk's anger, something she thought could be as overwhelming as his body. When he knelt down in front of her, she pressed back hard against the uneven wall, trembling uncontrollably, tears burning her eyes. Black robes still haunted her dreams, and now they'd come back to torment her waking hours.

The monk searched her face a moment, then sat back on his heels. "Why do you fear men who have taken God's vow?"

Katherine forced herself to look up into his eyes. "Because in my experience, they seldom keep it."

He remained close to her, staring at her with dark heavy brows lowered over eyes she still could not believe were true. He seemed perhaps honest, definitely determined, but Katherine could no longer find it in her heart to give away her trust.

But she knew when to give up the fight. What choice did she have? A woman alone would not last in this dangerous countryside, now that the threat of war inflamed men's minds. She smoothed the smock over her knees. "You said there was a gown to wear over this? And something about food?"

He smiled, and it transformed his face. He looked truly happy to be of service. Katherine should be thankful he seemed dedicated to his vows; instead the thought of them made her uneasy. He was large and strong, obviously not bred for the clergy.

"What is your name?" she finally asked.

The monk's dark head lifted as he reached into his sack. "Reynold."

"Brother Reynold," she said.

He nodded once.

"Brother Reynold, do you know how to reach Nottingham?"

"I do, but I am not convinced that you have relatives there."

Katherine forgot herself for a moment and smiled at him. "I don't. But I must arrive there soon. 'Tis either that or wander about on the moors, for I will not tell you where my family lives."

Brother Reynold tossed a brown woolen gown onto her knees and Katherine grimaced.

"And I should ask no more questions?" he said, rummaging once more in his sack.

She nodded as she stood and turned her back, drawing the sleeveless gown over her head and knotting the crude leather belt.

"My lady, though I am curious about your intentions, do not think that I will let you follow a whim."

Katherine combed her fingers through her hair as she faced him. "Then I will walk alone and you will follow if you like. But we will still go to Nottingham."

From his wallet of provisions, Brother Reynold brought out a round loaf of bread and a moldy piece of cheese, which Katherine pounced on. For once she did not care what someone thought of her appetite.

"Heaven help us," he said, eyeing her with a dubious frown.

*   *   *

The horse, big and dull from field work, kept its head down, following a faint path through the grasses of the moor. The red-haired man pushed a ragged wool cap off his forehead as he squinted up at the hot morning sun. He wiped sweat off his crooked nose, and rubbed the ache that had already settled into his neck. He was sure the girl had come this way, running back to Durham and her father.

The monk's aid had come as a surprise. He had been warned this could happen, but he had not heeded it. It mattered little. He was sure the monk would pose no problem. And he always finished the job. He had sworn to keep the girl safe, but nothing had been said about interfering fools. This one would be easy. The monastery didn't prepare a monk for life on the road with a hunted girl.

Katherine watched the monk gather up their old clothes and bury them at the back of the chasm. He was so broad and tall, all bone and hard muscle. He did not look like any priest she had known, with either their fat bellies full of good living, or bodies pale and slender with fanaticism. His short-sleeved tunic revealed arms that rippled with his movement. She had never allowed herself to study a man's arms before. His hands were stained with blotches of dark coloring, perhaps ink.

"What ails you?" she asked, pointing to the dirty rag wrapped around his elbow.

Brother Reynold's vivid eyes peered out at her.

"We had best begin moving, Lady Katherine. Your captor should assume that by now, we are long gone from the monastery. Can I conclude that if he thinks you will run home to your father's protection, it is somewhere other than Nottingham?"

After a moment, Katherine nodded. She would give away none of her secrets. She watched him draw on woolen stockings to his knees, then don rough leather boots with wooden soles. She wriggled her bare toes.

"Do you have any shoes in that magical sack for me?"

He glanced at her feet with a frown. "No boots to fit a small woman, but I found some heavy cloth shoes, more sturdy than those you were wearing."

Katherine laced her feet into them and straightened. The monk was watching her again and her shivers began as bumps that raced up her arms. She did not sense any menace in him. Then again, she thought bitterly, she was hardly a good judge of men.

Brother Reynold stepped outside their small chasm, and the sun turned him into a blazing statue. Katherine huddled into herself, waiting for her tormentors to find them, for arrows to pierce his chest. Instead he arched his back and looked up at the sun, as if soaking it in. Probably praying, she decided.

"Come, my lady. I see no one."

When the monk reached a hand to her, Katherine avoided it and stepped out into the sunshine.

The air was already hotter than normal, though the cool earth had shielded them.

Brother Reynold bowed and gestured ahead of himself. "You wished to lead, Lady Katherine?"

She raised her chin and walked a few steps beyond him, then turned when he did not follow.

"Unless you long for the wilds of Scotland, I suggest you come this way, my lady."

The monk began to walk in the opposite direction, leaving Katherine no choice but to catch up with him. She forgot about the gown which had not been tailored shorter than normal as her own were. She tripped over the hem and sprawled into the monk, her hands landing flat on his backside. She gasped in mortification and dropped to her knees. He caught her up, and before she could pull from his embrace, she saw him grimace. She quickly lifted her hands from the warm, contoured skin of his arms.

" 'Tis your elbow," Katherine said, dusting off her dress.

Brother Reynold hefted his sack over his shoulder. "Perhaps it would heal if someone would have taught you how to walk."

She squinted up into his dark face, haloed by the sun. Was he angry with her? She saw a flash of white teeth and relaxed, then caught herself. She mustn't relax, not ever.

Brother Reynold offered his arm but Katherine declined, holding up her skirt as she walked beside him. The air hung hot and sultry, and her hair clung to her neck. Before them stretched rolling hills covered in sparse grass, with occasional clusters of trees in the distance. No houses or people anywhere, just the two of them. Katherine swallowed hard and glanced at the monk.

"Your elbow . . . ?" she prompted.

"A bloodletting yesterday."

She grimaced, hugging her weak arm, which had many times suffered the same indignity. "Are you ill?"

"The brethren believe that an occasional bloodletting strengthens a man, purifies him." He glanced sidelong at her and Katherine looked away. " 'Twas the only way to be relieved from Night Offices. They would not miss me while I rescued you."

Katherine stumbled, but caught herself in time. "You did that for me?"

He shrugged and kept walking, forcing her to keep up with him.

"Why did you do it? What am I to you that you risked your health for me?"

"Someone in need of help," he said, slitted eyes gazing across the moor as if he could protect her from anything.

"But your calling—won't they miss you?"

He hesitated and once again a strange emotion darkened his face. "They will not miss me overly much."

"Will they take you back?"

"Almost certainly. I am the youngest and the strongest. They need me."

Katherine fell silent, and her thoughts turned to

her family. Her father must be terribly worried.
Did he think her dead, killed by wild animals? Did
he have men searching the forest for her body? But
her mother—Katherine doubted the woman even
cared that she was gone. She was probably on her
knees in her drafty, bare room, fasting, praying
that Katherine did not humiliate the family by being compromised by her abductor.

As Reynold walked along, he felt the springiness
of the ground beneath his feet, and the sun beating
down upon his head with ferocity. He did not
mind. For the first time in many a month, he was
content to wait for what the day would bring. The
air was fresh, not tainted with bitterness and neglect, as at Saint Anthony's. But that was the life
he must return to. It was all he deserved.

Far in the distance, he saw a large flock of sheep,
grazing slowly along a hillside. The shepherd saw
them, and Reynold waved. The woman beside him
stiffened.

"Brother Reynold, how could you call attention
to us? We are on a mission of utmost secrecy!"

"Are we?" he countered, looking askance at her
with amused tolerance. "Pray inform me."

He knew she would not. Instead Lady Katherine
straightened her shoulders and walked a little
ahead of him, as if she could possibly keep up the
pace.

"I waved because by not appearing friendly, we
appear suspicious. Would you have the youngster
tell whoever might follow us that he saw two
strangers to this countryside?"

Her chin lowered a notch. "I had not thought of that."

Reynold smiled at her, then almost laughed aloud as she stumbled again over the hem of her gown. He had never seen such a clumsy girl. Weren't they all taught to curtsy deeply and not fall on their faces? His own sister used to amaze him with feats of grace. Remembering his family brought a chilly bleakness to the day. He only hoped he could return to the monastery before his brother discovered his absence.

He thrust aside thoughts of the family he had not seen in eight months. He was free for a short while, the day was beautiful, and he was outside the walls of St. Anthony's. Although Lady Katherine guarded her secrets with a sincerity he found endearing, he would set her life to rights, for she needed him. The mystery of her intrigued Reynold. How could a naive woman, with a stumbling manner and a weak arm, be so feared that grown men would resort to kidnapping? And why were they so careful not to harm her?

That night, in a small grove of trees, Brother Reynold withdrew two blankets from his bottomless sack and handed one to Katherine.

She wrinkled her nose. "The night will be hot enough without that."

"You may sleep on bare earth with the insects, if you wish."

Katherine shivered and took the blanket. Brother Reynold irritated her. He dug the loaf of bread from his sack, and Katherine found it even harder than before. He gave her a handful of berries he had found amongst the trees, and she resisted the urge to complain that the fruit had not been cooked, as any sensible person should know.

Still, Katherine looked down at her meal bleakly. When she had been starving after their escape, it seemed like a feast. She ate every last crumb, but she imagined roast mutton, the tray dripping with gravy as the servant ladled it onto her plate. Katherine closed her eyes and pretended.

"You will not fall asleep and choke, I trust?"

She blinked and glared at the monk.

"You haven't told me whom to notify of your death."

The urge to stick out her tongue was so strong that she chewed vigorously in defense.

Brother Reynold stood up, towering over her. Katherine felt a momentary twinge of fear and some nameless unease. Yet she had to trust him. The monk had proven true so far. Unless he led her other than her destination. She frowned.

"A stream runs on the far side of the trees," he said, lifting up his sack and rummaging through it. He held up an object with obvious satisfaction. "Soap. I will bathe, and then you may do so."

"Bathe?" Was this monk actually worried about cleanliness at such a time?

"You have heard of it, have you not?" he called over his shoulder as he stepped into the trees.

Katherine sniffed. "They tease me for my unnatural cleanliness." The silence grew and the darkness seemed to fold itself around her. "I bathe once a week," she finished, then drew her knees up to her chest and shivered. Wasn't it she who had complained of the heat?

Katherine sat unmoving as the darkness thickened and the stars glittered above the overhang of trees. The wind picked up and the grass whispered to it. The moon was only beginning to crest the hills, and with its faint light, Katherine thought she saw a black shape in the distance. She squinted, wondering if it had moved, or if she'd imagined it. Something suddenly rose from the ground in front of her and she screamed.

Chapter 4

Reynold bowed his head, then stood up. Already the ritual of praying at the end of the day seemed ingrained in him, even in some ways easing his soul. The soft bank of the creek was a considerable improvement over the stone base of the choir stalls for his knees. He grudgingly admitted it could be comforting to cleanse his mind and think only of peace, rather than wishing he could change the past. He had not realized how bittersweet it would feel to be in the outside world again, to remember pleasures he did not deserve and tried to forget.

He kicked off the leather boots and stockings, then pulled the peasant's tunic over his head. The smell of the day's exertion assaulted his senses. He was often amazed at how well he had taken to the monastery's insistence on cleanliness. Now he could not imagine forgetting to bathe.

Reynold left on his braies, the thin strip of cloth around his hips, for the modesty of Lady Kather-

ine should she feel the need for his company. He
imagined the smallest squirrel could send her
shrieking into the woods. He chuckled at the image of her running in fright from the open moor
surrounding them. Of course, there were larger animals pursuing her, of the deadly human variety.

Uneasiness settled about Reynold like a lowland
fog. Perhaps he should not linger overlong. He
stepped into the waist-deep water and submerged
himself, shivering. He decided that although Katherine may be naive about some things, and very
foolish about others, she had a quiet courage he
admired. Noblewomen seldom lived through the
brutality she had experienced in the last week. Yet
she had not fallen apart and demanded to be taken
home to the safety of her family. Despite her fear
of him and what he was—and he sensed there was
a hidden reason for that—she had accepted his aid
and seemed to put her distrust aside for the present.

But not enough to reveal her secrets, he thought,
as he scrubbed his body with the soap. Not enough
to tell him what noble cause could drive an innocent girl away from her family and future husband—what did she say his name was? John?

Reynold dived below and scrubbed his scalp.
Through the gentle bubbling of the water around
him, he thought he heard a sound. He broke the
surface, and a piercing scream froze the blood in
his veins. *Katherine*.

Something primitive took hold of him, blotting
everything out in a haze of red rage. He had left a

woman with no fire to protect her from animals, for fear her enemies might spot them. All for the selfish pleasure of a bath. Reynold gritted his teeth together and a low growl of rage escaped his lips.

Katherine struggled with the man who grasped her arms, recognizing the stench of her captor.

"If ye scream again, I'll be forced t' hit ye, liedy," the man grunted out, using his weight to subdue her while he tried to tie her hands together.

Katherine knew she must keep her wits about her. She silently thrashed beneath the man, feeling his suffocating weight, remembering another man atop her, another man to whom she had trusted her young girl's emotions. The black terror of fear swallowed her whole. It was all happening again, and she was helpless to prevent it.

The man straddled her body and easily over-powered her weak arm, wrapping a length of rope about it. With her free hand, Katherine battered him, whispering, "No, no, no . . ." as if the words contained power. And they must have, because she heard a roar behind her that echoed over the moor and seemed to shake the earth. The kidnap-per froze and looked up, his face pale beneath the moon. He was knocked from her body by a force so powerful that she screamed in terror, then crawled backwards on her hands and feet, her backside scraping the ground. When she came up hard against a tree, Katherine went limp and stared with wide, frantic eyes. The beast from the trees could only be the monk.

She had never seen a man so close to nudity before, but she guessed he was no ordinary man. Water dripped from the hard contours of his body, past the wet cloth molded to his hips. Katherine knew she should blush, but his body was as beautiful as any tapestry's rendering of the ancient gods, every muscle bunching and straining as he pummeled her assailant. A knife suddenly glittered in Brother Reynold's hand. With a great arch of his back he lifted it over his head, prepared to strike down the enemy.

Katherine screamed. "Brother, no! He was trying not to hurt me."

He remained motionless, his muscles taut and straining, his broad chest heaving with each breath. Despair and anguish ripped across his face, and he looked at the knife in his hands as if it were a serpent. Just as he flung it into the dirt, the other man twisted and finally succeeding in grasping Reynold's arms. Katherine cried out in horror. Had she stopped Brother Reynold from murdering the man, only to have her rescuer die?

With a growl, Brother Reynold dealt his opponent a blow with one massive fist. The man went limp. The monk retrieved the knife, tossed it near Katherine's feet, called, "Wait here!" and disappeared into the blackness of the countryside.

Katherine remained huddled against the tree, watching the breathing of her kidnapper. She eyed the knife warily, knowing she would use it if she must. Every sound seemed distorted, sinister. The leaves of the tree bent over her, whispering their menace. The dark bulk of the kidnapper twitched and she jumped. The minutes dragged by until finally Brother Reynold reappeared, leading a horse.

Katherine got to her feet, feeling immense relief and a sudden shyness. Brother Reynold had risked his life in her defense, and all she had ever done was ridicule him and his calling.

"What should we do with him?" she asked in a small voice.

"Bind him and leave him," Brother Reynold said, and proceeded to use the assailant's rope to tie him with his arms behind his back, and his feet drawn up to meet them.

Katherine knew she should turn away. The monk must be embarrassed by his near nudity. Yet she continued to study him, fascinated by the muscles in his back.

"I must thank you," Brother Reynold said as he straightened.

Katherine found herself staring into the dark hair scattered across his chest. She reluctantly raised her gaze. "Thank me?"

"I would have killed him." His voice was hoarse, and she could only guess at the emotions he concealed.

"But surely you were only saving yourself."

"Murder is never necessary." Brother Reynold turned to the horse for a moment, patted its side, then slapped it soundly on the rump.

Katherine gasped as it galloped away. "We could have used that horse to travel faster!"

Brother Reynold smiled. It was becoming increasingly difficult to think of him as a monk, the longer he stood so brazenly before her. He almost glistened under the moonlight, the faint white scars across his torso hinting at another life.

"Peasants would not be riding such a fine animal. We would arouse suspicion."

"But I am in a great hurry."

His eyes narrowed. "Why?"

Katherine chewed the inside of her cheek as she thought about what to say. She didn't know him, couldn't possibly trust a stranger with royal warnings and treachery. And what if her words implicated her father? She couldn't risk that. She *knew* her father was innocent of the plot. She decided to change the subject. "Should not we have examined the contents of the saddle packs?"

Brother Reynold glanced skyward with a sigh. "And steal what is not ours?"

"Well surely we are allowed some . . . compensation."

"Perhaps, but I have everything we need."

Katherine sighed. "More moldy cheese."

"Your noble upbringing is becoming quite evident. Soon you will ask for a litter and slaves to carry you about."

She reddened. "You know that is not true. I merely wish to survive."

Brother Reynold regarded her with his piercing eyes, shadowed by moonlight. "I understand. I should not tease you. In some ways you remind me of my sister."

Katherine spoke sarcastically without thinking. "How comforting."

He arched one dark brow. "You do not wish to be treated as my sister?"

"No. I mean, yes! I—" Katherine whirled away in confusion and came upon the unconscious man. She hugged her arms and shivered. "Can we not leave now?"

"Of course."

Brother Reynold gathered his sack and their blankets, then led her through the stand of trees. His clothes and boots lay in a pile on the bank of the stream.

"Now that we are safe from your enemy for the moment, we'll sleep here. I will see to him in the morning."

"See to him?"

"I need to discover why he is determined to capture you."

Katherine looked away.

"Unless of course, you wish to tell me yourself."

She closed her eyes, feeling only the cool summer wind and hearing the soft babbling of the water at her feet. The monk's clothes whispered together almost seductively as he donned them behind her back. Brother Reynold had saved her life—again. Did he not deserve the truth?

Katherine turned and faced him. The moon had risen higher, leaving the man in shadows that disguised his strength, emphasized his remoteness. She sat down slowly, never taking her gaze from his immense figure. She drew her knees up to her chest and took a deep breath.

"Why did you become a monk? And why is not the top of your head shaved?"

Brother Reynold sighed heavily, then dropped to his knees beside her. It was dark and she should be frightened of him, but she wasn't. She no longer felt that he would attack her. Instead he braced his hands on his thighs, twice the size of hers.

"Lady Katherine, you must be tired. Could not this wait until morning?"

"No, I wish to know now. Unless you feel you must keep silent . . ."

He shook his head, then ran a hand through his close-cropped hair. "My head has not been ton-sured recently because no one insisted I submit. Most of the monks at St. Anthony's are old. They were content with my strong back."

She nodded in reluctant understanding. "You must have felt a calling early in life. They all seem to."

He chuckled. "My only calling early in life was to see what the dairymaid kept hidden beneath her skirt."

Katherine gasped, shocked, yet fascinated. She tried to imagine him as a young man, before the monastery, when girls were more important than prayers. Brother Reynold dropped onto his back, his knees raised, his head pillowed in his hands. The moon played over the contours and slopes of his body, until he seemed to rise like a shadowy mountain from the ground.

"No, Lady Katherine. You must already have guessed after tonight that I was no pious boy cloistered with the monks through childhood."

"But—"

Reynold interrupted her, his good humor gone. "I had a younger brother who accepted our father's decree that he should enter the monastery." Suddenly the words he had never said aloud were trying to burst from his lungs. "He seemed destined for the priesthood. He lived in his books."

Katherine's voice was soft, hesitant. "What happened to him?"

"He is dead." He made his tone deliberately harsh, hoping she would not ask for more. Reynold was desperately afraid that her sympathy would make it all come rushing from him, his culpability, his guilt.

"I am sorry," Katherine finally said. "You must miss him."

Reynold came up on one elbow. The anger in his voice was directed at himself, but she could not know that. She leaned back, and turned her glistening eyes away from him.

"I did not know him very well," he said. "He was my saintly younger brother, forever sickly as a child, destined at an early age for the church. We had nothing to talk about, nothing in common. I was fostered out to a noble family, like my older brother. But he was the eldest, the heir, while I was just . . . his brother." His laugh was forced. "An apt title for me, would you not say?"

"You were trained to be a knight."

She obviously wouldn't give it up. She laced her fingers together, staring at him, leaning forward intently. Reynold couldn't remember a woman besides his sister actually listening to what he had to say, unafraid of his monstrous size. She only feared his vows, something he still couldn't understand. He finally nodded to her question, remaining silent.

"Yet it is obvious that you took your brother's place at the monastery when he died. Why did you do it if you had no calling? You do not seem like other monks I have known."

Reynold rolled onto his stomach, nearer to Katherine, yet made no move to touch her. He reached into the stream and drank from his dripping hand, aghast that he was trembling.

"My family expected it of me," he said slowly. "I expected it of myself." The last he ground out in a harsh whisper, and regretted it when he heard her gasp. For a moment he relived the pain of his older brother's fists, the shame of standing still, taking the beating, because he deserved it.

"That was it?" she said in amazement. "You relinquished your station in the world just because your parents expected you to?"

"My parents are dead. Since I am a younger son, my marriage would not bring as much to the family as my older brother's will. But a son in the clergy can mean power for a family."

Reynold watched Katherine lean back on her arms, her head dropping back. The trees covered them like a dark tent. She murmured, "But to give up your whole life for your family . . ."

"Does that mean your betrothal was a love match, and your father remained uninvolved?"

She seemed to jump in surprise and only gave him the briefest glance. She sat up straighter and rubbed her arm. "But that is different. A woman must marry."

"So your father did not bring you and your suitor together."

"Of course he did, but I knew immediately that I could love him. I was fortunate he showed any interest in me at all."

Reynold's voice was quiet. "What do you mean?"

For a moment, Katherine forgot he was there. In her mind she saw only the great hall of her father's castle, and the man waiting before the hearth with her father. She was fourteen, and about to meet the man who would possibly take her to wife. But the room had been too warm, and she shook so badly that her well-practiced curtsy tottered. Yet the man with the golden halo of fire behind the dark curls of his hair had smiled at her, as if her arm didn't matter. But of course he didn't know what she truly was, he didn't know her sins. And he went away too soon.

Brother Reynold must have been speaking to her, because now he touched her arm and Katherine drew it away quickly, more out of habit than fright.

"Forgive me. What did you say?" she asked, trying to keep the quiver from her voice.

"I asked why you felt so fortunate that a man could fall in love with you."

"Such a personal question, Brother Reynold," Katherine said, reaching for a blanket and spreading it on the ground.

"You were the one who said it, Lady Katherine."

She lay down on her stomach and turned her head away from him. "I simply meant that because of my arm, which I am sure you have noticed by now, not many men would be willing to take me to wife."

"It sounds as if you were grateful, not in love."

"Of course I was grateful," she snapped back at him. "He was handsome and wealthy, and treated me courteously. What more could I want?"

She heard Brother Reynold roll over on the ground a few feet from her. "And you think only I settled for less because of my family."

Katherine was sure she was angry enough to debate this foolish monk for the rest of the night, but her eyelids were heavy, and the ground actually seemed soft. Just as she was about to drift into sleep, she heard Brother Reynold's voice, as if from far away.

"Do you not wish to bathe?"

She blinked slowly and rolled onto her back. The monk was seated beside her. "What did you say?"

"The water is refreshing. Did you not wish to bathe?"

Katherine shivered. The moon had slipped away behind the trees. The branches swayed above her, crowding out huge chunks of starry sky. Bathe out here, in the open?

"Perhaps another time," she said.

"You do not have to worry about the kidnapper. He is securely tied."

She sighed. "I had almost forgotten him."

"I will protect you."

His deep, gravelly voice hung in the air all around her. He seemed a giant against the night sky, a dark stranger who had rescued her for no apparent reason. And he expected her to trust him while she bathed?

Katherine shook her head and rolled away from him.

"I will stand near the trees with my back to you," he continued. "Remove your gown and leave on the smock if you must."

He got to his feet and walked away while Katherine gaped at him. He seemed to disappear into the night. Perhaps if she couldn't see him, he couldn't see her.

Katherine almost went to sleep just to spite him, but the soothing murmur of the water played with her senses. She was filthy from her days in captivity. She pushed up onto her knees. He had left the soft soap wrapped in a piece of cloth beside her blanket. Cautiously, Katherine removed the crude, sleeveless gown, then looked over her shoulder. The monk was nowhere to be seen and she felt a twinge of panic at the thought of being abandoned. But no, he had proven he wouldn't leave.

Katherine stood up and slowly walked to the

bank of the stream, feeling for the slope of the ground with her feet. The water was a dark, welcoming gurgle. She touched the folds of her smock draping from her neckline. What would she sleep in if she bathed in it? Taking a deep breath and trying not to panic, she pulled the garment over her head and stepped into the water.

When he heard the sound of splashing, Reynold tried to take a deep breath and relax. He stood facing the forest like a sentry, every sense attuned not to his duty, but to the sounds of Katherine bathing. He groaned and closed his eyes. He should not be having such thoughts. He tried to concentrate on the manuscript he had begun to copy so recently. A splash sounded behind him, then a giggle. A bead of sweat began a slow trickle down the side of Reynold's face. In his mind he saw water gliding down her bare arms as she lifted them to the starry sky. The water would be lapping at her breasts as she—

Reynold slammed his hand hard into the trunk of a tree. He could not allow himself to think this way. His old life was gone, forever dead to him. He was a monk now. He had taken his vows honestly, and he would not—could not—betray them.

Reynold suddenly remembered how he had felt when he heard Katherine scream but a few hours ago. He had forgotten the monastery, forgotten even the vows of knighthood he had sworn to the king on the battlefields of Scotland. No courtly knight would have burst forth from the water, feeling the need to crush bone and flesh for the sin of touching a woman under his protection. No courtly knight would have caught up his knife and run through the trees, intent on murder.

Murder—isn't that what he had done eight months ago? Besides his vows to God, hadn't he vowed to never harm another soul again? Violence and battle prowess had been so much a part of him, and all they'd done was rip him from his family, make him an outcast.

Reynold felt bewildered by it all. Was Katherine a test he must pass, to prove to God and to his family that he could be a monk, that he could do this honorable thing?

He heard a splash, then a muffled oath.

"I am finished," she called. "Just let me wipe the mud off my knee—I had a little fall."

A smile tugged at his lips though Reynold fought against it. She was so different, so refreshingly innocent. God could not have chosen this test better.

"I'm dressed, Brother Reynold."

He walked stiffly into the clearing and found her lying on her blanket in the darkness. Feeling that he couldn't trust the hoarseness of his voice, he silently spread his blanket beside hers. He lay down and remained unnaturally still, listening to her gentle breathing.

"Are you cold?" he asked. "Shall I make a fire?"

But she was already asleep.

Katherine came awake slowly, involved in the most wonderful dream. James had come to visit her again, instead of sending another message, or one of his occasional gifts. For once he had asked to see her alone, unchaperoned by her father. They stood on the battlements and looked out over the rolling countryside as the sunset bathed them in warmth. He put his arms around her and Katherine expected to feel revulsion, remembering that other man's arms. Instead she sighed and leaned back against him, felt the warmth of his breath on her neck. If only he'd kiss her, show her that he wasn't marrying her just for her dowry. And then he touched her, his hand sliding beneath her breast, and she moaned.

Katherine smiled, wishing it were all real. But parts of the dream didn't dissolve away. She still felt the solid strength of a man behind her. It all came to her in a rush, Brother Reynold going to sleep near her late the previous night. It was his body curled against her back and thighs, his hand that loosely cupped her breast. She opened her mouth to scream, but he snored.

Chapter 5

The elbow that slammed into Reynold's gut nearly stole the breath from his lungs. He groaned and rolled onto his back, away from the soft warmth he'd been drawn to. The "soft warmth" gave a screech and jumped to her feet.

"Brother Reynold! Please keep to your own blanket!"

He rubbed his stomach with one hand and struggled not to laugh, squinting up at the lovely face framed in morning sunlight and golden curls.

"Good morning to you, too, my lady."

"I am not your lady," she said, angrily tugging at the peasant dress that hung crookedly on her body. "If my betrothed ever heard where you just put your hand, he would challenge you to—to joust!"

Reynold grinned as he stood up and folded his blanket. "You mean my hand wandered, and I do not remember? How cruel."

"I certainly will not stay in the open tonight

since you cannot seem to control yourself."

Reynold merely shook his head and gathered her blanket when she seemed disinclined to do so. He found her a green twig to clean her teeth. When their gazes met, Katherine blushed. She flounced off into the bushes for privacy, then a moment later reappeared and hurried to his side.

"That man," she whispered. "The man who tried to—what will we do with him?"

Reynold sobered immediately, then walked towards their original camp with Katherine close behind. Her kidnapper was awake and struggling against his bonds. The man suddenly stilled and eyed him warily.

"Good morning," Reynold said. He squatted and removed the gag. "Are you ready to talk with me today?"

The kidnapper worked his jaw for a moment, then spat towards Reynold's feet.

"That was not very polite. Tell me who sent you to take the Lady Katherine."

His tongue wagged insolently between the spaces of his missing teeth. Reynold glanced at Katherine who stood across the clearing, watching her captor almost fearfully. Was she worried the man would reveal her secrets? Clearly she knew or guessed who had ordered her imprisonment. Perhaps this wonderful fiance wasn't so wonderful after all. He continued to study her until she lifted her gaze to his. She flushed and turned away. He wanted Katherine to tell him whatever truths needed to be told. He didn't want her forced into a confrontation she wasn't ready for. He needed her trust.

Reynold delivered a quick blow to the man's jaw.

Katherine gasped as he went limp. "Why did you do that?"

He unbound the man's legs and returned to Katherine's side. "I cannot just leave him to die."

He hurried her back to the stream to collect their things, not allowing her to eat her dried apple and bread until they were well on their way.

By mid-morning, storm clouds gathered above and the air was oppressively hot. Katherine's legs felt afire. As she took another two steps to Brother Reynold's one and stumbled on her hem, she yanked on his arm.

"Please slow down!"

He caught his elbow to his side, imprisoning her hand. "I thought you were in a hurry, your lady-ship. Have you not great wrongs to right?"

She blushed even more and tugged until he released her hand. Tucking a damp curl behind her ear, she attempted to walk before him and set the pace.

"Tell me, Lady Katherine, how did you injure your arm?"

Although she had been preparing herself for this, the question still shook her. Her inner vision slipped back five years, and she clutched the arm that always served to remind her of her folly.

"It might help to tell me," he said softly, looking

down at her as they walked side by side.

Katherine narrowed her eyes. "Are you my confessor today, Brother?"

He stiffened abruptly, all emotion leaving his face. He was the well-trained knight again, dispassionate and remote. Katherine winced and suddenly longed to see the violet eyes alight with warmth when he smiled at her. Had that become so important?

"I'm sorry," she said.

He glanced at her, then away, still stern, his brooding eyes deep beneath his brows.

" 'Tis not a subject I discuss. People usually pity me, but they seldom ask what happened. I was simply running where I should not have been. I tripped and fell, catching myself with my arm. I can still feel the snap." She did not mention what had caused her flight, although the thought was enough to make her shiver even in the heat.

His demeanor softened. "Could no one set it properly?"

"I imagine they tried, but 'tis all a blur to me. I only remember the pain."

Brother Reynold continued to stare at her, until out of sheer discomfort she met his gaze. She saw deep compassion there and was lost in his vivid eyes. For a moment, she did not even realize they had stopped walking, and were facing one another uncertainly in the middle of the road.

"Let me see your arm," he finally said.

"What? No!" she said furiously, trying to pull away from him. "I promise it will not slow us down. I can keep up!" But his strong hands already gripped her arm at elbow and wrist.

"I know you can keep up. But allow me to see," he insisted, his gaze earnest. "I, too, have been wounded many a time, and seen broken bones set when I thought 'twas hopeless. Perhaps it is not too late."

She knew there was nothing he could do, that he only meant to sway her to his demands. She felt ridiculous tears well into her eyes. Brother Reynold's grasp was firm but not painful. He merely waited patiently, while she struggled to suppress all the awkward pain of a girl who always felt different, worthless.

"Lady Katherine," he murmured, his voice low and soothing. "Surely many of your family have seen your arm."

She shook her head, grateful that she was still holding back her tears. Her hair had fallen into her eyes like a curtain, and she held her breath as Brother Reynold gently tucked the curls behind her ears.

"An injury is nothing to be ashamed of. Are you going to hide it from your husband?"

He was right, she thought, wanting to moan with dread. She went still, allowing him to hold her arm, but not seeing him anymore, just remembering the pitying stares of her father and the castle servants, and the cold reproach in her mother's eyes. James would hate her weakness, would pity her, maybe despise her.

Brother Reynold leaned towards her, almost

blocking out the sky. "Your face tells me how you feel, Lady Katherine, but you must not allow others' reactions to rule your life. You survived something many could not. Your husband will be proud."

She felt the tears spill down her cheeks as Brother Reynold gently pushed up the sleeves of her smock. He lifted her arm, turning it in the light, until she herself could see the horrible jagged scar on her upper arm where the bone had broken through the skin, the pale white slashes across her elbow where the physicians had bled her. Her stomach clenched tight with pain as she stared grimly at the reminders of her ruined youth, and what that other monk had done to her.

Brother Reynold began to trace the scars with his fingers, feeling the bone. Katherine barely held still. She wanted to hide, to sob.

"You were very brave," he said, lowering her arm but not releasing her. "I have seldom seen worse, and many knights had the arm taken off instead. A husband would be proud of a woman who could withstand such pain and live. And anyone who thinks less of you is not worth your consideration."

She stared almost in wonder at his harsh face, now gentled. The painful tightening in her chest eased away. Very slowly he lifted her arm again and bent forward, pressing his lips to the back of her hand. She was shocked into immobility, standing in an open road, allowing a man to touch her so intimately.

A moment later he dropped her hand and looked up at the darkening sky. "I hope this storm holds off until we find suitable shelter."

Katherine came out of her trance and quickly wiped the tears from her cheeks. She cleared her throat, unable to look at the monk who had just given her a compassionate gift she'd forever cherish.

She squinted, barely able to make out a dark curling ribbon between sheep pastures and fields of barley. "Is that a river ahead?" she asked hoarsely.

He picked up his pace. "Perhaps there will be a place nearby where we can wait out the worst of the storm."

As they neared the water, a small settlement came into view across the way, with its tiny cluster of houses around a village green, and a manor house farther away. An imposing mill straddled the river, with a foundation of stone beneath timber walls and thatched roof. Its wheel turned lazily through water that seemed unnaturally low.

"There will be a toll," Brother Reynold said in a low voice, waving to a few villagers who stood by the mill. "I do not wish to waste the few shillings I have, so I shall carry you across."

Katherine tried to pull away, but he thrust his sack and his boots into her arms, lifted her effortlessly, and pulled her close. His chest was warm and hard at her side, his fingers curled against her knees and the edge of her breast. A sudden image flashed into her mind, of Brother Reynold running almost naked through the woods to her rescue. Her dry mouth and pounding heart she attributed to the anxiety of a sheltered girl with little experience dealing with men.

"Laugh," he whispered, his breath warm on her cheek. "Do not arouse suspicion. Do you want them upset that we cannot pay their toll?"

He whirled her around in seeming abandon. Katherine's head dropped back and the first splash of rain hit her face, cooling her skin. He made as if to drop her, and she gave a little shriek and clutched his shoulders. He grinned and she suddenly grinned back, relaxing in his arms, trusting him. He began wading into the river while Katherine merrily kicked her legs and reached down to touch the water. Brother Reynold staggered.

"Let us not make this too real," he whispered.

Katherine splashed him.

The rain began to fall in soft waves and she laughed aloud, unlocking her arms from his wide shoulders and letting them dangle. Brother Reynold was so strong she had no fear he'd drop her— at least not by accident, she suddenly thought, as he dipped the back end of her dress in the river and grinned.

They staggered and laughed their way up onto the opposite shore, where Brother Reynold set her on the ground. He held her close for a moment, and the water from his legs dampened her gown. She thought she felt his lips touch her forehead, but she must have imagined it, because he waved to the miller, pointed up at the rumbling sky, then to the nearest shed.

The man waved back and nodded.

Brother Reynold dragged her forward by the hand.

Katherine resisted, feeling her heartbeat speed up. "Surely this is not necessary."

"Who knows how long this weather will last," he called, pushing through the sagging door.

Katherine peered around his arm, but in the dim, hazy light, all she saw were piles of what looked like long grass, and a scythe propped up in the corner.

"What is it?" she asked suspiciously.

"Grass, probably from the mill pond," Reynold replied, turning and falling backwards into the cuttings, arms outstretched.

Katherine saw more of his long, hairy thighs than she thought decent. "Brother Reynold!"

He suddenly grabbed a fistful of her skirt and pulled. Katherine shrieked as she fell.

Reynold stifled a groan and regretted his actions as she landed atop him. He could barely remember the last time a woman's thighs had entwined with his. It could not have been this memorable. Katherine was all warmth and smooth skin and flushed indignation as she squirmed until she lay beside him. Guilt hovered at the edges of his consciousness, but when she tried to get up, he caught her arm.

"Stay here. I will not have you soaked in the rain."

She removed his fingers from her arm with a huff, then sat up and showed him her stiff back.

"Brother Reynold, I don't think this is appropriate."

He almost begged her to stop using his title, but caught himself in time. For a tense moment, he stared at her slim back. Was that skin he saw between the laces of her dress? Gritting his teeth, he struggled to remember the holy vows that seemed to easily elude him. "Forgive my methods. I was caught up in our act."

"You seem to have had much practice," she said, still refusing to look at him. But the back of her neck had flushed red.

Reynold chuckled, crossed his ankles, and propped his arms behind his head. "I will only admit that the inside of a barn is hardly unfamiliar to me—although I shall not say if I was milking a cow or kissing a girl."

The sweet curve of her cheek rounded in a smile and she turned to look at him. "You are the most unusual monk I have ever met."

"Only because you never bothered to imagine that we all once had a life outside the monastery."

"How long have you been a monk?"

"Eight months."

"Oh, 'tis not so long."

Reynold groaned and closed his eyes. "Not long? When you have been raised to jousting and sword-fighting and court manners, not to mention pretty girls, eight months is an eternity. But I do not regret my decision."

She twisted to look at him, and Reynold's gaze was drawn to the plumpness of her breast pressed against one arm.

"Have you met any of the royal family?" she asked, her voice suddenly hesitant.

"Which family?" he countered sarcastically, thinking of the royal upheavals of the last few years, when Richard, once Protector for his young nephew the king, had assumed the crown on the grounds of the boy's supposed illegitimacy. Having grown up in the north, Reynold knew of Richard's legendary courage and intelligence. The men of Yorkshire followed him willingly. Who was he to say that the new king was not telling the truth? And a fourteen-year-old boy-king could not control a country with a hundred years of rebellion and war behind it.

"You know what I mean!" Katherine said, leaning forward and bringing Reynold's mind back to her lovely bosom. "Have you been to court?"

"Many times," he said absently, wondering how far her oversized peasant dress could gape. He was beginning to feel overwarm.

She leaned forward to an alarming degree. "Do you think you could help me past the courtiers to see King Richard?"

Reynold forgot about her breasts. "King Richard? Is that what this is all about? Do you have some silly notion he might attend your wedding?"

Katherine withdrew, her dark blue eyes turning to ice. "Do you think I would risk your life as well as my own on something so frivolous? You do not have a very high opinion of my intelligence, Brother Reynold."

He sat up. "What am I supposed to think? You will not tell me why we are going to Nottingham." He leaned on one arm, closer to her. "Why all the secrecy, Katherine? Why did those men imprison you? You must tell me."

Katherine almost forgot everything when his large hand, warm and callused with work, cupped her cheek. He turned her gently until their gazes met, and she could only stare. His strange-colored eyes were full of concern. The once-forbidding heaviness of his brow now made him look strong and secure, someone to depend upon—someone to trust.

But she could not risk trusting him, could not divulge her secret to anyone but King Richard. Some of his most favorite courtiers had plotted their treason while attending her father's hunt. Eleanor, her father's mistress, had overheard them, and trusted her with the information. She could not betray the only woman who had ever treated her like a daughter. And she would not listen to suggestions that her father might be guilty. No man would treat his own daughter the way she had been treated.

Katherine looked into Brother Reynold's eyes, so filled with concern. She wanted to speak, but words failed her. His gaze dropped to her mouth, and she felt a sudden, startling tightening in the depths of her body, a slow warmth that radiated outwards. Never had she felt such languorous

heat. All these new sensations just from a man's
eyes and hands—but this wasn't the man she
would be marrying. This was a monk.

Katherine turned her back on him and fought to
master her breathing. What was wrong with her?
She barely knew this man—this monk. Why did
she have to keep reminding herself what he was?

"I am sorry, Brother," she whispered hoarsely.
"I cannot tell you anything. I have people I must
protect. Please understand this and stop asking for
answers I cannot give."

She heard him sigh as he lay back in the grass.
Katherine sat stiffly, looking at the rough wood
wall.

"Lie back, Lady Katherine," he murmured.
"Rest."

Katherine slept deeply, unmoving, obviously exhausted from her unusual exertions. Reynold
propped his head on his arm and watched her,
studying her eyes with their flickering golden-
brown lashes, the rise and fall of ample breasts
which could not be hidden by an ill-fitting peasant
dress. Reynold inhaled deeply, struggling for control over emotions which ranged from protective-
ness to outright lust. And God help him, he did
lust after her, this fragile girl with a heart so big
she had to take on a man's cause, no matter what
the peril. Every other woman he had ever met or
wooed would have run straight to the man in her
life, be he father or suitor. He had never had much
use for women, except for baser needs. Sometimes

he felt pity for his older brother, who had to marry and produce heirs. Yet, had he met a woman like Katherine in his youth, perhaps his life would have turned out differently.

Reynold sighed. It was difficult to think rationally when her legs twisted in sleep, exposing the fair skin of her calves, when her lips pouted, then parted. He could only think of kissing her, of cupping one of those magnificent breasts in his shaking hand.

Stop this! he told himself angrily, rolling onto his back and covering his eyes with one arm. He tried to remember the monastery, the book he had been transcribing, but everything except the girl was a blur. Why was he allowing himself fantasies of making love to her? He knew it was impossible—not only was she engaged to some fool, but the monastery was where he belonged now. All he could cling to were the shreds of his honor. He remembered his older brother's contempt and disgust, his sister's sobs. Because of him, his youngest brother was dead. He had brought himself to this wretched life, but it did not mean he couldn't appreciate a beautiful woman.

He turned and looked once more at Katherine, at the curve of her cheek and those full lips, beckoning to him. She was a test to his honor and penance. He refused to fail.

The dream had not come to Katherine in many years. The old monk had been the only man to show her any kindness, besides her father's occasional remembrance that she was there. He wanted to know what she was studying, even what she was thinking. And he always hugged her, something her own father or mother seldom did. But once when they were alone, his hugs had turned to intimate touches. When she had finally realized that something was horribly wrong, she cried out in sudden shock and terror. He ignored her, his hands no longer gentle, but sweaty and hurtful.

Katherine's hoarse scream brought Reynold bolt upright out of a pleasant doze. Her contorted face was shiny with perspiration, and she lay unnaturally stiff, her limbs stretched outwards.

"Katherine," he called, reaching out to touch her shoulder. " 'Tis but a dream. Wake up!"

She screamed again, and the sound was so agonized that Reynold felt gooseflesh rise on his skin. He rolled up to his knees and shook both of her shoulders. She suddenly went limp and began to weep, huge sobs torn from her chest. He gathered her into his arms and she didn't protest. She simply clung to him, and he rocked her like a child, his hands combing through her tangled hair.

"Tell me your dream, my sweet," he whispered.

Katherine shook her head and sobbed harder, clutching his shoulders.

"Do you have this often?"

She began to quiet in his arms, and gave a shivery sigh. "No," she whispered. " 'Tis n-nothing. I'm sorry."

Reynold nodded, resigned to her silences. He re-

solved to himself that he would discover her secrets—all of them. He would help her heal,
because he had never bothered to help his brother.

"Do you wish to go back to sleep?" he asked.

She shook her head, then suddenly seemed to
realize where she was and how he held her. Instead of bolting from his arms, she studied him,
her blue eyes dark as the stormy skies outside.

"Brother Reynold?"

"Yes?"

"Why do you care about me? Why do you risk
your life for me? I tell you nothing, as if you are
untrustworthy."

He hesitated a moment, feeling the weight of her
head in the crook of his arm, her body across his
thighs. "You are frightened, but you will tell me
why eventually."

"You are so sure of yourself, then?" she said,
arching one eyebrow and showing more spirit.

"Sure of my power over women."

He winked, spoiling her outrage before it
started.

Chapter 6

❧

J ust before dusk they approached a castle, nestled in a valley along the banks of a river, with lush farm fields as far as the eye could see. Earlier they had passed through one of the outlying villages, and Reynold had inquired if the castle housed travelers.

"Is this not dangerous?" Katherine asked, pulling her hair back with a thin strip of leather. "What if someone is curious about us?"

"Better to answer simple questions, than to be attacked again."

She shivered and glanced over her shoulder. "Do you think we have been followed?"

"I will not take chances. That man seems determined to recapture you. Perhaps you would care to enlighten me as to his motives?" Reynold asked with a quirk of his brow.

Katherine rolled her eyes and sighed. She would tell him everything, if only her father weren't at risk.

The uneven ground sloped downward, and Katherine caught Reynold's arm to keep from tripping in a muddy hole.

He patted her hand. "Do not worry. I am a convincing actor."

"I've no doubt," she said dryly.

They walked along in silence, arm in arm, and for once Katherine didn't pull away. Her hand was caught in his elbow, where hard muscles bulged against one another. He felt solid and strong, like a man should feel. Did James feel this way? It had been three years since she'd seen her betrothed, three years of rare gifts and letters, but no wedding date. She remembered him as handsome and strong, but not so large as Brother Reynold. He'd never touched her, except to kiss her hand. Was not even her dowry an inducement for James to complete their vows? Had he forgotten her? Or perhaps he remembered only her physical flaws.

They approached the castle just before the gates closed for the night. The walls on each side of the gatehouse sloped outward towards the ground, but reared up to two towers which blocked out much of the sky. Brother Reynold smiled down at her and tightened his grip. Just in front of them, a man pulled a cart overflowing with children. A little girl with a thin face and a head of brown curls waved at them and giggled.

Somehow Katherine expected her knight-turned-monk would frown uneasily. Instead he grinned, wiggled his fingers in return, and crossed his eyes at her. The child shrieked with delight until the man told her to hush.

Katherine eyed the monk dubiously and he leaned down until his mouth was close to her ear.

"I love children," he whispered.

The words faded away as his lips brushed her ear and a shiver swept through her. His breath was warm against her neck and he seemed to linger there a moment, the stubble of his beard scraping her. Katherine remained immobile, caught up in the spell of his nearness.

"Don't you like children?" he murmured. "Or have your brothers and sisters soured you on them?"

"I am the only child," she replied uneasily, wishing he'd move away. She couldn't think straight.

"Ah, what a shame. No one to play with as a youth, no one to train with as you grew older." But his voice trailed off and he frowned.

She couldn't let such an opportunity go. "Why Brother Reynold, didn't you play with all the village girls?" She wanted to know everything about him, but didn't know how to begin. She expected him to laugh, but the anguish in his face only deepened before he could hide it.

"I was too big," he answered at last.

"Too big? What does that mean?"

"They were afraid of me." His deepset eyes were remote, almost wistful. "Sometimes I could not control my strength."

Her own smile died and her throat tightened in

sympathy, as she imagined a little boy, awkward in a too-large body, playing by himself. She wanted to kiss that little boy's brow, soothe his ruffled hair.

Katherine found herself sliding her hand into his much larger one. She saw the surprise on his face as he lifted their clasped fingers. With wide eyes, they stared at one another, then broke apart and looked away. Her skin suddenly felt too hot for her body, and the crowds seemed to press too close.

Katherine was grateful when the cart in front of them moved on. The guards who looked them over were not as tall as her monk, but big and broad, wearing plated brigandine instead of heavy armor. Each held a pike in one dirty hand. She had entered many gatehouses, but always in a litter, and the guards had bowed respectfully, afraid to look her in the face. Now they searched Brother Reynold and his sack, then actually patted her waist with their clumsy, rough hands. Katherine stiffened when the guard's arm brushed her breast. She heard a low wheeze of laughter. When he touched her again, she drew back a hand to slap him, only to have Brother Reynold grab it and tuck it safely into his elbow.

"Can my wife and I enter now?" he asked pointedly.

Katherine barely felt the last pat, or heard the onion-laced laugh the guard sent in her direction. Wife?

Brother Reynold led her beneath the portcullis, which was raised into the ceiling of the gatehouse.

Menacing, iron-tipped points hung above her head like teeth in a gaping maw. The darkness beneath the tower would have been absolute but for the open doors at each end. She saw the vaguest shadow of closed holes in the ceiling and arrow loops in the walls. She didn't need to be reminded to hurry. They passed two massive wooden doors propped open, and came into the outer ward, a bare yard between two sets of castle walls.

Following the cart of laughing children, they passed through a smaller gatehouse to the inner ward, which seemed to crawl with people. In the far corner the immense towers of the great stone hall rose high over the wooden buildings lining all sides of the inner ward. A pack of dogs went barking past and Katherine jumped back. Reynold pointed to her and shrugged, making the children laugh.

She gave him an ominous frown. Husband, was he? She longed to pull him aside and tell him what she really thought of his idea. But as it was, a man and woman traveling alone together would attract the least suspicion by being married. But that didn't mean she had to like it.

There had been no rain for days, and the dust hung heavy in the air, mixed with the smells of horses and overexerted men. She sighed her impatience when Brother Reynold insisted on waiting as all the children scrambled from the cart. She grimly hung on to him with her good arm and allowed herself to be swept along with the crowd and into the castle residence. Although she had

thought the day was hot, the interior of the great
hall engulfed her with smoky heat and her
breathing felt constricted. Rare windows had been
cut high into two walls, but their cloudy glass did
not let in much light at the end of the day. Instead
fireplaces at opposite ends of the room blazed as
high as a man, and candles and oil lamps hung in
brackets along the walls.

Trestle tables and benches cluttered the hall. A
servant impatiently directed them to a table close
to the main entrance, far from the raised dais.
Katherine suffered a sudden wave of homesickness as the noble family came out of their private
rooms and took their places for the chaplain's
prayer. The five children spanned the years from
infancy to adulthood. The oldest, a young man,
lounged in his chair as if bored. The women were
as colorful as flowers, and glittered in the torchlight. Butterfly veils on wire frames hid their hair,
leaving just the maidens bareheaded.

Although Katherine had always been curious
about her father's people below the salt, she had
never been allowed to sit with them. Now that she
was crowded onto a bench, pressed hip to hip with
Brother Reynold and a broad woman whose wimple hung askew, she would have given anything
to be seated with the marquess's family on comfortable chairs, waited on individually by deferent
servants.

Brother Reynold gave her a compassionate smile
and she felt hot tears gather behind her eyelids.
When he patted her thigh, she stiffened and

pushed his hand away. With a grin, he dug into his magic sack and handed her a knife and spoon. The room quieted as the chaplain prayed and thanked God and the marquess for supplying the evening meal. Katherine felt a quick pang of remorse, remembering that she was only eating due to the marquess's kindness.

She and Brother Reynold shared a thick bread trencher. A serving maid splashed in a generous amount of soup, and suddenly Katherine forgot her homesickness. Steam rose from the thick broth, and chunks of vegetables floated enticingly. She leaned forward to inhale at the same moment as Brother Reynold. Hot food. They looked at each other, nose to nose, and grinned.

The monk waited for the wooden trays of roast venison, but Katherine began to eat immediately. She paused only to allow him to set a piece of meat on top of the soup-soaked bread and cut himself a slice, before she attacked that as well, washing everything down with a tankard of ale. She knew Reynold watched her with amusement, but she ignored him, only clinking spoons occasionally as they tried to capture the same carrot.

When her stomach was full, she swayed in blissful complacency. Brother Reynold put a strong arm around her and she lazily allowed it, gazing at their tablemates in contentment. Children sleepily lowered their heads to their pillowing arms. Men and women leaned together much as she and Reynold were doing, talking in low voices.

Through half-closed eyes, Katherine looked

about the hall. Her gaze passed over the marquess's family, then swiftly back again. The eldest
son was staring at her.

Straightening her back, she glanced up at Reynold, but he was paying scant attention. He and
the little children were making faces at one another. Hesitantly, Katherine looked up and was
once again pierced by the son's insolent gaze. She
glanced side to side and over her shoulder, but
there was no one else paying the young lord any
attention. Blushing, she couldn't help but look
once more. He grinned at her.

Katherine dropped her gaze and did not look at
him again. Her stomach tightened with nervousness, and she could no longer relax.

Something cold and wet touched her hand. She
started, then quickly realized it was one of the castle dogs, gazing at her soulfully, its tongue hanging out in the heat. She was about to hand him the
last of the sopping trencher when the monk stayed
her hand.

"The almoner approaches. Save it for him."

She watched as a hunched little man in thread-
bare robes gathered uneaten food for the poor.

"Why don't they come in to eat like we did?"
she asked softly.

"The guards knew we were travelers. They do
not appreciate the same faces day after day, eating
their lord's food."

Someone pounded twice on a table across the
hall. Benches were suddenly pushed back, and the
tables folded up against the walls. Brother Reynold

wiped their spoons and knives as best he could before replacing them in his sack. People broke into little groups, talking and laughing, while the marquess's family seated themselves before one giant hearth. Colorful tapestries decorated the whitewashed walls over their heads. Katherine thought once or twice she felt the arrogant stare of the nobleman's son, but she firmly ignored him.

When she heard the first pluckings of lute strings and realized there would be entertainment, she banished her foolish nervousness. Excitement caught her up and she began to hum. Her mother had always made her retire after the meal, and she used to lie in bed forlornly and listen to the merrymaking. Once she had snuck in to watch people whirl and laugh and drink too much. Now she had a chance to be one of them.

She turned to ask Brother Reynold to dance with her, and found him on his hands and knees in the rushes, playing with the children he had befriended. She watched in bemusement as they tried to climb aboard his back. He growled and sent them tumbling. They were not afraid of his dark face with its heavy brows. In fact, Katherine thought as she looked around the room, the monk seemed to draw a lot of attention, and it wasn't only from the children. Women watched him speculatively, many sidling closer. Katherine fumed in silence. Could they not see he had a wife?

When she realized what she was thinking, Katherine almost gasped aloud. Was she actually jealous over a monk? The musician began a merry tune, and Brother Reynold grabbed her by the waist to dance. He kicked aside rushes, whirling her around until Katherine was forced to clasp his arms and trust his embrace. He was good, effortlessly teaching her the steps while grinning down into her face from his immense height. Always he seemed to show deference to her weak arm.

She told herself she was dizzy from spinning, not from the warmth of his violet eyes shining out of his face, or his hard arms encircling her.

Brother Reynold knew every step of the dance. Katherine leaned back in his embrace giddily as the room spun. The music ended and he stopped so quickly that she came up hard against his body and he held her close.

In that one moment, she could feel the muscles of his thighs entwined with hers, the expansion of his rib cage as he inhaled deeply, the press of his hips against her stomach. His face suddenly turned brooding, his eyes narrowed, and his lips compressed into a thin, hard line.

Katherine would have thought he was angry had she not sensed the yearning in him. Eight months in a monastery must have been difficult for a man who seemed to enjoy people as he did— especially women. Giving her a last tight squeeze, he pulled her to a bench and sat down stiffly beside her. She watched his cold profile as he stared unseeing at the dancers. Katherine felt a twinge of sympathy. Why should she care if he were in pain—but she did.

"You dance quite well." She glanced at him sideways.

He shrugged. "My fostering included practice with the earl's daughters."

"Practice?"

He met her gaze. "Dancing."

"Oh," Katherine said, feeling her face flame with embarrassment. How foolish she was behaving. She had a serious mission to reach the king, and she could have easily forgotten all about it and danced with Brother Reynold through the night. Instead she watched people whirling about by flickering torchlight, and thought only of the man beside her, and if he would ask her to dance again. And those women still stared at him!

Katherine shook her head, feeling hot and light-headed from the smoke. "If you will excuse me, I need a moment of privacy."

"I shall escort you," he said, taking her arm and standing up.

Katherine shook off his touch, unable to meet his gaze. "Please, I would rather go alone."

"Lady Katherine, we do not know these people."

"And I barely know you, do I?"

His lips tightened and Katherine winced, looking around to see if anyone had overheard.

"Forgive me—husband. I am simply tired and overheated. I will return in a moment."

She slipped out of his hands and weaved her way between the dancers, dodging a man's questing fingers. She murmured apologies until she reached a dark corridor, where flickering torches formed pools of light at regular intervals. She turned a corner, trying to find the exterior wall of the castle, where the garderobe would be. The noise of the dance was swallowed up almost immediately by the thick stone walls.

Katherine was conscious of being alone. It suddenly occurred to her that she and Brother Reynold had gained entrance to the castle very easily. What if her kidnapper had done the same, then hidden until he could find her alone?

Katherine looked over her shoulder in apprehension, but there was no one, only the damp stone floor and the smoky, wavering light of the torches. She hurried on, looking into each room for the garderobe, turning corners until she was dizzy. She suddenly stopped and swayed, holding her arm close to her body. She couldn't remember if she'd turned left or right at the last corner.

Covering her mouth so that she wouldn't giggle hysterically, Katherine tried to remember the way back. The garderobe no longer seemed more important than just finding Brother Reynold. While she stood immobile, eyes closed in concentration, she heard the faintest echo of voices.

Turning towards the sound eagerly, she started to run, then tripped over the hem of her skirt and fell against the wall. Her weak arm took the brunt of it, then collapsed so quickly she smacked hard into the stone. Her head blazing with pain, she swayed against the wall and closed her eyes.

Chapter 7

◇◇◇

The voices had come closer, and down the corridor she saw the bobbing of candlelight. The sounds blended suddenly, and Katherine realized that just one person came towards her, a man. He was singing. She shrank back against the damp stone wall, caught in the darkness between pools of torchlight. If she moved now, he would see her. Was it her kidnapper? Had he been following her?

The candlelight bobbed unnaturally, swaying back and forth down the corridor. The toneless singing grew louder. The man hiccupped and laughed to himself. He was drunk, Katherine thought in dismay and some relief. If he were following her he wouldn't have imbibed, would he? Perhaps it was a trick.

Breathing in quick, frightened gasps, Katherine remained pinned to the wall, hoping the darkness would conceal her. The singing man moved closer, reeling once or twice. The candle illuminated his face, and it was not her kidnapper's. Katherine sagged against the wall, feeling a rush of relief that lasted but a moment. It was the marquess's son.

"Where are you, little blond angel?" the young man called, continuing to sway as he came to a standstill. He shoved the candle forward, waving it wildly in the air. Katherine had no choice but to jump away from the spitting wax.

"There you are, angel," he said, coming closer to hold the candle near her face.

She forced herself to look serene and unafraid. His hand shook and his foul breath assaulted her face.

"What a sweet little miss you are," he murmured. "Left the party just for me, did ye?"

"No, my lord." She wanted to speak as little as possible, doubting he'd be rational with the amount of wine he must have consumed. His heavy-lidded gaze moved down her body, and she pressed back against the wall. Why had she so foolishly left the hall alone?

His face loomed near, youthful and soft. Katherine tried to edge away but he caught one arm and gripped her tightly. She struck his shoulder.

"Release me! My husband is waiting."

"Now, now, he won't mind sharing, angel. Come give me a kiss."

Katherine pulled hard against his grip. When she smacked him in the face he dropped his candle to restrain her other arm. The flame went out, leaving them in the shadowy darkness between torches. She tried to scream, but the sound was cut off by his hand over her mouth. She swung forward and hit him across the face.

His hands were no longer playful. He twisted her arms behind her back and Katherine cried out in pain. Her breasts were flattened against his chest, and his ragged, hot breathing struck her face.

"I'll scream!" she said, squirming against his body.

The man laughed. "No, you won't, unless you wish your husband to pay for your foolish error. After all, who will my father believe, you or me?"

Panic pounded through her veins, and pulsed through her wild thoughts. She twisted her face away. His wet lips touched her ear and cheek and finally the corner of her mouth. Katherine's stomach heaved and she barely controlled her nausea.

"Let her go," a deep voice said behind them.

She sagged in his grip as she recognized Reynold. But instead of defending himself or releasing her, the nobleman only laughed. He turned to face Reynold, pulling Katherine back against his chest. She stared up into Reynold's angry face, then cried out when the man crudely grabbed her breast.

"Whatever can you do, peasant boy?" His voice was as nasty as his drunken laugh. His head bumped Katherine's when he peered over her shoulder and pulled at the gown's neckline. "Why keep such treasure to yourself?"

He tried to plunge his hand down the front of her gown, straining the seams.

"Please," Katherine whispered, her body and

emotions bruised. Why did Reynold stand so still? In the shadowy torchlight, his face looked hard and angry, and his chest rose and fell rapidly. But still he did nothing.

The marquess's son released her body to grip her arm. "Your man knows, if you do not. He must sleep alone tonight. Come to heaven with me, angel."

He began to drag her down the corridor, and Katherine dug in her heels and tried to pull free. She stumbled forward, then flung herself back, her free hand stretched out to the monk.

Though she cried out, he did not look at her. As she was pulled relentlessly down the corridor, his dark form remained still, head bowed, fists clenched. She screamed again until her abductor covered her mouth, and dragged her around a corner. She could see Reynold no more.

The young man bent and flung her over his shoulder. He staggered to one side, and Katherine thought he'd bash her head into the wall. He steadied himself, and merely swayed as he took a torch down from the wall.

"We don't have all night," he complained, as if she were just as anxious to begin as he.

Katherine hung limply, barely able to breathe with his shoulder crushing her stomach. Reynold had abandoned her. She had only begun to trust him, and already he had betrayed her. She had thought he was different than any man she had ever known, his compassion and understanding changing her life.

Katherine was too despondent for tears. She hung there, feeling the blood rush to her head, hoping she would faint before she found herself beneath the nobleman.

She lost track of the corridors they wound through. Every staircase was an exercise in fear as the nobleman swayed on each step, threatening to tumble them backward. Finally he opened a door and threw her onto a musty bed, where dust flung into the air made her sneeze. Dazed, she watched him light candles with his torch, then toss it into the hearth.

What was she doing, lying here, waiting for the worst to happen? She sat up and he flung her back, then straddled her hips to pin them to the bed.

"Don't fight, angel," he whispered, slurring his words. "What's another man when you've had that big oaf in your bed?"

"Let me go," Katherine demanded, trying to push him off. He held her arms and kissed her until she twisted away. As he lifted his head to grin at her, the next moments became confused in her mind. She felt as if a shadow had detached itself from the wall, hovered above them, then struck swiftly. The young nobleman collapsed on top of Katherine, and she found herself staring into Reynold's hard face.

"You didn't leave me," she said softly. Relief surrounded her like a warm blanket, and she felt dizzy with happiness.

Reynold dragged the limp man away, then

straightened and frowned at her. "You thought I had abandoned you?"

She nodded, but he gave her no encouraging smile or reassuring word. He looked at her as coldly as he had the nobleman. She realized she had injured his pride.

"I was foolish and scared," she said quickly. "Forgive me for not thinking."

He rolled his eyes, and proceeded to toss the man on the bed beside her. Katherine scrambled off, and watched in shock as he began to remove the nobleman's clothes.

"Reynold, whatever are you doing?"

"The same thing I was doing when you thought I abandoned you—weaving a story he will believe."

"But—"

"We do not want the entire household chasing us in the middle of the night, do we?"

"Of course not. Yet—" She covered her eyes as Reynold stripped the man of his hose.

"You can look now. He is beneath the bedclothes."

The young man seemed to have fallen into a peaceful sleep. He snored heavily and rolled to his side.

Reynold picked up a pillow. "Hold still, Katherine."

He wiped the pillow up and down her body, especially into her hair. She grimaced and finally pushed him away.

"Whyever—"

"Because it will smell like a woman."

"Oh." She was quite impressed by his cleverness, but she cried out as he plucked a few strands of hair from her head and placed them atop the pillow. The nobleman continued to snore.

Taking Katherine's hand, Reynold pulled her from the room and led her down through empty castle corridors.

She caught up to walk beside him. "Can't we just leave the castle rather than resort to this farce?"

"The guards will not open the gates at this time of night, Katherine. If we ask them to, they shall merely become suspicious. Which means we must stay until morning."

"But when he awakens—"

"He will smell you and see the rumpled bed."

Katherine blushed. "You think he'll believe we were—together—even though he won't remember it?"

"I saw how much he was drinking." Reynold stopped and faced her. "I thought he was just a drunken boor. Then when I saw him follow you from the room—"

He broke off and stared deeply into her eyes. She shivered violently, remembering the man's hands on her. Reynold swept her into his arms and held her tightly. She relished his comfort and support, quietly glad that he had not abandoned her.

Reynold closed his eyes and gave a silent prayer of thanks that she was safe. But still she shook and burrowed closer to him, her soft hair tickling his chin. He took a deep breath and just held her, rubbing her back in what he hoped was a calming motion. She slowly quieted in his arms, and as his anger fled, the sensation of her body against his exploded in his brain. His vows and promises receded from memory, and all that was left was the crush of her rounded breasts against his chest, the soft indentation where her thighs met her hips.

He had a sudden mad desire to put his hands beneath her buttocks and lift her until their hips strained against one another. Instead he smoothed the tumble of curls from her cheek.

Katherine did not know what she had been expecting, but it wasn't the gentle touch she felt along her cheekbone. His fingertips brushed her lip, tracing the lower curve, and she quivered violently, wracked by emotions she had never known before. A small, sane recess of her mind told her to pull away, to stop this mad assault on her senses. Instead she was held immobile by a stab of fierce longing. She wanted his touch, his gentleness. She needed to hold the man people were afraid of. When his hands cupped her face she closed her eyes and a soft moan escaped her.

The shock of his lips touching hers made Katherine's knees weaken. She clung to him, her arms around his waist, pressed intimately against his body, so much harder and broader than hers. His mouth moved softly against her lips and she found herself imitating his movements, savoring the rasp of his chin against hers and the faintest taste of ale. His lips parted and she felt the gentle intrusion of his tongue. Katherine came to her senses with a rapidity that almost disappointed her. She had never even kissed her betrothed, and here she was, wantonly allowing what another had just tried to take by force.

Katherine groaned and pushed away from him. "No," she whispered, wiping a shaking hand over her mouth. "I can't—I won't—"

"Forgive my lack of manners, Lady Katherine," Reynold said stiffly. His features were weary, shadowed by sadness, and he looked over her head as if he didn't dare meet her eyes.

She could hardly slap his face and stalk away. He could not be blamed for kissing her when she threw herself against him. But as he silently led her back to the great hall, Katherine berated herself for her lack of control.

How could she allow a man she barely knew to kiss her like that? After her mother's monk, she had stayed far away from men and any chance of touching one. But since meeting Brother Reynold, she had embraced him more times than she could count, kissed him, and even seen most of his body. What kind of conduct was this for a betrothed woman?

She tried to concentrate on the face of James, but it had been three years since she'd seen him. For the first time, she admitted to herself that even his features had grown hazy in her mind. Why was it so easy to forget the only man who had ever wanted to marry her?

Reynold came to a halt and silently pointed to

what Katherine assumed was the entrance to the garderobe. Her face flushed red as she left him standing in the corridor, waiting for her.

Back in the great hall, the fire had dimmed, the music had ended, and the rest of the marquess's family had retired to their private quarters. Reynold led Katherine past benches where snoring men sprawled. Cloaks and blankets covered huddled lumps of people on the floor. He squinted into the shadows, trying to find a private place for Katherine to sleep. He retrieved his sack and settled for a spot near one hearth, between two other couples. No privacy, but at least the fire chased away the dampness of the castle.

He spread a blanket on the rushes, and bowed slightly to Katherine. She gave him an unreadable look and sat down stiffly. When he joined her, her eyes widened but she wisely held her tongue. He covered their legs with the remaining blanket.

With a heavy sigh, Reynold lay back, listening to the crackling of dry rushes beneath him. Katherine released her hair and it fell in waves down her back. He closed his eyes for a moment, but he could barely see his dead brother's face. Words like "duty" and "honor" floated behind his eyelids, becoming a meaningless string of letters next to Katherine's soft curls. All his vows, his promises of penance, meant little next a woman who actually wanted him, who kissed him with a passion he'd never experienced before. It made a mockery of every sexual encounter he'd ever had. He finally knew all he had given up.

Katherine lay back, taking special care to keep from touching him. Reynold drew his own half of the covers up to his waist, watching her pull her half right up to her chin as if it were a shield. The firelight flickered across the tip of her nose and touched golden strands of her hair. He deliberately turned his face away and tried to sleep.

The rushes crackled with the movements of the other occupants, and an occasional giggle or whispered conversation reached his ears. Then, in a moment of quiet, a languorous sigh rose from the couple to his left. Reynold felt every muscle in his body tighten. The rushes shifted and the man groaned.

Reynold desperately tried to think of something—anything—else. He pictured himself at his carrel in the monastery, painstakingly transcribing line after line. Though it had happened but a few days ago, that part of his life seemed hazy and unreal. Instead vivid images rose to mind of the smooth lengths of a woman's leg, the rounded edge of a breast slowly revealed as a bodice dropped away. Reynold's breathing quickened and he longed to wipe the sweat from his forehead, but he couldn't move. He used all his mental powers not to see the face of the woman in his dreams. A strand of golden hair curled at her throat, and before he could stop it, Katherine's face appeared above it, her head thrown back, her face severe in ecstasy. Reynold barely controlled the shudder that rippled through his body.

Why now? Why did he have to be so vividly reminded of the life he had forsworn? Why had he even helped this woman, whose body writhed in his mind, tempting him to forget all he had promised. Her mouth had been luscious and sweet beneath his, and it was easy now to imagine her lips parted, her tongue dueling with his.

In his dream the night was dark, the trees swayed above them and the firelight flickered across their naked bodies. He wanted to worship her breasts and lie within the warmth of her thighs. She would cry out her fulfillment and Reynold would always, always make her feel loved.

It was that thought that brought him out of the seductive trance and back to the damp hall, the prickly rushes, and the woman lying stiffly beside him. The other couple still groaned and fumbled beneath their blanket, but Reynold stared unseeing at the timbers of the roof and thought of her hand lying beside his.

Katherine felt a slow flush of mortification sweep from her chest to her forehead. She knew what that couple was doing beneath their blanket. Couldn't they wait until they reached their own home? Wasn't anyone else as embarrassed as she? But she only heard gentle snores or murmured words, even an occasional groan.

Katherine became aware of Brother Reynold, lying beside her on his back. She was too embarrassed to turn and see if he were awake, but she hoped he did not hear their neighbors. Though he'd been in a monastery, she knew he had been a worldly man once. His kiss proved that. She tried to forget, but her treacherous mind latched hold of the idea gleefully. It was not all that difficult imagining Reynold as a knight come to meet the daughters of a household. He had a hard, stern face which showed he could protect what was his.

But when he laughed—Katherine caught her breath as she pictured him grinning at her, the crease in his chin boyish, his eyes as bright as flowers. He did not laugh enough. Some secret tormented his soul, had made him retreat to the monastery. She could not even be angry that he had kissed her. She had wanted him to, betrothed though she was.

Katherine still felt the touch of his lips, so soft and gentle, making that other monk's hard, invading mouth recede from her mind. If she had not stopped Reynold, what would have happened? She had a sudden, vivid image of herself reclining on a soft bed in a tapestried room, candles glowing everywhere. She saw Reynold leaning over her, kissing her hands, her arms, her shoulders, her—

Katherine flopped over onto her stomach and squeezed her eyes tightly shut. She had to stop this. She was engaged to—to—

In disgust, she turned her head and suddenly saw the reflected firelight in Reynold's eyes as he watched her. She felt trapped by his silent, intense gaze and her own longings. Why did just being near him turn her into a quivering, confused girl?

He moved onto his side, facing her, and she put

out a hand to stop him from coming nearer. With a will of their own, her fingers remained on his chest, feeling his warmth and the hardness of muscle. He covered her hand with his own and lay there, watching her. The calluses of his palm were rough, and she imagined his hands caressing her in other, secret places, and her own touching him.

Although her mind told her this was madness, she wanted to be held, to be loved for herself and not her dowry. She rolled onto her side facing Reynold, her hand still caught in his. Her breathing was short and swift, her heartbeat frantic with uncertainty and desire. Her body quivered and tightened in places she'd never noticed before. Reynold's fingers slid along hers, stroking, setting her trembling with just his touch. He traced slowly up her inner arm, lingering at her elbow.

Katherine couldn't breathe enough air. Her blood shimmered with passion that seemed to intensify between her thighs. Reynold's fingers moved up her arm, ever closer to her body. The back of his hand brushed her breast and she shuddered. Somewhere in the depths of her mind, her logical self cried out a warning, but this time she could not obey. Her gaze was locked on the shadowy, harsh lines of his face and she heard his quick breathing. Was he similarly affected? Did he hover in this realm of pain and pleasure so exquisite she wanted to linger here forever? His large hand cupped her breast, lifting its fullness. She exhaled a moan, arching her back.

At the sound of her pleasure, Reynold shook

with the effort of holding still. She was warm and soft, her breast heavy in his palm. He rubbed his thumb gently over the wool-covered peak and was rewarded with a shiver and a sigh. His body raged with heat and a passion long unsatisfied. It was all he could do not to throw himself atop her and spread her thighs. There were too many secrets between them, yet his body urged him on. He came up on an elbow and watched her sweet face, her eyes closed, her head thrown back. The mounds of her breasts taunted him until the animal in him wanted to rip the clothes from her body.

He leaned over her, bracing his hand on the rush-covered floor. He buried his face in her warm, sweet-smelling neck, feeling her hands creep over his shoulders to clutch his back. He kissed the soft skin of her jaw and cheek, fluttered his lips over her eyelashes. He wanted to explore every inch of her, but this wasn't the time or place. He needed privacy to teach her lovemaking. That thought alone almost doused the flames of his need. Teach her lovemaking? When he would have to eventually leave her for the monastery? Leave her, when she lay soft and open to him, forgetting the man who would marry her?

Reynold kissed her brow, pressing his cheek there for a moment. He lifted his head and saw her watching him intently. He opened his mouth to tell her he was sorry, but she surprised him by sliding her hand into his hair and pulling his head down for a kiss.

Chapter 8

$\sim\!\infty\!\sim$

Katherine shook with need as she brought Reynold's mouth to hers. His hair was short and soft between her fingers, his chest a warm pressure against her breasts. Part of her mind whispered that she was leading him towards something she could not finish, but her sly inner self relished his passion and his strength. He wanted her just as she was, without her dowry, regardless of her weak arm.

When he slanted his mouth across hers, she willingly parted her lips beneath the thrust of his tongue. She matched his exploration with her own and felt him groan deep in his throat. He tasted like man and ale, and her body trembled and pressed closer to his.

He slid his hand around her rib cage and slowly upward, capturing her breast and kneading it gently. Katherine gasped against his mouth and arched her back, one hip caught beneath his. He shifted suddenly until she lay beneath him, her skirts holding her legs trapped by his. The laces of her gown and undergarment seemed to magically give way at her back. She felt his hot breath on the bare skin of one shoulder as he followed her receding garments with kisses. Expectation began to build deep within her until she grew still, holding her breath, waiting, waiting as the rough wool slid unbearably down her breasts.

She knew the moment she lay exposed to him. With a sigh she opened heavy-lidded eyes and watched him hover just above the peak of her breast. She gasped air into her starved lungs, but could not continue breathing, caught in the anticipation of his touch.

"Beautiful Katherine," he whispered.

His breath teased her nipple and Katherine jerked once and went still. When his tongue finally touched her, she shuddered with the explosion of sensation that started at her breast and radiated out to the far points of her body, then back to burn between her thighs. He ground his hips into hers and the hard length of him tormented her.

Both breasts were bared to him, and Katherine could only hold his head against her, shivering beneath the assault of his tongue against her flesh. He drew her nipple deep within his mouth and she inhaled sharply. In that moment of stillness, she heard a sound that was not from either of them.

The rest of the world seemed to crash down on Katherine in an instant. There were people all around her doing the same thing that she was. Her eyelids flew open as she stiffened, wondering what she displayed to the world. Reynold had pulled the blanket over his head, and somehow that made everything worse. He had had enough realization of the people around them to shield her from view. He knew where they were, what they were doing. And still he had tormented her body as if they were alone. Had he intended to complete this act in front of strangers? While she lost her soul and mind to the sensations, was he just taking advantage of her willingness, regardless of who might watch them?

"Brother Reynold!" she hissed.

His whole body stiffened and he suddenly seemed heavy enough to crush her. He rested his cheek for a moment against her breast, while she trembled in hot humiliation. He lifted his head and looked up at her, his eyes dark, full of pain. Katherine realized she could not only be angry at him. She had allowed all this to happen, even encouraged it.

"Please," she whispered, trying to shift beneath him, ever aware that his body still longed for what she had begun. When she tugged at her gown, he lifted himself off her and rolled away. Katherine covered herself and turned onto her side in a tight ball of misery. She fumbled behind her neck at the laces, but Reynold brushed her hands aside and swiftly tied them.

She covered her ears against the voices that screamed inside her that Reynold had his vows, and that she was betrothed. Would she roast in hell for her sins? Would this be her punishment for thinking she could do a man's work and warn the king?

Reynold lay on his back, listening to Katherine sob softly to herself. He wanted to comfort her, to tell her it was his fault alone, but he knew she would not welcome the intrusion. Why couldn't things be simple? Why couldn't they have met and courted, and been given permission to marry by their families? Maybe Edmund would still be alive.

Instead she would wed some fool who ignored the treasure he had, and Reynold would go back to the monastery to serve penance for his crimes. His sister would have his inheritance to increase her dowry, and his brother, the earl, would have the power of having a family member rise through the ranks of the church hierarchy. Did his brother even care if it were Reynold or Edmund? Did he even notice the difference?

Reynold realized he was being cruel and unfair. He would follow his brother's wishes, for he deserved no better. He would rise through the church. He could not linger in a ruined monastery. The slow pace of life would allow him too much time to think of Katherine. He would make everyone happy but himself.

Reynold slowly turned his head and allowed his gaze to feast once more on Katherine. She lay quiet with her back to him, finally at peace in sleep. He regretted that his selfishness caused her pain and wished he could take on all her guilt himself. Instead he touched her hair, winding a curl around his finger.

In the morning, Katherine arose as the bells rang out lauds, and readied herself for mass as best she could. She silently followed Reynold to the chapel tower, with its apse built in a large window recess, and a colored glass window high above. On her knees on the cold stone floor, she prayed for strength to resist her weakness where Reynold was concerned. She thanked God for the absence of the marquess's son.

Katherine could not bring herself to look at Reynold during mass, for fear she'd be struck dead for her sins. Yet afterwards, in the great hall, where they ate hard black bread and ale, she peeked at him once, expecting to feel embarrassment. Instead, as he chewed his food, she remembered what his mouth had done to her breasts. As his hands broke open bread, she felt again his skin on hers, bringing to life feelings she thought had died a violent death at the hands of another monk. Her body betrayed her by flushing with warmth, not just for what he'd done to her physically, but for all he'd sacrificed to help her. And she repaid him by refusing to answer his questions, by returning his kisses then turning him away. She was no foolish maid too naive to understand what she did to him.

Reynold caught her stare and Katherine blushed and turned away. She just didn't understand why he seemed drawn to her. Surely he'd been away from women so long he'd take anyone. Yet last night many women had sent looks his way and he'd ignored them. Even now one of those women plopped herself down on the other side of Reynold and leaned towards him, showing most of her breasts.

"For such a big man, ye dance right fair," the woman said, her smile exposing a missing tooth. " 'Tis too bad ye couldn't save one for me instead of running off after yer girl there."

Reynold stopped smiling. "My wife."

Katherine's heart contracted for a moment in guilt, but she was also grateful for his devotion. She slid her hand into the crook of his arm.

"And I'm feelin' sorry for ye, too," the woman answered with a laugh. "Eh, well, no harm tryin'."

When the woman slid off the bench and moved away, Katherine removed her hand without looking at Reynold.

"Thank you," she whispered, then stood up to follow the rest of the travelers. She saw Reynold slip the loaf of bread into his magic sack before following.

A moment later he gripped her hand. "He comes."

She knew who he meant. The young nobleman staggered to his place at the head table, his face ashen. He lifted his head, his gaze drifting over the crowd, and saw them. Katherine froze, waiting for a call to arms, and the sounds of running soldiers.

Reynold leaned into her face and whispered, "Cower from me."

She cringed at the sudden anger he displayed for their audience. He grasped her hand and pulled her towards the wide door. Katherine felt more and more relieved as their ploy seemed to be working. She turned and looked over her shoulder at the nobleman, who gave her a lopsided grin. She waved back.

Reynold pulled her closer. "Mayhap you should not have done that."

"But now he thinks he was a success last night. Won't that aid us even further?"

He smiled. "You think quickly, Lady Katherine."

At his praise she felt warm inside, and forgot all about the nobleman. She looked into Reynold's eyes, and down to his lips, and remembered only him and the things he had done to her. But she must forget her wicked, selfish thoughts. Her mission to the king was far too important.

Katherine heard the rumble of thunder before she reached the castle doors. As Reynold came up behind her, she stopped in dismay and watched heavy sheets of rain turn the gloomy inner ward into a sea of mud.

"We could wait here a few hours," he said into her ear. "Others are. And perhaps Lord Oaf will pass out."

Katherine watched a few travelers laugh and turn back towards the fire. The peasant woman with eyes for Reynold smirked in their direction, pulled a wimple over her head, and stepped out into the rain with her small ragged group.

"I must hurry." Still embarrassed by her conduct last night, she said, "I could go alone."

Reynold eyed her for a moment, no emotion in
his face. Her breath caught in sudden panic.
Would he truly leave her, now that she had dis-
graced herself? She had known him for but a scant
few days. Perhaps intimacy was all he truly
wanted of her. Katherine shivered.

Reynold briefly bowed his head. "Your servant,
my lady," he said, without meeting her gaze.

Biting her lip, Katherine took a step out into the
courtyard and sank up to her ankles in mud. She
slogged on through it, watching each step for fear
she'd lose the only shoes she had. Reynold took
her arm and she leaned against him, shielding her
face from the stinging rain.

Reynold felt her grip on him tighten. Was it all
too much for her? Would she give up this mad
notion to see the king and let him take her home?
He wondered if she truly would have traveled
alone. Maybe he frightened her now, disgusted
her. He well knew that look in a woman's eyes.

"Katherine?" he said uncertainly.

She looked up, and as the rain hit her face, he
saw that her expression was serene.

"I have never, ever done anything like this in
my life," she said softly. "I didn't know I could."

Reynold didn't know how to answer except with
silence. She'd say hello to the king, or whatever
she meant to do, and he'd go back—back to that
place where no one laughed, where there were no
families, no women, no Katherine. His mouth

tightened with bitterness and he looked away from her, ignoring the flash of pain in her eyes.

Hours later, thunder boomed above them and lightning crackled dangerously close. They caught up with four fellow travelers and walked together for protection from the elements. As they passed through a deserted village, where sheep pastures had taken over farmland, Reynold followed the group's lead into a thatched-roof hut built on higher ground. The six adults milled about for a few minutes, then settled down in respective corners.

Katherine was wide awake. She sat on a damp pile of straw next to Reynold, her legs folded beneath her, resisting the temptation to lean against his strong arm. She relied on him too much, and he helped her more than any other man ever had. He seemed to believe in her, to trust her even though she refused to tell him the whole truth. That must be why she lost control of her emotions when he touched her.

No, she could not lie to herself. Just looking at his strong face and dimpled chin sent shivers through her breasts and between her thighs. She shamed her upbringing with these dangerous feelings. She could not blame Reynold for a weakness she obviously shared with him. The few times she'd met her future husband, James, they'd been properly chaperoned, perfectly polite and restrained. She looked back now and wondered why he never wanted to be alone with her, why he did not look at her with intensity like Reynold did. She knew it was because of her arm. James saw it as her weakness, her mark of imperfection.

Yet Reynold was ever concerned, giving aid when she needed it. With a shiver she remembered his arms crushing her against him, forceful but never hurtful, powerful but not overpowering. He had made her feel desired, needed, something she never thought she'd have. Though she knew little of James, she understood she was merely his means of begetting heirs. Would it be different with a man like Reynold? Although he seemed to desire her, he also respected her opinions, even enjoyed talking to her.

Katherine forgot herself and glanced at Reynold, not bothering to mask her anguish and her need to be loved and appreciated. He caught her gaze and they stared at one another. In his eyes she saw bitterness and longing. A moment later it was as if a mask dropped over the harsh lines of his face and he turned away.

Katherine ached for him. She understood what was it was like to know you had to follow your family's wishes. He was trapped the same way she was, but at least she would marry, perhaps have children. Reynold—he'd be locked behind high walls, with no one to love him. She knew there was something else that bothered him, but how could she ask him to trust her with all his secrets, when she didn't show her own trust?

Katherine reached up and touched Reynold's hair, knowing of no other way to soothe him. He stiffened but did not move away. She ran her fingers gently over his head, feeling the shape of his skull, the curls behind his ears. She heard him release a shuddering sigh as his head dropped forward.

"Should we stand out in the rain so ye can go at it?"

Katherine pulled her hand away and blushed in mortification as the peasant woman gave a raucous laugh. Her men snickered.

"What do ye say, love?" she continued, eyeing Reynold. "Forget that pale young thing. You and me can give 'em a day to remember."

Katherine didn't resist as Reynold drew her against his side.

"Enough, woman!" he commanded in a hard voice. "If you cannot speak politely to my wife, then hold your tongue."

The woman seemed to hiss at them as she straightened from her slouch. "Yer tongue may know some fancy tricks, I can't be doubtin', but 'tis yer speech that's got me thinkin'. Ye don't sound like one of us."

"I am happy to hear that."

Katherine winced, wishing he wouldn't have spoken so abruptly. The tension was palpable now, and the low, angry murmurs made her uneasy. She closed her eyes and prayed the rain would let up soon.

The clouds rolled back to reveal the half moon just after sunset. Katherine was so tense she thought she'd jump out of her skin at every cough from their companions across the hut. The group watched in sullen silence as Reynold lit a fire from dry bits of wood.

When he sat down beside her, Katherine spoke in a whisper. "Reynold, I need to go outside. I will return in but a moment."

He caught her arm as she rose. "I shall come with you."

"No! No, please, I am nervous enough. Just stay and watch them. I do not wish to be surprised."

"I can guard you best out there," he insisted, getting to his knees.

Katherine pushed him back. "Give me this moment of privacy—please!"

He hesitated, then slowly sank back down. As Katherine straightened, the group along the far wall broke into noisy laughter.

"She don't want ye, man, can't ye see," the woman said loudly.

They elbowed each other and guffawed. Katherine sent a worried gaze to Reynold and slipped quickly out the door.

After taking care of her needs, she leaned against a tree in the overgrown yard behind the hut, breathing in the moist, cool air, happy to be alone with her thoughts. She wished she could ask Reynold how far they still were from Nottingham, but their companions made speaking impossible. Katherine felt that her mind and heart were warring within her, one urging that she warn the king with all haste, the other wanting to linger on this journey and savor these stirrings she'd never felt before.

Her peace was suddenly shattered by the sound of rustling grasses nearby. The yard was so overgrown that an animal—or a man—could easily surprise her.

Katherine silently ran the opposite way, around the sagging walls of the hut to the front entrance. As she slowed down to catch her breath, she heard the peasant woman's unpleasant laugh.

"She's not coming back, ye know," the woman said.

Katherine heard a thud and a moan. She flattened herself against the wall, heart pounding.

"I sent Jack out to find her. He likes a good hump in the grass."

Biting her lips against a moan of terror, she gazed wildly about the overgrown village, where the wind whistled and the leaves whispered their menace. Someone was looking for her.

Chapter 9

The silence frightened Katherine more than anything. A man was looking for her, and Reynold was ominously quiet. What had they done to him? Holding her breath, she leaned over to take a quick peek inside and straightened with a smothered gasp. By the firelight she'd seen the villagers grouped around a body on the floor.

Her breath came in frightening pants that threatened her with dizziness. Reynold couldn't be dead—they were speaking to him as if they expected an answer. But he wasn't answering. Two tears slid down her cheeks before she remembered that there was a man out here somewhere. If she let herself be captured, she couldn't help Reynold.

Katherine sunk down to her hands and knees, slowly crawling back the way she'd come. The man hunting her wouldn't expect that, would he? The wet grass swished about her body, stinging her several times in the eyes and face, but she kept moving, stopping every few minutes to listen. She hit her hand on a piece of firewood someone had abandoned long ago, then gripped it like a weapon and continued to crawl.

A moment later she heard a branch crack directly in front of her. She dropped onto her side and held the firewood against her chest, waiting. He loomed above her in the grass as he trudged by, his head swinging from right to left.

Katherine held her breath until he'd passed, then scrambled up and hit him as hard as she could in the head. The sound of the wood connecting with his skull made her gag, but there was nothing in her stomach to lose. He crumpled at her feet and Katherine didn't check to see if he were alive or dead. Although it sickened her, she forced herself to search his body until she found a knife near his outstretched hand.

With a weapon, Katherine felt almost invincible. Yet she could hardly walk in the front door and confront two men and a woman by herself. She leaned against the wall in consternation and rising panic. She'd never had to defend someone else before. Did she have the strength to kill?

The wattle and daub wall seemed to give way beneath her weight and Katherine straightened rapidly. Frowning, she stared at it a moment, then dropped to her knees and began to scrape at the dried mud between the wood sticks in the wall. The mud crumbled to the ground and she dug faster, ignoring the slivers of wood that cut her hands. Soon she'd opened a small hole to which she pressed her eye. Her sight blurred for a moment then adjusted to the flickering firelight and the bodies moving about Reynold. He came up on his elbows and a man kicked him for his effort.

The woman emptied Reynold's sack onto the floor and dropped to her knees to root through his treasures. She gave a screech and flung the bag at her victim.

"Ye got nothin' but two shillin's? Ye're 'olding out on us. Search 'is clothes!"

Katherine gasped as the two men rolled Reynold onto his back and began to tug and pull at his tunic. Reynold groaned. Outraged, Katherine jumped to her feet and ran towards the front of the hut. She stood next to the crooked door frame and began to shriek at the top of her lungs.

From inside she heard the woman curse.

"Go tell Jack to shut 'er up!"

One of the men came lumbering through the door and Katherine hit him hard with her piece of firewood. He dropped to his knees, but it took another swing to send him into the mud. She turned in time to see the two remaining peasants charging towards her.

Katherine stumbled back in shock and raised her knife and branch, wondering how she would fight either of them, let alone two. But the man went down on his stomach before he even reached the door. She glimpsed Reynold raising himself up from the man's legs just as the woman launched herself into the air. Katherine fell backwards, squashed into the dank mud by the woman's solid body.

Katherine gasped and tried to bring the knife up, but the woman grappled for it. The mud made everything slippery, and the knife was caught at an awkward angle near Katherine's hip. She could smell the woman's foul breath, feel her own mind go foggy with lack of air. Just as the knife slipped from her fingers, the woman was yanked away. Reynold, angry and very intimidating, shook the peasant until she dropped the knife, then flung her to the ground.

"Go!" he shouted into the woman's pale mud-spattered face. "Go now before I change my mind and punish you as you deserve!"

The woman crawled through the mud before stumbling to her feet, then pulled at two of her groggy friends until they stood and reeled. The third man tripped over Katherine in his haste to leave the hut. The four thieves propelled each other down the mud road.

Reynold could hear the woman's cackling laugh. "I still got yer shillin's, lad!"

He took one menacing step in their direction, and the woman shrieked and dragged her men into a run.

"Katherine, are you hurt?" he demanded, feeling as if his head and heart were on fire at the same time. If she were injured, it would be his fault. Once again he had not protected her. He fell to his knees beside her and she surprised him by sitting up quickly and throwing her arms around his neck.

"Oh, Reynold, when I saw you just lying there, and I thought they had k-killed you—"

She made a funny, muffled sound and clung to him even tighter. Reynold picked her up and allowed himself the painful joy of just holding her, feeling her warmth and the weight of her against his chest. She shuddered and sighed in his arms, all the while dripping mud.

Reynold lifted his head from hers. "Did you see a well behind the hut?"

"Severely overgrown, I fear."

"It will do." He stomped through the high grass, feeling a sharp ache in his ribs with each step. He set Katherine down with great reluctance.

At the well, she removed her muddy gown and Reynold scrubbed it in a bucket of water, while she dabbed at the smock's dirty sleeves. Once they returned to the hut, Reynold had Katherine lay her gown near the fire as he added wood. His head ached, his side felt tight and painful, and he staggered when he rose to his feet.

"Reynold, you're hurt," she cried, sliding an arm about his waist. "Lay back in the straw."

He sat down heavily. She bent over him and he watched the flickering light through the strands of her hair. What had happened while she was alone with that cur?

"After they hit me, I thought I heard you scream," he said. Images he didn't want to imagine flickered through his mind. "Did he—"

"Oh, no, I had already seen to him."

He smiled in relief. " 'Seen to him'?"

"I hit him over the head." She blushed and lowered her face. "I screamed to lure one of them out. I hope I did not frighten you."

Reynold watched the curve of her cheek, and the dipping of her lashes. "You did, but it seemed to work."

"Show me where they hurt you," she said, pushing his shoulders back into the straw.

" 'Tis nothing but a bump on the head and some bruises. I do not remember much. I think I tried to get up."

"I saw them kick you. Oh, Reynold, your ribs could be broken."

Before he could stop her, she was pushing his tunic up over his stomach, ordering him to lift his hips when the garment caught. He couldn't have resisted her command for all the gold in the royal treasury.

"Katherine," he said, and his voice sounded ridiculously hoarse. He saw that she looked away from his hips. His genitals were only covered by his braies, a scant piece of linen. He was embarrassed by how obvious his desire was. "Katherine, do not—"

She hushed him and pressed along his chest. "Does anything I do hurt?"

He groaned and closed his eyes. Everything hurt. He was on fire for her, burning with his sin and his need, but the need was fast outpacing everything else. Her hands were cool on his flesh.

Her fingers brushed his nipple and his body betrayed him with a sudden shudder.

Katherine jerked her hands back, fearful that his injuries were worse than she had surmised. "Oh Reynold, I have hurt you. Show me where the pain is."

His words were muffled, almost a moan.

"Please, do not suffer in silence. Mayhap I can help you." She leaned forward over his chest, trying to keep her gaze on his face, but her hands shook and she couldn't seem to breathe deeply enough. She kept remembering the lean strength of his hips as he lifted them, and the dark hair on his chest that had dwindled down to . . . there. Though his tunic was caught beneath his arms, enough of his chest was visible for her to see up close the hills and valleys of muscle, the scars that dotted it like rivers across the earth.

He caught her upper arms and she gasped.

"Katherine," he whispered, then pulled her mouth down to his.

She quivered, off-balance and disoriented. She gasped air as his teeth and tongue devoured her mouth as if she were his first food after a long fast. She put her hands on his chest to push herself away, but one touch of his bare, hot flesh and she felt suddenly lost, drained of her will to resist. His kisses covered her cheeks and nose and eyelids and Katherine rubbed her skin against his stubbled cheeks. All her cares melted away in a haze of passion. Reynold wanted her, Reynold needed her. And she needed him, his strength, his devotion.

He moved his hands up her shoulders and over her back, pulling her down onto him, cupping her buttocks and grinding her hips into his.

Katherine cried out softly against his lips. When he hesitated, she slanted her open mouth, letting her tongue trace the lean curve of his lips. Her world reeled as Reynold rolled her onto her back and rose above her, shedding his tunic. She kneaded the hard muscles of his shoulders as she welcomed his weight. Her blood flowed quickly through her veins and a restless, aching yearning built inside her for Reynold's touch. The rough skin of his palm slid up her inner thigh and Katherine gasped and arched her body against him wanting—wanting—

The air was suddenly cool against her stomach and Katherine realized that the folds of her smock were being dragged up her body. It was unbearably exciting to feel the scratch of linen across her breasts, to see the firelight flicker over their bare skin. She raised her arms when he pulled the gown over her head. As he paused to look at her body, blind panic and self-doubt warred with her passion. She wanted to cover herself in shame but he caught her hands and kissed each palm.

"You are so beautiful," he murmured, spreading her arms wide as he leaned over her.

His mouth paused above one breast and she shivered at the warmth of his breath. His tongue darted out to lick her just once, and she felt as if her body were no longer her own as it shook beneath him.

"Reynold, please," she said with a gasp, and he rewarded her by sucking her nipple deep within his mouth. He lavished each breast with kisses until Katherine was mindlessly rolling her head back and forth, eyes closed in ecstasy. She never dreamed a man's touches could make her burn and writhe as if pleasure were a terrible torment.

His kisses seared her ribs, her navel, the upthrust bones of her hips. He gently spread her knees apart, and for a moment, Katherine was swept with such keen embarrassment she tried to force her legs closed.

Reynold held them apart, pressing kisses to the tender flesh of each thigh. Katherine shivered and shook, unable to stand more, but wishing it would never end. He pressed his mouth between her thighs and a bolt of the most delicious pleasure arched her back. She cried his name and he rose above her, lowering his weight between her legs. She should have been crushed; instead she felt fragile and feminine as he adjusted his body to hers. The firelight danced across the harsh lines of his face, the dominant brows, those magnificent eyes.

"Reynold," she whispered again in wonder, unable to believe the joyous things he made her feel. She felt the hard length of him probing her, and she was suddenly shy again, awkward, an innocent. What was she supposed to do? She raised her knees. He groaned and eased slowly inside her until the pressure became stretching, and the stretching, pain. With one thrust he sheathed himself fully, and Katherine bit back a cry of pain.

Reynold cradled her face between his hands, kissing her gently. "Sweet, sweet Katherine, it only hurts the first time."

The thought that she was no longer a virgin almost chilled her passion, but he picked that moment to lift himself and then slide back inside again, even deeper. Katherine groaned as his body slid roughly against hers, making her skin tingle with awareness and life, feeling again the vibrations of desire that only moments before had consumed her. She writhed against him and heard his quick intake of breath. Boldly nibbling his collarbone and neck, she let her hands slide from his shoulders and trail over the muscles of his chest. She caressed his nipples as he had done to hers, and was rewarded when he slid in and out of her, quickening, thrusting deeper and deeper, until Katherine forgot all about her exploration and fell into the mindlessness of pleasure.

The world retreated until it was only the two of them in growing darkness, their bodies undulating together, their breaths mingled, his hands caressing her breasts. Her body seemed to tighten in around itself, the pressure mounted, and after one more thrust of his hips, she was rocked by wave upon wave of such pure bliss that she shuddered for endless moments. He drove into her again and again, then with a hoarse groan stiffened above her. Katherine held him as he shook, then with tender care guided his head down beside hers, and put her arms around his shoulders. She kissed his warm chest, and the damp side of his neck. She felt fragile and protected by his body all around and inside her.

"I must be crushing you," he murmured into her ear.

Katherine shook her head, then sighed in dismay when he lifted himself off her and to one side. She looked down at herself and saw with a bit of shock that she was totally and completely naked, except for red marks of passion across her breasts. While she gaped at her body, Reynold drew their discarded garments over them. He reached to pull her closer and left his arm resting across her chest, his head pillowed in the straw next to hers, his breath soft and warm against her ear.

Katherine felt the first strains of panic begin to tug at her mind. The straw itched her back and his breath tickled her ear and his arm hugged her breasts and she felt so . . . sticky. While she debated what she should say, Reynold snored once, softly.

Katherine groaned. She should push him away, leave, do something, but he was so warm. She simply lay there, realizing with growing dismay that she had just allowed a man she'd only known four days to take her virginity, the one prize every husband expected as his due. Her lower lip began to tremble and she bit it. Perhaps this was why her mother spent each day in prayer. Did she sense how sinful Katherine was? Did she somehow know that her daughter would one day turn her back on all she'd been taught, even forget that a monk had almost raped her once? A hysterical giggle bubbled in her throat. She'd let another monk have her, and willingly, too. She threw an arm across her eyes and listened to Reynold breathe.

Katherine awoke with a start, panicking in the darkness, relaxing when she saw the dull embers of the dying fire. Cool air chilled her side and she realized that Reynold no longer lay beside her. For a moment she thought he'd left her, after taking all that he had wanted, but she couldn't believe such things of him. She propped herself up on one elbow and saw him at once, kneeling beside the fire, head bowed, unmoving.

Chapter 10

Reynold was filled with remorse, his eyes burning as they stared hard into the fire. What had he done? What horrible selfishness, what evil, had taken over his mind and soul again? He had ravaged Katherine's gift of virginity, meant for her husband. She had not understood where desire would lead her; none of this was her fault.

But he had known, Reynold thought, clapping his palms over his eyes and arching his head back in agony. He had known, and allowed the passion to overtake his conscience and his will, destroying his vow to God and himself and his family. Had he no honor? Had his brother's death meant nothing to him? He looked down at his body with a virulent hatred. If only he could beat it out of himself, this terrible weakness, this hunger for Katherine.

I have failed, he thought, gripped by a despair so bleak it was painful. He sat back on his heels, head bowed, and found himself sinking to the floor, his cheek pressed to the cold dirt, eyes squeezed tightly shut. He had betrayed himself, but mostly he had betrayed Katherine.

Tears streamed down Katherine's face as she watched Reynold collapse to the floor. Her chest ached with the sobs that built inside her, yet had to be repressed. Horrible guilt twisted her heart, blotting out all of the good she thought she'd done with her life. Her own self-pity seemed to pale beside the torment Reynold was suffering. She had broken a vow to her betrothed, but he had broken a vow to God. She ached to comfort him, to tell him it was all her fault. But he would not want her pity.

I am so sorry, she thought over and over again, wishing she could take back their sin. She had always known there was something . . . tarnished inside her.

She never thought she'd be able to sleep, watching Reynold huddled by the fire. But suddenly it was morning and Katherine was alone in the hut. She did not worry that in his grief, Reynold had left her. She knew him too well, her fondness for him tainted with sorrow.

Reynold stood at the edge of the road, staring out across the rolling, mist-drenched fields. He felt alone and friendless, a sinful man who deserved nothing more than that. It seemed hard to expect anything decent of himself anymore. He was no sooner fifty feet from the monastery, than he was lusting after an innocent virgin, a girl betrothed.

Gritting his teeth, he rubbed the ache building across his forehead. Had he forced her to accept his help, while some hidden part of him had rubbed its hands gleefully, ready for seduction?

Reynold refused to accept it. He could not believe he would use any excuse for sex. There was something about Katherine, with her clumsiness and her bravery when any other woman would have run home to her father. She was convinced of the rightness of her cause, whatever it truly was, and no danger could stop her. And she was not afraid of him.

Reynold grimaced and kicked at a tall stalk of grass. She hadn't counted on him and his uncontrollable lust. Even now, as she appeared hesitantly in the doorway, he had the dark urge to throw her to the ground and part her legs and—

"Reynold?"

Katherine heard her voice crack. She must force aside this nervousness, this sorrow. Reynold was suffering, but she must not add to it. He looked so alone as he stood there in the fog, his face impassive yet tired, as if he'd remained awake the entire night. She suddenly didn't know what else to say, how to atone for their sin. She could only stare at him, but he wouldn't meet her gaze.

He began to walk towards her, his head down. Katherine remained frozen in the doorway, afraid of what he would do. Would Reynold berate her? Would he leave her at the next village? But as he continued to move closer, her heart pounded with the anticipation that he might touch her, might hold her, might even—she shook her head to banish such dark, tormentingly sweet thoughts.

Reynold halted before her, and Katherine found herself staring into his broad chest. She was afraid to look up and see her punishment written across his face.

Suddenly he dropped to his knees before her, his bowed head level with her chest. Katherine could only tremble as he took her hands in his and pressed his face to them.

"Forgive me, my lady," he said, his voice a husky whisper. "I have violated the trust you have shown me."

Katherine's sorrow spilled out in hot tears that fell from her eyes. She wanted to touch his soft hair, to pull his head to her breast and comfort him. But still he squeezed her hands in tight desperation.

"Reynold," she whispered, taking painful pleasure in the mere sound of his name on her lips. "I, too, have sinned and you must not take all the blame."

He lifted his head. "You but sinned in ignorance," he said passionately, his blazing eyes burning into hers. "But I—I knew what I was doing. I should have stopped—"

She covered his mouth with her fingers, then snatched them away when he stiffened. "Regrets are futile. It is done. Stand, Reynold. Lead me to the king. Then you will not have to bother with me."

"Bother?" He seemed to choke on the word, but said no more.

He rose to his feet, a dark mountain of a man she once feared, but now she—she thrust such thoughts away. What had she been thinking, what foolish dreams had threatened her plans? Her own life was not to be thought of—she must get to the king.

The midday sun had finally burned away the last of the fog, leaving the ground steaming with mud. Reynold, morose and tired, tried to hang back from the group of peasants ahead of them. He had known he would have to be very careful in this remote section of Nottinghamshire. He had deliberately avoided the toll roads, where they might be seen by unfriendly eyes. It had entailed a slight risk, coming this close to Bolton lands. He'd only passed through a few times on his way to Oxford, so he prayed he would not be recognized.

He couldn't understand why there were so many groups of peasants on the road. The ones before them pushed carts piled with freshly picked vegetables. A young girl in a dirty brown dress turned to stare at them, her face brightening with a smile. Reynold looked away, wishing he wore a hat for protection from curious girls. He hoped his two-day growth of whiskers would be disguise enough. An older woman admonished the girl, who turned away with a giggle. But soon she looked back again, and gave them a small wave. Katherine returned the gesture.

"What are you doing?" Reynold demanded in a tight voice. "You but call attention to us."

Katherine kept her gaze on the road. "I thought I had learned my lesson. If we act suspiciously, they will suspect us, is that not correct?"

Reynold could have bitten his own tongue. He hated having his words thrown back in his face. Farther north their presence did not matter, but here—

"From now on, keep your head down and ignore them."

Her deep, blue eyes flashed at him once, then she raised her chin and kept walking. Reynold tried to slow their pace, but short of crawling, they couldn't help but catch up with the peasants. He groaned softly when the young girl immediately tried to make conversation with Katherine. Even he felt the sweet tug of the girl's youth, with the freckles across her nose and two of her teeth missing. Reynold hung back and tried not to be drawn in. He morosely watched the trees on either side.

Katherine slowed her pace just as the group veered down another road. "Let us go with them, Reynold."

"No."

"They are bound for the earl's castle. They said it is just down this road. Perhaps we can spend the night."

Reynold stared at her, his bitterness almost overwhelming. "Are you afraid to be alone with me?"

She looked down, and her long lashes swept her cheeks, hiding those magnificent eyes. "I am afraid of myself."

"Katherine—"

"Please, let us be warm and dry and safe to-night."

He watched the retreating backs of the peasants, saw the girl turn and entreat them to follow. "If I thought it were wise, we would. But Katherine—"

"I am going with them, Reynold. I have to." She straightened, looking up into his eyes. "We shall have help from the earl."

Reynold came to a halt in a mud puddle that felt like it was sucking on his feet. He saw the faint blush across her cheeks, the way she clasped her hands together.

"You do not trust that I can protect you?"

" 'Tis not that! Here we can acquire money, horses, an escort. James will help me—I know he will!"

Katherine tugged on his arm, but Reynold barely felt it. He stared at her, feeling his soul sinking deeper and deeper into torment so foul he thought he'd be sick. Of course. James. He should have known. She was Lady Katherine Berkeley, and she was betrothed to the Earl of Bolton—his half-brother.

Katherine continued to pull on his arm, and Reynold stumbled along, too despairing to resist any longer. How the hell had she ended up at his monastery? What mystery was she the center of?

The guilt of all he'd wrought pounded his headache to blazing proportions. As if he hadn't already done enough to James, he'd seduced his betrothed. He'd taken her virginity, something his rigid brother would prize highly. Katherine didn't seem to notice that anything was wrong with him, though he felt his eyes were bulging out of his head as he stared desperately at her for what felt like the last time. Already she was leaving him, pulling him toward her future husband's home. He wanted to crush her to him, whisper his sorrow and his apologies, inhale the scent of her one last time.

The smile she bestowed on him was fraught with tension. If only she didn't have to know. She'd hate herself even more for what they'd shared the past night. Reynold knew the servants weren't likely to recognize him. He and his brother were never close, and he'd seldom visited. James was the product of their mother's first marriage, and he'd been fostered out at a young age to train for the earldom he'd already inherited from his dead father. Reynold had mostly grown up in his own father's home, when he wasn't being fostered at his cousin's. Though Reynold had inherited a few manors when his father died, James had never let him forget the difference in their status. It hardly made Reynold feel brotherly. Besides, he had known how it upset James to have his younger brother bigger and stronger than him. He had never felt comfortable in Bolton castle, so his few visits had only been when he needed a place to stay for a night. In the mornings he had quickly gone.

Yet if he could stay in the background, disguised by his clothes and the ragged beginnings of a beard, there was a good chance James wouldn't see him. Trying desperately to ease his conscience, Reynold thought perhaps he could accomplish this one last deed for Katherine. He would quickly return to the monastery, and she would never know with whom she'd committed her only sin.

The memory of their dark night together stirred in him unholy thoughts. How he still wanted her. He watched her back, knowing what the baggy clothes hid. If he closed his eyes he could see her breasts by firelight, feel the silkiness of her thigh, hear the soft, feminine gasps of her pleasure. He was hard just remembering how she'd touched him. He so wanted to believe that in some part of her heart she had loved him, even just a little.

"Reynold!"

He glanced up, sighing as he watched the wind dance with her blond hair. She was so beautiful he ached with the sight. But she wasn't his. This pain was just one more thing he would have to suffer because he took Edmund's life.

"Hurry!" she said. "Soon it shall be dark and they will close the gate!"

Katherine only spared one last glance for Reynold, and even that silly mistake cost her a twisted ankle. She frowned at her clumsy limbs, but the pain was slight and she was used to it. Nothing could stop her. She was close to knights and armor

and horses, all of which could help King Richard.
Katherine grew cold at the thought of facing
James. Would she tell him of her sin? Perhaps
she'd know what to say after they'd helped the
king.

She tried to think how close she was to accom-
plishing her mission, but the thought of her sin
had brought the night rushing back like some
darkly tormented dream. There had been nothing
frightening about what Reynold had done to her.
In fact, it seemed like she'd been another woman,
a woman whose flesh burned for a man.

Katherine looked back once more to find Reynold watching her, with those eyes that shone out
from beneath his heavy brows as if he could see
everything about her. And he had. She blushed
and turned forward, following the excited young
girl. She could no longer compare Reynold to that
other monk. That man had deliberately misled an
innocent. Katherine was not innocent any more.
And Reynold had never lied to her or tried to
thrust upon her something she wasn't prepared
for. She flushed in shame as she remembered
pushing his garments aside. Had she truly been
concerned for his injuries? Or could she only think
of his body?

No, no, no, she was confusing everything. She
cared for him, she worried about him, and all of
those emotions had weakened her ability to resist
what she should have. She should have saved herself for her husband. Katherine tried to picture
what lovemaking would be like with James. But

he had never shown any passion, never held her hand for more than a moment to press his lips there. She had always told herself it was because of her arm and her clumsiness, but that did not seem to matter to Reynold.

Katherine lost a shoe in ankle-deep mud. She bent over to retrieve it and hopped as she tried to put it back on. She felt a hand clasp her elbow and knew Reynold was there once more, as he always was. She slowly straightened and looked up, up, into his hooded amethyst eyes. He looked at her without speaking, and Katherine couldn't tear her gaze away. His hand burned the flesh of her arm. She remembered his fingers inside her body, his mouth plundering hers. Katherine caught her breath and found herself staring at his lips. Would he kiss her? Would she let him, here under the bright sun?

Instead, Reynold seemed to break away with a violence she didn't associate with him. He pulled his magic sack off his shoulder, and began to root through it, his movements abrupt. They partially blocked the road and people streamed by them, jostling Katherine.

"Reynold, what are you doing?" she finally whispered.

He ignored her as he pulled out a handful of wadded material. With no warning, he tossed the sack at her and she caught it hard against her chest. He separated his prize into two handfuls, one of which he tucked under his arm, while the other he pulled over his head. Her mouth dropped

open in stunned surprise as he arranged the peasant hood under his neck and partially down his
back. The other bundle of material he spread open
to reveal a wrinkled black cloth hat with a sad-
looking brim. He jammed it on top of his head,
pulled it down as far as it could go, then took back
his sack.

Katherine finally found words. "Why are you
wearing that on such a hot day?"

Reynold gave her a look of impatience, something she'd never seen on his face. "I was a knight
well-traveled throughout the kingdom. How long
do you think our luck will hold and no one rec-
ognizes me?"

She had no answer, for he made perfect sense.
But she sensed something else was wrong, something deeper, darker. He gave her a black look and
strode on ahead of her, not waiting to see if she
tripped or kept up with him. Perhaps he blamed
her for leading him from his religious vows, but it
had not seemed so last night. Katherine frowned
as she picked up her skirts to hurry, wishing that
she had not complicated everything by surrender-
ing to her darker side.

They came around a stand of trees to see a castle
pointing up to the heavens with high towers con-
nected by walkways and battlements. Guards
marched, or stood imposingly silent, keeping
watch. Twin stone towers flanked the gatehouse
and appeared to stand in judgment as they looked
down upon her.

Reynold stared broodingly at the ground. She

missed his reassuring smile. Everything about him seemed like a different person. What had she done to him?

The peasants in front of them grew quiet as they lined up in twos to pass through the gatehouse. The wait was long and each step forward slow. The sky reddened as the sun set, and the wind took on a chill.

Katherine's nerves began to fail her. The dark tunnel of the gatehouse was an open mouth, with the portcullis like teeth about to crush her from above. Would any of these people let her see James, dressed as she was? She knew she looked filthy and her hair blew wildly about her face. Perhaps she shouldn't announce her identity immediately. She could wait until she saw James, and he would recognize her. She wondered how guilty she'd feel when she saw her betrothed. Her stomach plummeted back to her toes again.

The tunnel arched above her for a moment, then everything seemed to fade away to black. Katherine felt Reynold's presence beside her, heard the coughs of the people ahead. Wind whistled through arrow loops. Katherine felt as if all the guards were peering at her through the holes, knowing that she'd betrayed their lord.

The evening sky appeared once again above her and Katherine breathed a sigh of relief. Up ahead, guards were digging through the possessions of every peasant, confiscating anything larger than an eating knife.

Katherine watched Reynold open his sack with

apparent resignation, but he kept his head low-ered, as if the guards awed or frightened him. Katherine knew this was an act, yet he hadn't felt the need before. Why now? What was different about this place? He'd been very adamant about staying away from Bolton's castle.

She frowned as she watched the guards yank the sack from Reynold's hands and dump the contents onto the ground. As they kicked through it, Rey-nold remained silent, even his fists unclenched, as if watching their invasion provoked no reaction in him. But Katherine could sense the wild violence building inside him, the restraint he barely held onto. He seemed consumed with anger. What had one night of passion done to him? Was this one more sin to add to her growing list?

When the guards dropped the sack and returned to the gatehouse, Katherine went down on her knees to pack Reynold's things. He stood beside her, unmoving, making no effort to help. She looked up once to catch his gaze burning down upon her. She saw the hunger and the pain for only a moment before his face formed once more into lines of stubborn silence and bitterness.

Katherine suddenly shivered as if winter were descending instead of a cool summer evening. All because of one glance from Reynold. She dropped a coil of rope she was holding, appalled by the way her hands tingled.

She gasped as Reynold squatted down beside her, swept everything into the sack with one well-muscled arm, and then stalked away from her towards the castle residence. Katherine stared after him, her mouth hung open in shock. What had she done to turn her chivalrous monk into this cold stranger?

Chapter 11

~~~OGO~~~

Katherine bit back a startled cry as rough hands grasped her under the arms and helped her up. She turned to meet the warm gaze of the peasant girl's mother, a coarse old woman who barely reached Katherine's chin.

The woman clucked and rolled her eyes. "Husbands," she grunted in sympathy. "Don't ever try to figure 'em out."

With that wisdom, she pushed Katherine on ahead of her, towards the massive double doors through which Reynold had disappeared.

Katherine took the stairs up into the great hall on the second floor and stopped in sheer dismay. The smells and noise of what must be a hundred people were like a wall keeping her out. Table after table overflowed with villagers and travelers and soldiers, laughing and shouting. Serving girls bustled about like bees in a hive, carrying massive platters stacked with meat. The whitewashed walls soared high above her head, and were decorated with magnificently stitched wall hangings of exotic colors. Stone hearths higher than a man dominated each end of the room, giving off their smoky light.

But that was not the only source of light. Arching her neck, Katherine looked high above and saw the faint reddish glow of the setting sun through a massive glazed window. She couldn't help gaping at it as if she were a peasant, not the daughter of an earl.

A solid bump across Katherine's legs made her lose her balance. She caught the door beams for support just as one of the castle dogs scurried away. She held onto the doorway tightly and gazed with dismay on everything before her. She should be elated. Her betrothed appeared a rich man, not one who needed her solely for her money. But Katherine was terrified. She had never seen so many people in her life. How would the mistress of this castle control everything? Her upbringing only involved the gentle country life of a small estate. James Markham, Earl of Bolton, might as well ask her to be mayor of London!

Katherine felt lost, unsure, and suddenly ridiculous for thinking she could run off and warn the king about noble traitors. Look what she'd gotten herself into! She'd lost her virginity, seduced a monk from his vows, and her betrothed would probably never speak to her again.

All she wanted to do was run. She turned and smashed her nose into the metal-plated chest of a soldier. He leered down at her out of a face made homely by a broken nose and only one ear. Katherine didn't want to faint. But the room was so hot and smoky, and she was being pushed and elbowed.

"Katherine?"

She sagged in relief and Reynold caught her from behind. She turned and put her arms around him, not caring what he must think after she'd sworn to put their past behind her.

"Reynold," she whispered against his neck. My protector, she thought.

"Are you ill?"

She shook her head, remaining still, wondering what was wrong. Then she understood. Reynold kept his arms by his sides, not returning her embrace. *He must hate me*, Katherine thought, squeezing her eyes shut to force back the tears. *I've not only ruined my life, I've ruined his*.

She stepped away and looked up into his face. He didn't appear angry; he showed no emotion at all except perhaps polite concern.

"I am fine," she said, cursing her hoarse voice. "My stomach is merely protesting its emptiness."

"I have found us a place to sit," he said, walking ahead to lead the way.

Katherine saw his magic sack perched on the edge of a crowded table, as if daring someone to steal it. She touched the cloth bag briefly before sitting down. Reynold squeezed in beside her, murmuring his apologies. Katherine's evening was already a failure, and she still hadn't thought about how she should inquire after the earl.

*　　*　　*

As the evening revelry began, Reynold slouched on a bench beside Katherine, his back propped against the wall, his chin on his chest. He tried to give the appearance of a man longing for sleep, but his eyes were so watchful beneath the brim of his hat that they ached. He wondered when Katherine was going to begin her search for the family's private apartments, but she seemed in no hurry, and that was just fine with him. She sat beside him with her back straight, her hands folded delicately in her lap, her golden hair flowing down her shoulders and over her breasts. He should procure her a wimple to cover her hair—she looked like a young maiden, instead of his wife.

He turned away and crossed his arms over his chest, trying to let his anger and bitterness dissolve. He was so torn with these emotions that his head ached constantly. His neck hurt from keeping his face hidden from the servants, though none even looked familiar to him.

With growing dread he watched the hall that led to the family's apartments, feeling every moment that his brother would stride in and spot them immediately. Which was exactly what Katherine wanted. When James found her, Reynold would just have to fade into the background.

Katherine finally gathered her last bit of courage and stood up. She turned to Reynold, who watched her with what seemed like resignation.

"I'll find James by myself," she said, wincing when he didn't offer his aid. "It will be better if he doesn't question you. If—if you wish, you could slip away during the night. I'll never tell anyone."

Tears stung Katherine's eyes at the thought of never seeing him again. She had given to him what she'd never given another man, spent every moment of the last four days in his company. Her life wouldn't be the same without him trailing her every step.

"I shall not leave until I know you are protected," Reynold said, sitting up straighter, his face just beneath hers.

Katherine found herself entranced, staring into his hard face with its burning eyes. She longed to trace those heavy brows with a finger, ease the tension she saw there. She wanted to hold him, perhaps for the last time.

She gently rested her hands on his shoulders, rubbing them for a moment, then touched his jaw with trembling fingers. Reynold clenched his eyes shut as if in pain, then with a groan he wrapped his arms around her and pressed his face between her breasts. Katherine rested her cheek against his head and closed her eyes. She didn't know why she inspired such feeling in Reynold, but she thanked heaven she had experienced it at least once in her life.

"I must go," she whispered. "I don't know how to thank you for all that you've done for me."

When she would have broken away, Reynold held her tighter. He looked into her face for a moment, then sighed. "The stairs to the family's apartments are over there," he said, pointing to the center of the far wall, where a blaze of torches dwindled up a staircase that wound into the depths of the castle.

"How did you—"

He touched her lips with his finger. "I knew whom to ask. Just go, Katherine."

She kissed him quickly, then walked away.

As she walked down the deserted hall, Katherine began to think Reynold had been given the wrong directions. She passed no one on her journey, neither a servant, nor a finely dressed member of the family. She began to open doors along the passage and found nothing but simple bedrooms with bare beds and plain walls. Where were all the people? Where was her betrothed?

From down the corridor she heard the faintest echo of footsteps on the stairs. Katherine quickly pulled a candle and its holder from a recessed stone shelf and stepped into the final room. It was wide, with high ceilings, and a large window cut deep into the opposite stone wall. Dark curtains hung from the bed, and every chair was cushioned. But it was also deserted; no earl, no family, no fire in the hearth. James must be away.

Katherine closed her eyes as weariness assailed her. She would have no horses or armies to help her save the king. It would be just her and Reynold. At the thought of him, she felt a glimmer of hope. He was more than capable of protecting her and seeing her safely to King Richard. Now if only she could forget what had happened between them.

She would try to keep the image of this room, someday to be hers, in her mind. This is where she would sleep, where her children would be born. She couldn't help thinking how dark and depressing it looked by gloomy candlelight. She would just have to arrange things to her own taste—if James would let her. Katherine sighed and turned to leave.

The door was suddenly flung open and then banged shut. The draft blew out the candle. Terrified at being discovered, Katherine dropped the useless candle and began to back up.

"I've found ye, liedy."

At the sound of his voice, she bit back a moan. It was him, the man who had breathed into her ear for two days, and held her waist with crude delight.

Her pounding heart seemed to echo through the room as Katherine tripped over a chair, then righted herself. Her only advantage was that she could still remember the layout of the room. She held her breath and eased her way towards the bed.

"Come, liedy, let's not make this 'ard on yourself. I'm mad enough 'bout whot your friend did to me. Hit me right 'ard, he did."

Her leg bumped the edge of the bed.

"I'm sick o' followin' you, liedy. And I'm losin' me temper. Just give up, and I'll go easy on ye."

Katherine's hand skimmed a bedpost and she

latched onto it in desperation. Could she lure him this way, scramble across the bed and reach the door before he did? She heard his dreadful breathing and held her own breath to keep from whimpering aloud.

The door suddenly opened again.

"Katherine?"

"Watch out!" she screamed as the kidnapper flung himself at Reynold, slamming his body into the door frame. She couldn't see much by the hall torches except their bodies entwined and rolling on the stone floor. She turned and felt along the table beside the bed, looking for something, anything to use as a weapon. She found a heavy candleholder and raised it above her head. But how could she tell which was the thief and which was Reynold?

The shuffle of heavy boots in the hall preceded the sudden blinding thrust of torchlight into the room. Katherine shielded her eyes.

"Halt!" someone cried.

She saw firelight glitter on drawn swords. Two soldiers pulled Reynold and the man apart.

"Thieves!" the kidnapper cried. "I followed 'em up here to see whot they was doin'. They were goin' to kill me!"

" 'Tis a lie," Reynold insisted, his voice dignified and calm. His hood was askew, and she saw the silly hat clenched tightly in his fist.

Katherine thought they had a chance at being believed until the red-haired man pointed directly at her.

"Look whot she's got!"

In dismay, she saw that she still clutched the candleholder, and it shone silver by torchlight.

"But I was trying to—"

Two soldiers clasped her by the arms, yanking away her only weapon of defense. The sergeant appeared to be the only one dressed in armor, ancient though it was even by Katherine's poor standards.

"We'll let 'is lordship decide which of you three is thieves. To the dungeon!"

"Wait!" Katherine cried, trying to give her voice a depth of authority. "My name is Lady Katherine Berkeley and I am the future wife of Lord Bolton."

The room remained silent as Katherine bit her lip and deliberately avoided looking at Reynold. How she hated to hurt him like this! But it was best he knew the truth. Now she would be in a position to help him, to help the king.

Then the laughter started, each man following the other until the room rang with it, pounding into her head. Only Reynold was still, his head lowered.

"You don't believe me?" she demanded, struggling against her captors.

The sergeant wiped a gloved hand across his mouth. "Now, girl, it's not that ye couldn't look real pretty if ye were . . . cleaned up a bit. It's a shame ye didn't think out your plan sooner. You could have—washed."

Katherine felt her face flush with humiliation as they continued to laugh at her. "I'm telling you the truth! When his lordship returns, he'll have you all—" She struggled to think of the worst torture they could endure, but her sheltered experiences left her at a loss. "—severely punished!"

They continued to laugh uproariously as they led her away.

Reynold looked at her once, then turned his head.

The walk through the depths of the castle was one of the most humiliating moments of Katherine's life. Everyone stared or smirked until she had no choice but to raise her chin and try to look unjustly accused.

At the rear of the giant residence, the ground sloped sharply downward. The group walked beside a high wall, and the chill of the stone made Katherine shiver. Finally they were led into a round tower in a corner of the curtain wall. Before her, Katherine saw two wooden doors imbedded into the dirt. She raised her puzzled gaze to Reynold, and felt herself chill as she saw the taut line of his jaw and the clenched fists.

One of the guards raised the trap door and the foul odor that rose from the pit made Katherine's knees weak with the beginnings of pure terror.

"You can't put a lady down there," Reynold said.

"No, we can't," agreed the guard. "But then she's not a liedy. Unless ye'd like 'er to keep us company?"

A choking sound escaped Katherine's throat.

"There are only two dungeons?" Reynold asked. The sergeant nodded.

"Then she goes down with me."

"Men separate from the women. We can't give ye all the fun, now can we?"

The kidnapper snorted his agreement.

But Reynold was watching Katherine. He saw the instinctive terror in her eyes, the way her body shook. He felt a sudden need to get the negotiations over with, because she didn't look as if she could hold back her screams another minute.

"Look at her!" he shouted. "Do you want to be responsible for what happens to her down there? What if she's who she says she is?"

They all snickered and elbowed each other.

"Can you take the chance of mistreating her? I'll protect her. I'll keep her safe."

The sergeant turned to watch as Katherine sagged in her captors' arms, backing away from the pit.

"Oh all right. The two go in together. You first." He pointed to Reynold.

"No," he said. "I cannot trust that you will send her down after me. She goes in first and I shall follow."

"No," Katherine whispered, as they dragged her toward the pit. "No, please! I can't go in there!"

Chapter 12

❝**I** am coming, I promise,❞ Reynold said, willing Katherine to obey him this once. While his fear for her grew, his bitterness and anger fled.

She clawed at the arm of one of the soldiers as he tried to release her near the edge. He slapped her hard and with a cry, she swayed out over the gaping hole. Reynold surged forward and staggered as the two soldiers gripped his arms.

The sergeant put a hand on Reynold's chest, and spoke over his shoulder to his men. "Leave the girl alone. Bring up the rope."

Katherine wept, hands covering her face, shoulders trembling. Reynold's throat tightened. This was all his fault. If only he'd trusted his instincts and dragged Katherine away from his brother's castle. Watching her defeat was almost unbearable.

"She will not be able to climb down," he said. "She has a weak arm."

Katherine lowered her hands from her face and glared at him. Ahh, some spirit, Reynold thought with relief.

The soldier pulled up the rope which was attached to a stake near the trap door. He displayed a loop on the end. "We'll lower 'er in."

"You're making a mistake," Katherine said with a hoarse voice. "I am truly Lady Katherine Berkeley, and I'm here for Lord Bolton's help!"

"Save yer pretty speech for 'is lordship," said the sergeant as he fitted the loop around the arch of her foot.

"When will the earl return?" Reynold asked.

The red-haired kidnapper laughed. "Not soon enough for you, Brother." He lounged against the soldiers' restraint, then poked his tongue out between the hole where his two front teeth should be. Reynold gave him a cool stare.

Two guards stood on either side of Katherine and lifted the rope straight up in front of her, directing her to hold onto it. A moment later they lifted and suspended her over the pit. Katherine screamed as the rope swayed and spun.

"Hold on tight!" Reynold yelled.

"Help me!" Her voice sounded feeble as she sank into the depths of the pit. Then he heard nothing but her soft weeping.

"Pull up the rope!" Reynold shrugged off the guards and stood at the edge of the pit, looking down into the blackness. He straightened his hood and jammed the hat back in place. "Can we have a torch?"

"What, so ye can set a fire we'd have to haul ye out of?" The sergeant laughed.

Reynold stood at the opening, watching as a soldier drew up the rope. For one wild moment he thought about taking them all on. His arm trembled with the need to grip a sword; his heart pounded with the lust for bloodshed. Yet he stepped back from his old ways. One against five armed men would not give him victory. And then Katherine would be left to satisfy their anger.

Reynold put his foot in the loop and turned his back to the pit, watching as three men braced themselves for his weight. He eased his foot over the edge and stepped onto the rope. They grunted and the rope slipped through their hands. Reynold lurched to a halt, feeling his stomach plummet to his feet. If they dropped him, Katherine would be alone. Inch by inch, the creaking rope lowered him.

"Move, Katherine. I do not wish to land on you."

The air grew cooler as he descended. The foul odor wafted around him, yet didn't overpower. When he touched the ground, Reynold released the rope and listened as it swished through the air on its way up. The hatch slammed shut, rendering the darkness complete.

"Katherine?" Reynold shuffled his feet through what must be layers of straw and debris. He heard the distant skittering of tiny creatures. "Katherine, where are you?"

"Here," she whispered.

He reached out towards the sound of her voice and found her shaking body. He drew her into his arms and let her weep against his chest.

"I am so sorry," he said into the hair above her ear. "I wish I could have protected you from this."

" 'Tis my fault," she whispered, clutching him even more tightly. "I should have told you . . . everything. I should have—"

He touched her lips to still her voice. When his fingers lingered, he pulled them away. "Shall we explore our new quarters and see what we can sit upon?"

Katherine nodded, and her hair caressed his chin.

"Here, hold my hand."

He grasped her fingers in one hand and held the other one straight out in front of him. Before he hit a wall, Katherine stumbled. He yanked her upright.

"Let me guess," Reynold said. "Was it your gown, your shoes, your—"

Katherine hit him in the arm. " 'Tis a wooden bucket, I think. Let me see."

"Do not touch it! You never know who has been here before us."

Katherine made a choking sound. "I had not thought of that."

Reynold stuck out a toe until he tapped the object. The smell that arose made him turn away. "Let us hope for rescue before we must resort to this." He kicked the offending bucket away.

"Reynold," she whispered.

He could hear the tears just beneath her words. Sliding an arm around her shoulders, he guided her forward. "We shall think about everything else later. I found a wall."

Together they patted the wet, uneven stone and moved towards their right. Soon Reynold banged his shin on a rickety pallet. He ran his hands along it and found the ragged remains of one woolen blanket.

"How thoughtful of them," he murmured.

"What is it?" Katherine asked from the darkness beside him.

"A blanket—I think." He shook it out as best he could, then offered it to her.

"No, thank you."

Her distaste made Reynold smile. He turned the pallet upside down, kicked it twice, then righted it. "There. Would you like to sit while I continue to explore?"

She found his arm and then clutched his elbow. "My thanks once again, but no."

Reynold chuckled and patted her hand. "You are very brave, Katherine."

She sighed. "No, I'm not. If alone, I would probably be quite mad by now."

"You underestimate yourself," he said, stroking her delicate hand. He remembered the firelight flickering across her fingers as he'd kissed each one. He shivered and still felt the way her nails had grazed his back when she'd cried out in pleasure. Was it only last night?

"How long do you think we'll be here?" she asked, interrupting Reynold's memories.

"Who can say? They seem to expect the earl

back soon, or I assume they would have dealt with us themselves. Perhaps your betrothed likes to wield all the power."

He regretted the sarcasm the instant he spoke. Where had such bitterness come from? Hadn't he always known she was not for one such as he?

Katherine stiffened and removed her hand from his arm. "You must be very angry with me."

Reynold shrugged. "I knew you had your secrets. I knew you were to be—married." He choked the last word out, sickened by an image of his brother and Katherine locked in a naked embrace.

Katherine remained silent for a moment, torn between wanting to tell him everything, and sparing him the knowledge. "At the monastery, I didn't reveal my full name because I was afraid you would take me home."

"You were right."

"I couldn't go there! 'Tis where the kidnapper would have expected me to go. He'd have been waiting, putting my whole family in danger."

"Why?" he demanded, gripping her shoulders hard.

Katherine stared into the inky blackness that was his face.

"Enough of your pretenses," he said. "What do you have to warn the king about?"

Katherine opened her mouth, but nothing would come out. Reynold shook her once and her arm began to ache.

"You're hurting me," she said.

"What do you think you have done to me?"

She had no answer for that except the truth. "Friends of my father—fellow noblemen—had gathered at our home to hunt. Someone overheard them discussing how they would support Henry Tudor, but not openly."

"Traitors?" The hiss of that word made the pit seem darker.

"They said they would pretend to support King Richard, then turn to Henry at the king's weakest moment."

Reynold said nothing for a moment, and Katherine waited for him to commend her bravery and devotion.

"Could you not have sent a letter?"

She shoved away his hands. "I might have, but the choice was denied me. They discovered what I knew and had me kidnapped! What was I supposed to do, allow them to intimidate me? King Richard needed my help. His wife, Anne, was my cousin. I could not just go home and allow them to be betrayed."

"I still do not understand the secrecy. You could have stayed safely in hiding and allowed me or someone else to carry your message. Why did you not trust me?"

Katherine kicked at the straw beneath her feet. "Reynold, I knew nothing of you. I could not risk my father's life on a stranger."

He groaned. "What does your father have to do with this?"

"Do you not see? These men were gathered at

my father's estate. People might suspect that he was also a traitor, although he is not."

"You are certain of that?"

"Reynold! We are related to King Richard's wife! Why would my father want to do harm to her husband?"

"You said 'someone' overheard the traitors. Was it your father?"

"No. His mistress."

"And you wish to protect her?" Reynold asked.

Katherine could hear the irony in his voice. She knew how unusual her family was. "Eleanor is . . . more a mother to me than my own. If the traitors find out who overheard them, they'll kill her."

"You do not know that," he said. "They did not kill you."

"I'm not a man's mistress, nor a commoner."

Startled, Katherine realized what she'd just said. She was no better than Eleanor, her father's mistress; they'd committed the same sins.

"Katherine—"

"Have I answered enough questions for tonight? Could we keep exploring?"

When she would have gone around him, Reynold moved on, holding her hand. Together they discovered an arrow loop in the far wall, the source of cool air and relief from the stench. They stood at the opening and simply breathed.

"I thought we were underground," Katherine murmured, squinting out at the dark countryside.

"The land sloped down as we approached the

tower. The walls of this pit are uneven enough to have been dug out of rock."

Together they dragged the rickety pallet over to the arrow loop. Katherine heard Reynold test the pallet with his weight, then he gently pulled her down beside him. She shifted uncomfortably.

"Reynold, you must know that nothing has changed."

He didn't answer, or draw away.

"When James returns, I'll be cleared of these charges."

"Will he believe who you are? Did he see you often enough to memorize every curve of your face, as I have?"

Some deep part of Katherine feared that what Reynold had said might prove true. "He may not recognize me dressed like this, but it will not take me long to convince him. Then you'll be free to go. You will not have to risk yourself for me anymore."

" 'Twas not by force that I left the monastery, Katherine."

She allowed herself to lean back, ever closer to the warmth of his side. "Will you go back?"

She heard the dull thud of his head dropping back against the wall. "I have to." He was silent for a moment. "Katherine, who were the traitors?"

"Will you not answer my question?"

"Tell me."

She heard the bitterness that was once again laced through his words. He had every right to be angry with her and his situation. She had practically seduced him herself, then led him to the home of her future husband. Why should he confide his plans to her?

"The Earl of Northumberland. And Lord Stanley—"

"No surprise there," Reynold interrupted. "He took Henry Tudor's mother to wife."

"But he pledged loyalty to King Richard. He is one of the king's councilors. How can he go back on his word?"

"When their own necks are concerned, many men have no problem with dishonor. Anyone else?"

"Only the Duke of Suffolk."

"The Duke—" Reynold broke off with a soft curse. "His son is Richard's heir."

"I know," she whispered. "Doesn't anyone believe in loyalty any more?"

"You do."

His voice rumbled softly, deeply, in his chest, stirring an answering shudder that seemed to begin between her thighs. Her skin flushed with warmth. The wool gown and smock trapped the heat of her body until her breasts burned with it. She scrambled up onto her knees and turned her face into the draft of cool air from the arrow loop. Pressing the front of her body against the rock wall, she tried to will her flesh into submission.

She would not allow herself to repeat her sins of the previous night. She was at the home of her betrothed—admittedly in the dungeon, but that would soon be rectified. She could not allow this weakness, this languor, to steal over her again. It would only hurt Reynold more when James returned, demanding his future wife. And Katherine would be that woman, and suffer silently for her sins for the rest of her life. She could not go against her father's wishes in choosing the earl for her husband.

She remained still, silent, struggling to clear her mind of all but her mission. Yet Reynold breathed beside her, his big body restless on the pallet, his heat as necessary as fire in a winter storm. 'Tis what he stirred inside her, a storm of desire and sin so wicked and compelling that she couldn't think, couldn't connect the reasons why she shouldn't touch him. She felt his head lean against her hip and she shuddered.

"Katherine," he said, and her name sounded exotic in his deep, hoarse voice.

"No, oh no," she whispered. To her mortification, her voice trailed off into a moan as Reynold's hand touched the back of her thigh and slid slowly upward, rubbing linen and wool against her sensitive flesh. He cupped her buttock in one large hand and kneaded the muscle gently, rhythmically.

Katherine clutched the wall, trying with all her might not to collapse in his arms and beg him to ease this anguished wanting she could not control.

"I may burn in hell for this," he said, his face pressed against her hip, "but nothing can be worse than this fire I feel whenever I am near you."

The fire that he spoke of burned and consumed

her, until not even the darkness of the pit could reach her. Every sense was riveted to this man below her who made her feel more a woman than she ever had in her life.

Katherine knew she should hit him, scream, do something, but she remained immobile, shivering uncontrollably, held in place by the gentle pressure of his hand on her backside. She felt him touch her bare knee with the other hand and begin a torturous slide upward. His fingers brushed the curls between her thighs and she convulsed in his grip.

"Open for me," he whispered.

Still kneeling beside him, clutching the stone base of the arrow loop for support, Katherine allowed her shaking knees to part the smallest bit. She smothered a groan against her arm as his fingers slid between her thighs until they found the hottest center of her and began to stroke. Katherine's head fell back as a mild convulsion rippled out to her breasts and thighs. She remembered every moment of last night—remembered and relived and prayed for that stunning release she had not believed really existed.

Katherine's belt fell to the pallet. Reynold's hand descended the back of her thigh and slipped beneath her gown. She cried out softly as his rough hands cupped her naked hips, front and back. She shivered and would have fallen had she not held the stone window ledge with a death grip. She wanted him now. She wanted to feel the release, the drawing away, the end to this insatiable, painful, pleasurable desire for him.

Chapter 13

~~~◦◦◦~~~

Reynold's palms came together and flattened over her smooth, soft stomach. He shook with the effort of holding himself back from taking everything from her this moment. Instead he pressed his face into her wool skirt where it gathered at her waist. He allowed himself the touch of her, memorizing the way her bones sculpted the flesh of her hips. He allowed his hands to roam higher until his fingers teased the undersides of her breasts. Her soft gasp sent the blood pounding through his veins, making his erection so hard it was painful. Still, he teased her breasts, just touching the hard nipples and retreating. He froze at the sound of her voice.

"Please, Reynold, I can't take much more."

He knew how much it cost her to admit her desire. His own seemed to rage out of control as his arms went around her hips and pulled her body against his. With one hand he roughly yanked his tunic and braies aside. He guided her body over his, poised above him. He wanted to mindlessly sheath himself in her, to be released from this agony, but he felt her trembling and he soothed her with his hands.

"Touch me, Katherine. Guide me inside you."

She shuddered and clutched his shoulders. "I— I—"

"Are you afraid to touch me as I have touched you?"

She seemed to hesitate as she knelt above him, her knees on either side of his hips. At the first tentative brush of her fingers on his stomach, Reynold shuddered with a near loss of control.

"Do you know what you do to me?" His breathless voice sounded unrecognizable. Her fingers slid lower and he grew deathly still, until she touched him and the world seemed to explode.

"Did I harm you?" she cried, withdrawing her hand.

The effort of chuckling hurt his chest. "Do not stop! Do not ever stop, my sweet."

Her fingers encircled his penis, lifting it up towards her body. "How—what do I—"

"Inside you, Katherine," he said with a groan. When he felt the wet, warm, opening between her thighs, he grasped her hips in both hands and brought her down hard, sheathing himself deep inside her. Katherine gasped, and Reynold lifted her gown and smock up over her head. His tunic quickly followed. When free of the dress, her hair fell down about them like a silken waterfall.

He pressed kisses across her breasts, teasing her

nipples to hard peaks. He felt her arms about his shoulders, her fingers in his hair. She tugged gently until he lifted his face. She lowered her open mouth to his and Reynold drew in her tongue. He lifted her hips and lowered her again, feeling her erratic breaths mingle with his.

They moved as one, lifting and releasing, soft breast sliding against hard chest. The pallet swayed and creaked beneath them, but Reynold gave no thought to falling. His world was the heat of her body surrounding him, the softness of her lips, the clutch of her hands. As she shuddered her release against him, he gave one final thrust, exploding inside her, moving slowly, revelling in each lingering ripple of pleasure that shook him to the core. Never, never, had he felt the sexual act more deeply, more poignantly. Katherine would never give of herself to him again. His cursed brother would come to take her away.

Reynold kissed her once more, then buried his face in her neck, crushing her body against his. All his self-hatred mattered naught when she touched him. His vows and despair disappeared beneath the rush of feelings aroused by the smell of her skin.

Katherine's ribs ached from the strength of Reynold's embrace, but she didn't move from his lap. She kissed his hair and caressed his shoulders and tried not to think about where she was or who she would soon have to face. She wanted their bodies to remain joined together for as long as possible. Her breathing eased and she rested her head on

his shoulder. A sudden draft of air blew across her
bare back and she shivered.

"Katherine, your clothes."

His voice was so gentle, so resigned, she had to
will herself not to cry. He handed her a bundle of
wool garments, then helped her climb off him onto
the pallet. Katherine clutched her knees together
and bowed her head in grief. She'd never felt more
empty and alone. Was this how her whole life
would be? Would she ever again know the joy she
felt in Reynold's arms?

In a daze she donned her linen smock, then the
peasant gown. Where was her belt? As she
searched for it, her fingers touched Reynold's bare
thigh. His hand covered hers for a brief moment.

"Sleep in my arms, my lady," he murmured.
"This pallet is not fit for you."

She hesitated only a moment, listening as he
donned his tunic. Crawling into his lap, she allowed him to cradle her against his chest. She fell
asleep listening to the reassuring beat of his heart.

Reynold could not sleep so easily. Instead he
thought of the reasons why a man would support
Henry Tudor against an unpopular king. Uneasiness stirred in his stomach. He had always found
it suspicious that the kidnapper had done his best
not to hurt Katherine—almost as if someone had
ordered him, someone who didn't want her
harmed. A stranger wouldn't care. A relative—her
father?—would. Treason did strange things to a
man's mind. But Reynold could not rule out the
traitors themselves, men who might eventually

want the Earl of Durham's support, and wouldn't risk hurting his daughter.

The sun had barely topped the trees when James Markham, fourth Earl of Bolton, threw open the doors to the great hall and strode inside. Two of his knights kept pace behind him. He ignored the dutiful nods of his servants and the villagers who came to do business with the estate. He halted in the center of the hall, doffed his felt hat, and tried to imagine what he could possibly sell next.

And then it came to him. It was time to send for the girl. James shuddered at the mere thought of the skinny, plain, crippled thing he would wed. He'd tried to avoid it as many years as he possibly could, but living a life of nobility grew expensive. One more bad harvest and he'd be no better than his serfs. It was time to be married, time to collect the dowry.

The castle steward tentatively approached, bowing and bobbing his bald little head, already listing the things that needed James's attention. But he wasn't in the mood to listen, and gave thanks when his sergeant-at-arms approached and stood stiffly at his elbow.

James turned his back on the steward and nodded to Galway.

"Milord, we surprised thieves in yer bedchamber last night."

James grimaced and almost wondered aloud what they could possibly find to steal. "I'm sure you handled the matter. Why bring it to my attention?"

The blond giant grinned and shrugged beneath his tunic. "It were two men and a girl. This girl . . . well, she says she's Lady Katherine Berkeley."

James's brows shot up. But he very well knew she could not be who she said she was.

"Yer betrothed."

"I know the name," he said dryly.

"The girl is lyin'," Galway continued, "but I thought ye'd want to know before I punished 'er."

"What does she look like?" James asked, beginning to grin.

" 'Ard to tell beneath all the dirt, milord."

James shuddered with distaste. "An amusing story just the same. I trust she's being confined."

"In the dungeon, milord, although I thought we'd never get 'er down there."

James chuckled. "Didn't like the smell, did she?"

"She took that fine. 'Twas the rope. She 'as a bad arm and I didn't think she'd—"

"What did you say?" James interrupted, feeling a sudden cold sweat break out on his brow.

Galway blinked. "I wasn't sure we'd—"

"No, you fool, her arm! How badly crippled?"

"Nothing I could see."

"Damn!" James swore as he dropped his leather gloves on a bench by the hearth. It couldn't be. "I'd better see the girl."

Galway nodded, his eyes wide with surprise. James ignored the look and followed the sergeant to the tower reserved for prisoners. He seethed with anger and hoped for the girl's sake she was not who she claimed to be.

Katherine came awake slowly, feeling soft lips against her forehead. She blinked, sighed, and snuggled closer to his warmth. Then she realized the dungeon was no longer dark. She sat up on Reynold's thighs, looking at the shaft of light that poured in the arrow loop. Their prison had roughly carved walls, wet in places, barren of everything but straw and a pallet.

"A good morning," Reynold said.

Katherine looked into his face and wished she hadn't. His smile was tight with pain.

"Reynold—"

He shook his head, then handed over her belt. "Up, Katherine. Perhaps they shall drop us food."

"Do you think we'll be released today?"

"They are waiting for Bolton."

Katherine winced. "They didn't sound like they knew when to expect him."

Reynold lifted her to her feet and stood up. "I shall give a shout."

Just as he reached the center of the pit, the trap door opened, sending a shower of dirt down on his upturned face. He staggered to one side, rubbing his hands across his eyes.

Katherine stepped forward to help, then froze as she heard the voice which had lived in her daydreams for five years.

"Girl, tell me your name."

She gasped and ran beneath the trap door. "My lord Bolton? It is I, Katherine."

She saw Reynold turn away, and though a part of her died in misery, she had to fight her weakness for him. She needed to do everything in her power to convince James to help her warn King Richard, and to keep Reynold and his identity a secret. She didn't know James well enough to trust he would not harm the man who'd helped her.

She heard the sound of male voices in the tower above, but no one spoke to her. "My lord?" she called again.

The rope slithered down and Katherine put her foot in the loop, holding on tightly with her good arm. She looked over her shoulder at Reynold, who stood impassive as a statue.

"Trust me!" she whispered, then held on for dear life as she swung into the air. The bright light of the tower blinded her, as hands grasped her beneath the shoulders and dragged her out of the pit. She staggered when set on her feet, then lifted her chin in a fake show of strength.

Katherine saw James immediately, his face so full of contempt and distaste that she inwardly cringed. She was dirty and disheveled, but her betrothed was dressed in the height of fashion. He wore a deep blue doublet cut low to emphasize the brilliant white of his shirt. His black hose molded tightly to his thighs, while a black cloak, lined with spotted lynx fur was thrown back over his broad shoulders. Katherine knew she was staring, but she couldn't help it. Truly, he must be too wealthy to need her dowry.

James turned away. "Punish her as you see fit."

"My lord!" She darted forward to grab his sleeve.

He pulled away.

"Forgive this unannounced arrival, but I must speak with you."

He continued out the tower door into the inner ward.

"I was kidnapped!" she cried after him.

He halted and slowly turned to face her. "What did you say?"

"I was kidnapped a week ago from my father's home. I need your help."

James hesitated.

"What can I do to make you believe me?" she asked desperately.

"Bathe."

Katherine gave him a grateful smile. "I would love to."

James nodded to his sergeant. "She'll come with me."

Reynold remained flat against the dungeon wall, listening to their conversation. He wished he would have told Katherine not to mention him by name. If she called attention to him, his brother would discover his identity, and probably inform Katherine. But she didn't even seem to remember him as she went off with James. Reynold bitterly kicked back against the wall. The pain knifed through him, startling him with its intensity. This was what he wanted, wasn't it?

The trap door suddenly swung shut and the end of the rope dropped to his feet. They'd forgotten all about him. Reynold cursed as he hadn't done in months.

This was as it should be, he kept telling himself. He had to protect Katherine from the knowledge of his identity. He didn't want to hurt her any more than he already had. Clinging to that thought, he slowly began to climb up the rope, using the muscles of his arms. When he reached the top, he twisted the rope around one leg to give himself leverage, then pressed one palm to the trap door. It lifted barely an inch.

Reynold groaned and maneuvered himself higher, his head and shoulders bowed against the wood. He slid the fingers of one hand between the trap door and the frame, braced his weight there, then shoved hard against the door. It fell open with a loud thump. He boosted himself out, and crouched back against the wall. He was alone. Quietly, he shut the trap door.

Katherine stood alone in one of the bare rooms she had searched through just the past night. The walls were whitewashed, but empty. A bed and a chest occupied one corner. She sighed and thought about her betrothed. James couldn't seem to get rid of her soon enough. He'd left a guard outside her door. He doubted her story, but was willing to be absolutely sure. For that she was grateful.

The door opened a minute later and two kitchen boys carried in a wooden tub between them. They leered at her and Katherine returned the most frigid glare she could. She was the daughter of an earl, their future mistress, not some conquest of their master. She regarded them in icy silence as they started a small fire in the hearth.

Four more buckets of tepid water were soon added, which barely filled the tub halfway. A silent maid brought in a towel and a clean dress which had obviously been borrowed from a servant. When Katherine was finally alone, she stripped off the wool gown, washed her hair, then scrubbed herself raw with coarse soap. It felt good to be clean.

And then she remembered Reynold. She stood frozen in the drafty room, the towel clutched to her wet skin. Did Reynold think she had abandoned him? She had to convince James to let him go, without exposing Reynold to danger. Would her betrothed feel the need to avenge himself on the man who'd been alone with her for days? Tears stung her eyes and she put a hand over her trembling mouth. Reynold deserved all the protection she could give him. What would she say to James when he asked how she got here?

Chapter 14

⌒⟞◯◯⟞⌒

J ames paced before the hearth in the great hall, a tankard of ale in one fist. The girl couldn't be Katherine. Her face was a grimy mess and her hair all tangles. And that peasant dress hung on her like a sack! No, he was being a fool. She was merely a serf looking for a few days of amusement and good food. And when he looked into her face and was sure it wasn't Katherine, he'd give her all the amusement she wanted. Provided she was half decent. He thought he had glimpsed white teeth, a rarity among his villagers. She might have quite a kissable little mouth.

He looked up and saw her descending the stairs, wearing the gown of a much smaller woman. She came towards him, eyes downcast, damp golden ringlets of hair falling over her shoulders. She blushed as she stopped before him, but he could not keep his gaze from wandering down her body in frank admiration. The dress was too tight, hugging her bountiful breasts almost indecently. Her waist was elegantly trim, her wrists and hands delicate, her exposed ankles tiny.

"My lord Bolton," she murmured.

She finally raised her gaze, and James was struck mute. Those vivid, storm-blue eyes. The one thing memorable about her. He looked down her body again. But not the only thing memorable any more. Perhaps this marriage would prove interesting.

"My lady," he said, and brought her hand to his lips.

Katherine was so relieved she could have melted into the floor. "You believe me," she breathed, watching his dark head bent over her hand.

He looked up and grinned. Katherine tried to relive the excitement of their first meeting, how dashing he was, with his proud face and blue eyes. But five years had passed, five years of a young girl's life as she waited daily for her future husband. The joy she thought she'd feel when she saw him was gone, leaving only nervousness.

On the other side of Lord Bolton, a group of servants were gathered, whispering and pointing. Katherine would have paid them scant attention, but then she was struck by a familiar pair of amethyst eyes, cold as the gems they reminded her of. He towered above the servants, a dark, impassive mountain of a man, his head smothered in that ridiculous hood and hat. She shivered with the remembered sensations of what his hands had done, of how she had touched him. *Please, Reynold*, she thought, *please keep quiet and let me help you in my own way.* If she could keep James's attention solely on her, perhaps he wouldn't inquire too much about how she came to be here.

"Lady Katherine, you have blossomed into a true beauty," James said.

She tried to give him a ladylike blush, but inwardly she rejected his meaningless words. She was no beauty, and he could have seen for himself if he'd have visited more than three times in five years.

Katherine sighed. Where did such rebellious thoughts come from? Even a week ago she would have been grateful for any crumb of his attention. But that was before she had been rescued by a man who gave everything he had for her and her cause. A man who cared.

"Lady Katherine?"

She was startled out of her reverie. "I'm sorry, my lord, my thoughts are wandering from the stress of all that's happened to me in the last week." She winced at her coy words.

"It must have been quite trying. I apologize that my soldiers and I didn't believe your story. Perhaps you could tell me everything."

He took her left elbow to guide her to a cushioned chair before the hearth. Katherine's instinctive reaction was to draw her arm away and hold it close to her body, but she fought her old habits. She seated herself and wondered just where to begin. Would he believe her news of treason?

Katherine looked up and saw the servants dispersing, leaving Reynold no choice but to follow.

Don't leave me! her mind cried, but she knew she had to move on with her life, and he could not be a part of it. Her father had a contract with Bolton to marry her, and Reynold had to return to the monastery. But her stomach twisted into knots at the thought of never seeing him again.

"Lord Bolton," she began.

"Call me James."

His voice was low and pleasant, his manner courtly, his looks as handsome as she remembered. And yet—

She managed a smile. "James. If it wouldn't be too much trouble, could I have a morsel to eat? I have had nothing since the previous night's meal."

His face was full of concern. "Of course, my dear! You should have said something before your bath."

You'd have laughed in my face, she thought wryly.

A hunch-shouldered serving woman wearing a stained apron brought Katherine a bowl of soup, a loaf of bread, and a spoon. She ate as sedately as possible, knowing James watched her. Was he still unconvinced?

When she was finished, she pushed the bowl aside and met his intense gaze. She tilted her head and studied him for a moment. He seemed suddenly more familiar to her. Her memories of his brief visits must be returning.

James sat back in his chair. "You mentioned something about being kidnapped. Was that merely to capture my attention?"

"No, my lo—James," she said, folding her hands

in her lap to hide their trembling. "I was kidnapped because I have information about houses which are secretly turning against our king."

James's brows shot up. "That is a serious accusation."

She smiled. "Which is why they had me kidnapped."

" 'They'?"

"I'm not sure which nobleman paid the thieves."

"Did these men bring you here?"

"After a two-day journey from my father's home, I was held prisoner at Saint Anthony's Priory."

James spat ale back into his tankard. "A monastery? Surely you must be mistaken."

"No, my lord."

"James."

"James," she repeated, smiling. She felt as if her lips must be visibly twitching with nervousness.

"How long were you there?"

"A few hours only. I was rescued." Her gaze slid from him to her lap, a mistake, she knew. It only made her look guilty.

"Your family discovered your whereabouts?"

"No, one of the monastery's laborers. He saw me dragged in at night. He guided me this far." Katherine took a deep breath, waiting for his reaction to her story.

James slowly set his tankard on the trestle table. "You were alone with a strange man for the entire journey?" he asked with no emotion.

Katherine raised her chin. "It was either that, or

remain a prisoner in a filthy, deserted undercroft, waiting for my jailers to return." She knew many men would prefer that fate to their women being unchaperoned. She bitterly waited for his censure.

"This stranger wanted nothing from you in return for his help?"

"Nothing, James," she answered honestly. Reynold had asked for nothing. She had given everything.

"Where is this hero now?"

She thought she heard sarcasm in his voice, but pretended not to. "When you brought me out of the dungeon, he was still there."

James's dark gaze sharpened. "You were even in the dungeon together?"

"Your men wanted to put him in the second pit, with the man who accused us of thievery. But I— my lord, I couldn't be alone in that dark hole! I heard things moving down there. I—" She broke off, trying hard to recapture her initial fears of the place. But Reynold's memory was now entwined with the darkness.

"I understand, my dear," he said, awkwardly patting her hand.

He probably didn't, but at least he was willing to accept her tale. James looked to his sergeant-at-arms, who came forward.

"Milord, the man's gone."

Katherine gasped on cue. "But I didn't have a chance to thank him!"

"Gone?" James demanded. "How did he escape the pit?"

The blond man lowered his gaze. "After the girl—Lady Katherine—come up, no one pulled up the rope."

"And the other man?"

"Still there, milord."

"His accusations were obviously lies. Punish him as you see fit."

"Yes, milord."

Katherine's relief was so great she could have wept. Reynold was free to leave without pursuit. She spoke quickly before James could remember him. "I have a favor to ask of you. I need your help to warn the king."

He smiled. "I think His Grace can take care of himself, Katherine. It was very noble of you to want to help."

"But you don't understand! These men were of the nobility. Richard's own councilors. He will not be expecting their betrayal."

James sipped his ale, looking at her over the rim. "Who are these men?"

"Lord Stanley, along with the Duke of Suffolk, and the Earl of Northumberland."

"God's teeth," he murmured, his face sobering as he stared at her.

"You must see why I need your help. Can you send a message to the king?"

"I'll not only send a message, but also a detachment of soldiers as escort."

"Thank you, James," Katherine whispered, sinking back in her chair. She felt drained, exhausted, and very relieved that the burden of the secret was off her shoulders.

"You look tired," he said. "Would you care to rest for a few hours?"

"Yes, thank you." She stood up and he followed.

"I'm sure my dungeon is hardly a comfortable place for a lady. Forgive our disbelief."

Katherine nodded quickly, unable to meet his eyes. His dungeon was not a subject she wanted to converse about.

"Would you like me to send a maid to keep you company? You'll feel safer with her sleeping at your door."

"No, James, but thank you."

He caught up her hand for another kiss to her fingers. She darted a glance to the stairs, impatient to be alone, to sleep and not have to think any more.

James watched the sway of Katherine's hips as she ascended the stone staircase. He didn't think he was going to be a very patient bridegroom. He had dreaded the wedding for so long, and now his reversal of feelings was rather overwhelming. Though no rare beauty, Katherine was a stunning young woman, and he regretted not marrying her years before. He called for his secretary to write a missive to Lord Durham. The old man deserved to know that his daughter was safe, and ready to be wed. James's plans couldn't have worked out better. Except for the mystery of her rescuer . . .

*   *   *

Katherine slept the afternoon away, came downstairs for a quick evening meal, and bid James an early goodnight. He seemed disappointed, and she knew she should be thrilled that he wanted to spend time with her, but all she could feel was unease. It was hard to look him in the eyes. Did her guilt show?

Now that her duty to King Richard had been lifted from her thoughts, all she could think about was Reynold. She had lain with a man not her husband—not merely one uncontrolled time, but twice! How could she possibly enter a marriage based on a lie? James thought he was marrying a virginal, sheltered girl. Instead she was a wanton who could not control her own body. What kind of woman did that make her?

Just as Katherine reached her room, she heard James calling her from the stairway. She turned and saw him enter the corridor. Every step he took made Katherine's heart pound faster. What could he want, beyond what had already been said?

He stopped before her and took both her hands in his. "I was not a very proper bridegroom tonight."

She smiled nervously. "James, you are very kind to me."

"But kind is not all I want to be."

He leaned towards her and pressed his lips to her cheek. Katherine held her breath, controlling her instinctive urge to push him away.

"Do not be frightened," he murmured. "I won't hurt you."

Katherine was trapped. She could not very well refuse her betrothed a kiss goodnight. But his arms around her produced none of the sensations she experienced with Reynold. When his mouth touched hers, she panicked and turned her face away.

"James, please!" she cried, pushing at his chest. "We are not yet married."

He let her go and grinned. "Forgive me, my dear. I forget you are yet an innocent."

He leaned forward once more and she allowed a kiss to her cheek.

"Goodnight, Katherine."

Giving him a forced smile, she opened her door and closed it quickly behind her. With a sigh of relief, she slumped against it, eyes closed. That was much too close. She could not continue to hold him off without raising his suspicions. She shouldn't be resisting him at all! Hadn't she dreamed of his kisses at night? But she couldn't remember her girlhood dreams anymore; there was only Reynold.

She opened her eyes and stood still in surprise. Someone had been here while she was gone, leaving bed curtains to keep out the chill, and rugs to warm her feet. Across the bed, a new gown lay, one obviously not borrowed from a servant. A single cushioned chair had been placed near the fire. Katherine sank down on it and covered her eyes.

She was so confused. At supper she had kept her eyes downcast, fearing that she would see Reynold and give his identity away. Yet in one moment of bravery, she had looked and never saw his face. Was he already gone?

She knew his calling was important to him, but wasn't she? After what they'd shared, he couldn't just escape with no word. She was suddenly flooded with the image of Reynold kneeling in agony on the floor of the hut. Perhaps she had finally hurt him too much.

Would he come tonight, when the others had gone to sleep? Katherine stole a glance at the bed, then angrily berated herself. No, she would not give in to the urges of her body. She was contracted to marry a man, and she had already dishonored herself.

She paced the room as hour after hour slipped by. The noises of the castle quieted then disappeared. Outside her shuttered window, the moon began its rise. Reynold did not come.

Finally Katherine undressed to her linen smock and got into bed. She left the bed curtains open, drew the coverlet up to her chin, and waited.

Katherine jerked awake and winced as her neck protested the abrupt movement. She rubbed it for a moment, then sighed as she realized it was dawn, and Reynold had not come.

He's gone, she thought, as her eyes stung and her throat seemed to choke her. She wanted to protect him; she should be happy that he had escaped. Instead she felt more alone than she ever had in her life.

If she gave James a chance, he might be gentle,

but always her secret would lie between them. Should she tell him the truth, that she was a virgin no longer? It might ease her conscience, but he would demand revenge upon Reynold, and possibly her father, for she had broken the vows of the contract. Now was not the time. Reynold was still too close, too vulnerable.

Katherine donned a wine-colored gown with a fitted bodice and low-slung jeweled girdle. A maid silently brushed out her hair and covered it with a soft golden hood and a veil falling down her back. Katherine looked sedate and respectable, a lady, not a peasant. Why was she so miserable? Why did she feel such a fraud?

After mass in the chapel, Katherine sat on the raised dais next to James, picking at her morning meal of porridge, bread, and ale. She felt uncomfortable being the center of attention, uneasy, as if everyone could guess all the terrible things she had done in her life. James sat beside her, occasionally conversing with his steward or the sergeant-at-arms.

She stared listlessly at her food, wishing that her longed-for meeting with James had never happened. She hugged her arm to her chest.

"Katherine?"

She lifted her head with a start. "Yes, James."

"You seem very distracted this morning. I hope your journey is not weighing on your mind."

She smiled weakly.

"You've done a brave thing, and I'm sure the king will appreciate it." James took a sip of ale, but his gaze remained on her. "What did you say the name of your benefactor was?"

Katherine forced a chunk of bread down her dry throat. "He wouldn't tell me his name."

"No? Didn't you consider that odd?"

"He rarely spoke at all. I think he was worried someone at the monastery would find out he had aided me."

James nodded thoughtfully, with the faintest frown etching his brow. Katherine prayed for a release from these embarrassing questions, prayed that James would forget a man had ever helped her. But her prayers only produced Reynold himself.

He sat at the farthest trestle table from hers. She ached with longing to be sitting thigh to thigh with him, not on display. Only the crown of his cloth hat was visible as he bent over his meal. He wasn't eating. With a sudden stab of pain, Katherine realized he was praying. Her guilt doubled and she prayed that God would understand that everything was her fault. Reynold suddenly looked up, and Katherine's emotions swung to fear. His beard had thickened, making him seem even more like a stranger, remote, cold. He gave her a glare that would frost a desert.

Chapter 15

Reynold clutched the eating knife loaned to him by one of the servants. He had never realized how truly painful it would be to watch Katherine laugh and talk and flirt with his brother. Her dark red gown emphasized the creamy flesh above her breasts, something only his eyes and mouth had touched. Katherine hid her golden curls beneath a veil, but in his mind he saw them tumbling across his skin—a sight James would soon see.

Reynold looked down at his trencher, willing himself to eat for strength, but his stomach seemed overfull with the emotions he could never show again. James would have everything he'd ever wanted, a wealthy, beautiful bride. Their sister Margery would have Reynold's holdings for her dowry.

And Reynold? He would have the church as his penance. With that he would have to comfort himself at night in his cold, lonely bed. He would have no wife, no children.

Reynold gripped the knife with white-knuckled violence, barely keeping himself from glaring at his brother. He stared at his hands instead. When he realized that violence raged through him, he dropped the knife in disgust.

He heaved a sigh and slumped lower on the bench, resting his elbows on the table. None of this was James's fault. Reynold's own arrogance had been his downfall, and caused his brother's death. He remembered the sound of James's hoarse cry of pain when Edmund breathed his last. Reynold knew he did not deserve Katherine, but he wasn't sure James did either. Would he make her happy? Would he cherish her for her strength, her loyalty? Even her sweet clumsiness plucked at Reynold's heart.

He frowned and picked at his food. Why had James barely visited Katherine during their betrothal? For once he wished he and his brother were closer, that he knew his brother's mind.

Perhaps Reynold really did belong cloistered away. Regardless of his sins, he could not stop this envy of his brother, which feasted on his soul and tore him apart. He stood up, stepped over the bench behind him, and left without another glance at Katherine.

Katherine gladly waved good-bye to James as he and his men rode out to hunt. She needed to be alone. Only then would Reynold come to say good-bye, as she knew he must. She spent the afternoon in her room, with a frame, cloth, and thread given to her by a serving woman. The needlework was mind-numbing in its monotony, and as Katherine stared at it, she realized the rest of her life would be like this. Oh, she would live in grander rooms, dress in fine clothes, even rule the servants, if she were lucky. She would be the wife of an earl and bear his heirs.

Katherine sniffed and dabbed at her wet eyes. At least she would have children to comfort her. Suddenly all the air seemed to leave her lungs and Katherine stifled a cry. Heirs. She dropped a hand to her stomach and felt it twist into knots. She could already be pregnant with Reynold's child.

Gasping in air, she covered her mouth and squeezed her eyes tightly shut. Tears dripped down her cheeks. Unless she married James soon, her shame would be known by everyone, her dowry forfeit, her family dishonored. Why had none of this seemed important when Reynold held her in his arms? She buried her face in her arms and sobbed.

That night sleep eluded Katherine with a subtlety that was exhausting. She would doze off, only to see Reynold's face, hear his voice in her ear as they lay in a naked embrace. She tossed and turned for a comfortable position. Again, he appeared in her dreams, this time glaring his hatred.

Katherine groaned and rolled onto her back. A large hand suddenly covered her mouth, pressing her lips against her teeth. She stiffened in wide-eyed terror, then relaxed as she saw Reynold's face looming over her.

He released her and stepped away from the bed. He was tall and broad, filling the small room with his forbidding presence. His face with its low brows was shadowed by flickering firelight, his expression unreadable.

"I knew you'd come," she breathed, unable to stop herself from staring at him.

"You think I am so enamored of you that I have no will of my own?" His low voice was laced with bitterness.

Katherine lowered her gaze, feeling his pain as her own. "You know that's not true. I only hoped that I would be able to say good-bye, to thank you for all that you've done for me."

"You wish to thank me for stripping you of your prized virginity?"

"That was more my fault than yours," she said, wishing she could take away his bitterness.

"I do not see it that way."

"You should!" She covered her mouth and looked quickly at the door.

"Katherine—"

"Can we not say good-bye in a civilized manner, instead of hating ourselves for the sins we've committed?"

"I try not to hate myself!" he answered fiercely, bracing himself on one knee beside her. "I hate that you must give yourself to him."

"Give—but Reynold, you act as if I have a choice." Katherine leaned back, looking up as he filled her vision. "There is a contract between our families. I cannot turn my back on it and bring shame on my father."

"Perhaps he's brought shame on you."

"What are you saying?"

"Have you not considered how careful your kidnapper was not to hurt you? Do you think a stranger would have ordered such treatment?"

"But I am an earl's daughter!" she insisted.

"Perhaps the earl has a secret to hide," he said.

Katherine felt anger well up inside her. "Are you implying that my own father had me stolen away, locked up?"

Reynold still loomed above her, but she wouldn't back down, even in the face of his ominous silence.

"Not for a moment do I believe my father had anything to do with this. One of the traitors arranged this and I hope to discover who. Please do not bring up such foolishness again."

He looked away from her, absently rubbing the skirt of her smock between his fingers. She watched his strong hands, and saw that they were trembling.

"Reynold—"

"I am sorry for upsetting you." He turned earnest, violet eyes on her face. "When I watch you with him, I am not myself. I see you sitting close to him, wearing garments he gave you—"

"But I have nothing else!"

"—laughing at his stories—"

"Do I have a choice?" she demanded, pulling

her skirt away from his hand and inching backwards on the bed. "He is my future husband. He has the power to kill you for what we've done. Do you think I want him to have time to remember you, to wonder who you are and where you've gone?"

Reynold brought his other knee onto the bed and leaned forward, bracing himself on his arms. His body hovered over her legs, and Katherine drew them up as close to her body as she could. Her breathing quickened and her flesh began to tingle, remembering his hands upon her. She couldn't allow this to happen again.

"Reynold—"

"You do this for me?" he asked softly, his breath touching her hair, her face. "You worry for me?"

"You're wrong," she said, but her voice was unconvincing. She was having trouble remembering their conversation. All she could think about were his muscled arms on either side of her legs, trapping her in the bed.

"Why are you shaking, my lady?" he whispered, leaning nearer.

Katherine saw him in her memory, naked, his body covering hers, pressing into her flesh until they were joined.

"I'm c-cold," she said without thinking—and immediately regretted it.

"Allow me to warm you."

She sank back on her pillow in excited dismay as he rose above her. Cool lips touched her cheek, stubbled chin brushed against her own. He

smelled as sharp and clean as the outdoors. She
tried to push him away, and he kissed her fingers,
her palms, until she cupped his head between her
hands.

"Reynold." She whispered his name with
pained regret, suddenly wishing with new understanding that he was her betrothed.

His mouth covered hers, his lips soft, yet insistent. She kissed him back with no restraint, saying
good-bye the only way she could. Their tongues
met and dueled with desperation, while his body
pressed hers down into the coverlet. But when he
touched her breast through the thin linen, she
shoved hard against him and turned her face
away.

"I can't betray him again," she whispered, more
to herself than to Reynold. His body lifted off hers
and she closed her eyes in relief, willing her tears
to remain hidden.

"I am always apologizing," Reynold said, moving away from the bed.

"Then let this be the last time."

He bowed his head. "As you wish, my lady. I
shall be gone in the morning."

" 'Tis for the best," she said, unable to look at
him. "Every moment you stay you risk discovery.
James did not like the idea of my being alone with
a strange man."

"Did he threaten you?"

"No. I just don't wish to give him the chance to
question my story."

"Good-bye, Katherine."

Her throat tightened and her eyes misted over. She blinked and slowly looked up at him. Her heart twisted and seemed to die within her. "Farewell, Reynold."

"Brother Reynold," he said.

Katherine could feel the tears pushing at her eyes, the sobs catching in her throat. And then he was gone, as silent as a cat. She sank back in the bed, pulled the coverlet over her head, and let the tears come.

Before dawn, Reynold knelt on the cold stone floor of the chapel, his head bowed as he asked the Almighty for forgiveness. Just one more sin, he thought, clutching the habit he had stolen from the priest. By meager candlelight, he dressed and slipped out the door.

In the gray light, the castle dogs gathered around him, whining for his attention. He patted them absently, nodding to the passing soldiers who staggered to their pallets after a night on duty. They bowed to his black Benedictine robe and Reynold's smile turned grim beneath the cowl. He no longer deserved the respect they accorded him. He would have to earn it all over again, and the thought was hardly pleasant.

At the gatehouse, the guards retreated a step when he walked by. As the first sunlight touched the trees, Reynold began his journey to the monastery, back to his search for family power, back to loneliness and atonement for even more sins.

*   *   *

James paced before the hearth as he awaited Katherine's appearance. He wondered if he could find a moment alone with her, taste more of her kisses. But he had not been the only one alone with her, he thought, frowning.

Sipping a tankard of ale, he watched the servants stack the trestle tables against the wall after the morning meal. Katherine had claimed her traveling companion innocent of touching her. From his first impressions of her many years ago, he could have believed a man would not be tempted.

But now, when he watched the mysterious depths of her blue eyes, the swell of her breasts—a lone man would have trouble resisting such temptation. But Katherine had not seemed frightened or even guilty. Still, the man had asked for no reward. James didn't believe in good deeds. And he had a very bad feeling about it. It couldn't possibly be—

He gulped down the rest of his ale and called for his sergeant-at-arms. A few moments later, Galway appeared, breathing heavily from his morning broadsword practice.

"Yes, milord?"

"The man who accompanied Katherine—you said he escaped the dungeon by himself?"

"Aye, milord."

"Did he leave the castle immediately?"

" 'E was seen at a meal or two, milord. Should I 'ave watched him?"

James shook his head. "Has he been seen today?"

"Not by me."

"What does he look like?" he asked, then waved away the question. "Just bring him here."

An hour later, as James walked through the lady's garden with Katherine on his arm, Galway stopped outside the gate and waited.

"I'll be back in a moment, my dear," James said, leading her to a bench. As she leaned over to admire the flowers, he sighed. How could a woman always be content in a garden? Flowers—just sat there.

Galway walked along the curtain wall with him. "Milord, the man 'asn't been seen since yesterday afternoon."

James cursed softly.

"I did find out somethin'. A monk left 'ere at dawn today. Father Carstairs doesn't know 'im."

James felt disaster creeping all around him. "Katherine says a laborer from the monastery helped her escape. Perhaps. . . ." He headed for the stables at a fast walk, calling over his shoulder, "Give the lady an excuse for my absence."

At the sound of horse's hooves on the deserted dirt road, Reynold cursed his luck. There was no time to hide. But why should he? Katherine was safe, and he was merely a monk once again. The horse slowed to a walk as it approached him, and he resisted looking over his shoulder.

"Brother!"

As he recognized the voice, Reynold grimaced, knowing his luck had turned. He felt an irrational urge to flee, but he could hardly outrun a horse. He glanced desperately towards the trees, then gave up the thought of escape.

James's voice was cold. "Are you the man who helped my betrothed, Lady Katherine Berkeley?"

Ducking his head so the cowl draped over his face, Reynold nodded. He kept putting one foot in front of the other.

The horse moved up alongside him, and he could smell the sweat of the animal, hear the breathing that sounded as ragged as his own. Why this fear of confronting his brother? Was he afraid James would read the guilt on his face? Or was it that Reynold would be hard pressed to quell the bitterness on his tongue?

"Brother, the morning is hot," James said. "Allow me to share a horn of ale with you."

With a sigh, Reynold halted. Resistance was useless. James dismounted with a squeak of leather. Perhaps Reynold could sip the ale quickly, without showing his face, and be on his way. He watched in dismay as James drained half the container himself. Reynold was trying to imagine how he could keep his face hidden and still drink, when James suddenly jerked the cowl backwards and tossed the contents into his face.

Chapter 16

~~~~~∽◯◯◯~~~~~

"What the hell did you do that for?" Reynold demanded, sputtering ale.

James looked at him coldly. "You were alone with my betrothed for how many days?"

"I saved your betrothed's *life!*" he shot back. "Unless, of course, you knew she did not need to be saved."

James threw up his hands. "What are you talking about? I didn't even know she'd been kidnapped!"

They glared at each other, and Reynold found he couldn't really believe what he'd been thinking. He took a step backwards, and wiped his hands across his face. "Do you have more ale? I was actually thirsty."

James folded his arms across his chest. "How do you have the gall to face me after what you've done?"

"To Katherine?"

"To Edmund! I thought we agreed never to see one another again."

"You agreed. I did not." Reynold looked away from his brother, feeling a cold ache of loneliness settle in his heart.

They remained silent, frozen though it was a summer day.

James cleared his throat. "I guess I should thank you for delivering her to me," he said, no warmth in his voice.

"You can thank Lady Katherine, not I. She led me here."

James frowned. "But when you recognized her—"

"I had never met your betrothed, remember. I seem to recall you never wanted her near you. When I rescued her, she was too frightened to tell me her full name."

"But why didn't you tell my men who you were?" James asked. "Or for that matter, come to me?"

"And receive this kind of gratitude?" Reynold said, then closed his eyes and tried to rein in his temper. It was his own fault that James hated him. He continued in a controlled voice. "Lady Katherine tried to tell your men who she was, and they merely laughed. I never thought I would have better luck. And then once you returned, I did not wish to intrude. I knew you would not want to see me. And now I must return to St. Anthony's and give an explanation for my sudden disappearance."

"Damn," James said, tapping his toe on the ground. "You can't leave."

"Why ever not?" Reynold demanded, so close to victory he could feel its breath. "Lady Katherine is safe with you, her secret as well. You can help her."

James laughed grimly. "You don't honestly think that His Majesty would believe a word of this?"

"Whether I believe it or not, he should be warned."

"The man has enough on his mind. The Tudor has landed in Wales."

Reynold nodded slowly. "I knew it would come, but so soon?"

"He's marching into England, gathering his supporters. Katherine's news—if it's true, and I have my doubts—will probably be useless by now."

"You told her you had sent men."

"I've told no lies, Reynold," James insisted angrily. "I did send men, but they won't be trying to see the king. Yet Katherine's lovely soul will have peace. After all, I can't have her worrying when she should be preparing herself for our wedding."

Reynold felt his heart shrivel painfully in his cold chest. "You delayed the wedding for so many years."

"Not any longer. She's a hot-blooded wench. Not that you're interested in that sort of thing anymore, Brother Reynold."

James was deliberately toying with him, and Reynold had had a bellyful. He tried to remember the grief they both shared over their brother's death. James had a right to be angry.

"I have a long journey ahead of me," Reynold said between gritted teeth. "Have a joyous wedding, James."

"Won't you return to officiate?"

The sarcasm grated on Reynold, but he tried to ignore it. "You forget I am but a novice."

"Aye, well, you still can't leave."

"But you want me gone."

"Of course I do—you're a bitter reminder, Reynold." He sighed. "But I'm sure Galway will let slip to Katherine that I'm pursuing her rescuer. The girl will probably wish to thank you properly."

"Did she say that?"

"I don't think she realized you had left." Cold satisfaction laced James's voice. "Did you tell her about our family history?"

"Of course not."

"I'm not surprised. Since I don't want to upset her before the wedding, I will not mention it—for the moment."

Reynold nodded coolly, despite the threat.

"I wish I could leave you to walk, but I could hardly explain that either. Ride behind me." James mounted but didn't offer a hand.

Katherine awaited her midday dinner, trying her best to pay attention to stories regaled to her by each of the knights. Yet the door drew her eye every time it opened. Was Reynold still here? Would he wish to speak with her? Her heartbeat quickened, her breathing grew rough. How she longed to see him again, to watch his eyes alight when he looked at her, to remember his strength and gentleness.

She tried to rally her anger, her disgust about what she had done with a man who was not her husband. Yet hard emotions slipped away beneath the gentle memories of Reynold loving her.

The double door of the great hall opened again. Katherine gave it a single preoccupied glance, then went back to her brooding. The image of two men suddenly flashed into her brain and she looked up with a gasp. A cowled monk walked beside James.

Katherine began to shake. She could no longer protect Reynold. His identity would be exposed, perhaps his life in danger. Could she hide her guilt when its cause stood before her?

They walked towards her, and still Reynold did not drop his cowl. He was a study in black and shadows, an image she trembled from only a few days before. She still trembled, but not from loathing. There was anticipation and yearning and guilt.

"Katherine!" James's voice boomed loudly through the hall. Servants picked up their pace, laying out bread and butter on immaculate tablecloths.

Katherine licked her lips and attempted a smile. Her gaze was riveted on Reynold, the way his robe scattered the rushes at his feet, the breadth of his shoulders beneath the coarse wool habit. The cowl remained in place, a dark cavern where his face should be. She clutched her goblet tighter and tried to remain calm.

"Katherine," James said, coming to a halt before her, "I found your protector trying to leave without a proper good-bye."

She sipped her wine to hide her trembling lips. "How nice," she murmured, struggling to keep her gaze on James, and not the silent man behind him.

James pulled a chair out from the table. "Reynold, sit and eat with us."

Katherine's eyes widened. James knew Reynold's name. His identity was no longer a secret. Would her enemies seek him out? Were they already watching, waiting to pounce? She looked around nervously, wondering which of the servants were new.

In her need to protect Reynold, she forgot about her guilt for a moment. Then her wide-eyed gaze returned to James.

Could he tell? Did her face give her secret away? Perhaps that was why Reynold hid his.

Reynold lifted his hands and slowly removed the cowl from his head. Katherine watched in horrified fascination, as she had the first time. His face was oddly still, even pale, and he didn't meet her eyes. James called for a servant to bring him the platter of venison.

"I must admit the coincidence is startling," James was saying.

Katherine dragged her gaze from Reynold and blinked. "Coincidence?"

"I had forgotten Reynold had been sent to St. Anthony's."

Katherine suddenly had trouble swallowing. "You know him?"

"I admit our last names are deceptive. My father died when I was but an infant. Our mother then married Reynold's father."

Katherine shook her head in bewilderment. "My father," "his father," "our mother"? And then it all came together with a clash of thunder that seemed to reverberate through Katherine's head.

They were brothers.

She stared anywhere but at the dark monk and the well-dressed earl. Brothers. And Reynold hadn't told her.

The last thought threatened to cut off her breathing. Katherine gasped, then took a quick drink of wine, only to end up coughing like a fool.

"Are you all right, Katherine dear?"

She nodded to James, but couldn't look at him. Then she would have to see Reynold, the man who lured her to betray his own brother in a dungeon.

Katherine shuddered with self-loathing and closed her eyes. Reynold had known from the moment they'd arrived, and never told her. He had allowed Katherine to be locked in a pit, when a simple word from him would have freed her. But then, of course, she would not have debased herself by mating with him again.

Katherine's stomach threatened to rebel and she put a hand to her mouth. She interrupted whatever James was saying. "Excuse me, I'm not feeling well. I think I'll retire. A good evening, James, B-Brother Reynold."

Of its own volition, her gaze lifted momentarily to Reynold. If possible, his face was whiter than before, and his eyes seemed to shine with a terrible intensity. Katherine whirled from him and walked away as quickly as she dared.

Reynold bowed his head, his eyes squeezed shut as he surrendered to the pain in his heart. Katherine's feelings were overly apparent. She'd never forgive him for his lie. He had tried to keep her from all harm, including the knowledge of his identity, and in the end it had demolished every feeling they'd shared.

James studied him, eyes narrowed. "You know what she's been through this past week."

"Yes."

"She doesn't like to speak of your journey. Tell me about it."

Reynold told him the barest details, trying to keep his mind from wandering to the woman upstairs. James didn't look satisfied.

"I'll be leaving in the morning," Reynold said.

"She might insist my brother should be here for the wedding. I wonder how I can get around it."

Reynold struggled for impassivity. "Married so quickly, James? Your last words about her were not kind."

"She's matured into quite a beauty, don't you think? Oh, so sorry," he added insincerely. "You're not supposed to think that anymore." He watched Reynold with angry intensity. "I have a hard time imagining what it must be like to be raised as you and I were, only to give it all up. The women in particular. How do you stand it?"

Reynold opened his mouth, but the words seemed stuck in his throat.

"I know, I know," James continued, clearly enjoying himself. "Family loyalty and all that. And of course we mustn't forget Edmund's death."

Reynold's guilt seemed to batter the heart inside his chest. "I am no better than any man, James," he said. "This isn't worthy of you. I am going to bed."

James had the grace to redden. "Allow me to show you to a room."

Reynold listened without comment as James pointed out the plate and jewels he had amassed in the great hall. He knew most of it was a show for James's people. He could tell even James's heart wasn't in the performance. But once upstairs, Reynold noticed how sparsely furnished the corridor was. No luxuries adorned the room James showed him to.

James looked him directly in the eyes. "Yes, it's time I married the girl. These rooms need to be furnished."

Reynold closed the door.

Katherine lifted her wet, hot face from the pillow and gasped fresh air into her lungs. Strands of hair clung to her tear-dampened cheek. With shaking fingers she pushed them away and sat up. Her throat hurt and her eyes were swollen. She must cease her pointless crying.

Sniffing, she gathered a blanket around her

shoulders and got out of bed, sinking into the thick carpet. Every time she came into her room, something new had been added. The comfort was nice, but it made her uneasy. Why such a show of wealth below stairs with so little above?

She sank into a cushioned chair before the bare fireplace and tried to think of anything but her predicament. Her mind was a blank pool of water, with much going on beneath the surface, but nothing rising for her to think about. Just Reynold.

Katherine shuddered. He had lied to her. She took a shaky breath and forced back the ever-threatening tears. She didn't blame him for not revealing his identity during their first few days together—after all, she hadn't told him hers. She remembered his hesitation about journeying to the earl's castle, how she'd practically had to drag him here. Now she knew why.

A flood of anger overpowered her teary emotions. Of course Reynold hadn't wanted to approach his brother's castle. He knew his sexual appetites would no longer be appeased.

Katherine groaned in shame. How easily she had given in. She would have traveled on for weeks, not knowing how close they could be to Nottingham, endlessly allowing his seduction until she was with child. Then what would have happened? She could hardly picture Reynold on his knees begging to marry her. And James would have dissolved the contract. She would have had to return to her father in total humiliation.

Katherine stood and began to pace. Thank God

she had come upon James's castle when she had. Although her conduct in the dungeon mortified her, at least she now knew what kind of man Reynold was. A man who could continue to betray his own brother.

Just as Katherine was about to blow out the smoking rushlight, she heard a knock on her door. She straightened with a feeling of dread.

"Who is it?"

A soft voice answered, "It is I."

She practically flew to the door and pressed her lips near the crack. "How dare you!" she hissed. "What if your brother sees you pawing at my door?"

"He is already abed. I must speak with you."

"The servants—"

"No one has seen me. Open the door before someone comes!"

Katherine put her back against the door, spread her legs for balance and held her position. "Go away!"

The latch lifted and the door began to swing slowly open. Her feet slid along the stone floor, then her toes caught on the carpet. She gave up her struggle and whirled to face him, holding the blanket around her like a shield.

"Your gall astounds me," she said, trying to send him the most menacing of looks while her heart pounded erratically.

Reynold closed the door behind him and leaned against it, watching her with his dark, shadowed eyes. The monk's robes hung about his tall, powerful body.

"Did you hear me?" she demanded.

"Aye, I heard. I need to speak with you."

"I wish never to speak with you again! Leave me in peace and go back where you came from!"

"To the monastery?" he said shortly. "I shall go back because I must, but not before you hear my words."

She tried to laugh. "What could you possibly say to me? You can make no excuses for your deception. The moment you realized where we were going, you should have told me your identity!"

"How?" he asked, taking a step towards her.

Katherine shrank back against the bed.

"When I realized who your betrothed was, I was stunned, heartsick. You were blithely following those young travelers. Was I supposed to drag you off into the woods and tell you my horrible secret?"

"It would have been preferable!" Katherine clutched the blanket higher beneath her chin. "By not telling me, you allowed me to—to—" She closed her eyes in misery as she relived their dark coupling in the dungeon. "How could you do it?" she whispered past the ache in her chest. "How could you betray your own brother in his household?"

Chapter 17

Reynold took another step closer, and grasped the bedpost beside Katherine's head. He regretted the fear in her eyes, but could not stop the words that tumbled from his lips.

"I know I have sinned!" he said in a hoarse voice. "But do not dare put all the blame on me. I knew he was my brother, and you damn well knew he was your betrothed!"

Katherine slapped him hard across the face, then gasped and held her hand to her chest. The blanket slipped to the floor, revealing her linen nightdress.

"You are no saint, my lady. I will not be made to take all the blame myself!" Reynold stared into the stark whiteness of her face and felt a momentary twinge of regret.

"Get out of my room."

He heard the icy chill in her voice. He had had his whole apology rehearsed. How had it dissolved into angry accusations?

"Katherine, please—"

"Just leave!" she cried softly, a tear tracing a path down her cheek.

Reynold reached out to wipe it away and she cringed from him. His self-disgust threatening to choke him, he walked towards the door. He put a hand on the latch and looked back at the ghostly whiteness of her gown and the flowing gold curls he would never touch again.

"I am truly sorry, Katherine." He slipped into the hall and closed the door behind him.

Keeping her head held high, Katherine left her chambers at dawn and descended the stairs into the great hall. She heaved a thankful sigh on spotting neither brother, then hurried to the chapel for mass. She didn't walk up the center of the aisle to where James knelt near the altar. Instead she dropped to her knees on the rough stone floor beside the castle servants, who eyed her nervously as they moved aside.

Katherine was embarrassed that her garments so outshone theirs. James had gifted her with another gown, this one of deep blue brocade embroidered in gold. The jeweled belt she wore twinkled in the chapel's smoky rushlight. She had not wanted his expensive gifts, which had obviously kept the village seamstresses up all night. Guilty and ashamed, she bowed her head and prayed, asking God to help her out of this disaster she had brought on herself.

For no matter how angry Katherine was with Reynold's deception, she was just as guilty in their sin. She, too, had known whose home they'd violated. She could not understand why God did not strike her dead for kneeling in His house of worship.

Raising her eyes to the altar, she saw Reynold's back. He knelt near the aisle, away from his brother. His head was bowed and his broad shoulders hunched forward. For a moment Katherine experienced a twinge of sympathy, but she immediately banished it. She had been an innocent before "Brother" Reynold had rescued her.

After mass, Katherine broke the fast with James and Reynold. She ignored the younger brother and focused all her attention on the man she would marry.

"Katherine, my dear," James was saying, "today I will take my best knights on the hunt. If we bring back that cursed stag which yet eludes me, we'll celebrate our impending nuptials with a grand meal."

Katherine nodded and smiled, sipped her wine, and tried to appear interested. His last sentence made her choke. "Impending?"

"I have waited too long to make you my wife. It is time you took your proper place."

It seemed so long ago, but when Katherine was innocent, she would not have read a second meaning into James's words. Now she reddened with anger and only spared Reynold a brief heated glance. The monk tore off a handful of bread and ate it without looking up.

"I have dispatched a messenger to your father,

telling him you are here, safe, and that we desire to wed as soon as possible. No doubt he and your mother will arrive shortly."

Katherine's mouth slowly dropped open, and a wedge of bread seemed to stick in her throat. Someone kicked her hard on the shin with a booted foot. She jumped and tried to ignore Reynold's blazing eyes.

Katherine swallowed the lump of bread. "So soon? But I must prepare—"

"I'm sure during the many years we've been betrothed, you and your mother have prepared your bridal wardrobe."

"Of course, but—"

"And your mother will no doubt bring it. We will not have to wait a moment longer to be wed." James leaned forward and took her shaking hand. "Does this not make you happy?"

Katherine looked down at his hand engulfing hers. In her mind she saw another hand upon her flesh, an image forever burned on her brain. "Yes, of course I am happy," she said between her teeth. A sudden concern for her father wiped all else from her mind. "James, what did you say to my parents?"

Both brothers looked at her, and she couldn't help but remember Reynold's unkind references to her father.

James shrugged. "I told of your abduction, naturally, and that you were now safe with me and ready to be wed."

She lowered her voice and glanced about to see

if anyone was listening. "Did you mention the traitors?"

James reached over to pat her hand. "I understand, my dear. Your father's safety is the reason you did not have Reynold bring you home. I respected your confidences and did not tell him of his friends' plotting. The decision to tell him is up to you."

Katherine sat back in her chair as a wave of relief left her weak. "Please keep this a secret, both of you."

They glanced at one another.

"It is much to ask, I know, but I wish my father to remain untouched by the traitors' disloyalty." She frowned at the doubt both brothers tried to mask. She knew they were not yet convinced of her father's innocence. Doubts crept into her own heart, but she put them aside.

Reynold said, "My lady, you cannot forever protect him as you would a child. War is coming, and soon he will know all."

"I understand." She clasped her hands before her and gave them each a direct look. "Allow him to find out when the traitors are unmasked by the king, when no disloyalty can be attributed to him. I have risked my life to protect him, and I don't wish it to be for naught."

The brothers nodded. Katherine could tell Reynold disagreed with her, but thankfully, he held his tongue. James eyed her but said nothing as he lifted a tankard of ale to his mouth. A ring glittered on his finger. Like the one she would soon wear. She sighed.

The day had not gone at all as she'd expected. She'd wanted to punish Reynold for his deception, to hurt him for all the sins she'd imagined he'd committed against her, by flirting with James and ignoring Reynold. But James had disrupted all her plans.

Marriage? So soon? She tried to imagine her wedding night with James, and could only shudder. Would she be able to carry off her deception of virginity? Or should she tell the truth and accept her punishment?

Katherine looked at the two brothers, so dissimilar in face and build, but for the dark hair. If she told the truth, James might demand revenge on his brother. She could not bear to be the force that split an entire family, although she'd like to split their heads from their bodies.

"Katherine," James said, bringing her out of her dark thoughts, "allow Reynold to keep you company while my men and I hunt. My poor brother has closed himself off from such blood sports. And heaven forbid, we might see a pretty village maiden!"

Katherine gritted her teeth. Reynold's face remained impassive as if he were used to such treatment.

"Forgive my wit, my dear. As I've told Reynold many a time, he is a better man than I to give up life for God."

Katherine sensed a dark undercurrent between

them, but could make no sense of it. James left the table in search of his knights. Katherine glared after him, thinking that she hated all men.

"Lady Katherine?"

She composed herself, then slowly looked up into Reynold's eyes, as bright and hard as jewels.

"Shall we take a walk in the lady's garden?"

"My needlework—"

"There will be plenty of daylight for your ladylike pursuits." Reynold, as reserved as a stranger, stood up in his black habit to tower above her. "Come, my lady, I must speak with you."

Katherine pushed back her chair and smiled weakly at the serving girl who cleared away her goblet and plate. Reynold made no attempt to take her arm, even when she stumbled on her hem. They walked side by side into the warm sunshine. Dust rose high into the air as the inner ward came to life. A pack of dogs chased a stray chicken, and she heard the insistent clank of hammer on anvil as the blacksmith plied his trade.

She followed Reynold towards the back of the castle, where the sounds of the soldiers' barracks faded into the distance, and once again she heard the twittering of birds. The lady's garden, its white gate hanging ajar, was a precious retreat for the lady of the castle. And that would soon be her. Katherine sighed at the garden's weedy disarray.

In silence she walked beside Reynold down the dirt path, winding past an apple tree and flowering rose bushes. A breeze whipped a stray curl into Katherine's eyes and she tucked it behind her ear. She glanced from beneath her lashes at Reynold, so dark and forbidding and out of place in the lady's garden. She had a sudden image of the priest who used to follow at her mother's heels as she walked through her garden. Whispering some evil, Katherine had no doubt. But not Reynold. No matter her anger, she knew he was unlike the monks she'd known.

"You have nothing to say, no hidden purpose for our walk, Brother Reynold?" she asked, then regretted her use of his title.

"No purpose, my lady. I would have been gone but for my brother's interference." He hesitated. "I had hoped you would never need know my identity."

Katherine stared at him in outrage. "How do you think I would have felt upon learning it years from now?"

"I had not considered that," he said softly.

"My anger would have been magnified a thousand fold!"

"I only thought to spare you from the hurt."

"You thought too late to spare me, Brother Reynold."

He stiffened and turned to face her. "Then perhaps I should tell you all. King Richard—"

He broke off and stared over her head with a frown. Katherine turned and spied a division of archers running excitedly for the main gate.

"What is it?" Katherine asked.

"Someone must be approaching," he said, his face hard and closed against her.

Katherine turned and left the garden, walking quickly towards the gatehouse. The archers and other soldiers made way for her until she stopped short in their midst. Up ahead a confusion of horses and carts and litters were distributed all across the inner ward. Armed guards dismounted and she recognized their colors immediately. Katherine caught a glimpse of the one person who could make her day worse. Her father.

Shocked and disoriented, clutching her arm, she took a step backwards, tripped over her hem and landed heavily against Reynold. He held her up and she allowed it for a moment, trying to regain her strength for the days to come. It appeared her marriage was closer than she had thought.

Reynold told himself he could not leave Katherine. She seemed almost immobile as she watched the soldiers dismount.

"You know these men?" he asked near her ear. Before she could answer, the lord's pennant unfurled and he understood. "Your father travels quickly."

"Too quickly," she murmured, or had Reynold imagined her words? Did perhaps she, too, wonder who masterminded her kidnapping?

She remained still and Reynold kept his place at her back as they watched the curtains part on an austere litter. No sooner had a woman's gown rippled forward, than a priest hurried to her side to help her alight. Reynold felt the tension that surrounded Katherine like a wall against him. Was this one of the monks who'd turned her against all holy men?

A tall thin woman emerged and squinted in the glare of the sun. She was dressed in a plain black gown and her hair was invisible beneath an unadorned headdress and veil. She glanced around the ward impassively, then lent an ear to her priest.

Before him, Katherine shuddered. Reynold laid a hand on her shoulder and squeezed once. She allowed the contact for a moment, then started forward through the crowd. He followed at a discreet distance, watching in satisfaction as her father enveloped her in a bone-squeezing hug. He hoped for Katherine's sake that her father was not involved in the treason.

Lord Durham cupped his daughter's face in his hands. "Katherine, dearest heart, we were so worried!" He hugged her close again, then held her at arm's length. "You look well, child. I'm so thankful that James rescued you."

"No, Father, his brother gave me aid until we reached James."

"James?" said a woman's cool voice.

Without looking, Reynold knew Katherine's mother had spoken. She moved forward fluidly, with her lapdog priest at her elbow. Katherine lowered her head briefly.

"Good day, Mother," she said. "My betrothed requested that I use his given name."

The woman nodded. "You are soon to be his

wife. It is only fitting. You are . . . well, Katherine?"

Reynold heard a wealth of meaning in those words, none of which he liked. Katherine tensed before him, and he saw her holding her weak arm, a habit she'd seemed to have forgotten with him. He began to wonder if perhaps Katherine's mother could be a traitor.

"I am well, Mother. Brother Reynold protected me."

Her parents suddenly looked over Katherine's head and saw him. He nodded respectfully, trying to appear serene, when what he felt like was a clumsy mountain. He was as tense as Katherine seemed to be, worried that they would see what was in his heart when he looked at their daughter. But the Earl of Durham only let out his breath in relief.

"Bolton mentioned you'd been imprisoned in a ruined monastery. I guess I assumed the monks had long since fled. I'm glad you had such good protection, child."

Reynold gritted his teeth. *You should be punching me, old man,* he thought angrily. *I ravished your daughter!* But a monk seemed above reproach in their household.

"Brother," Katherine said in the silence, "allow me to present my parents, Theobald Berkeley, Earl of Durham, and his wife, Lady Durham."

"Brother Reynold," the countess said, "could you tell me where the family chapel is located? The hasty journey did not leave me much time for prayer."

Heaven forbid she should worry about her daughter, Reynold thought darkly. He gave the woman directions and watched in amazement as her priest silently led her away. The earl seemed not to spare his wife another thought.

"Brother Reynold, do you know why Katherine was abducted?"

Reynold felt Katherine stiffen at his side, and his own unease made him hesitate. It was difficult to lie to a man who only wanted to help his daughter. But Reynold understood Katherine's motives.

"No, my lord. Lady Katherine and I thought perhaps a ransom might be demanded of you or my brother."

The gray-headed man nodded thoughtfully, but his trim body was still taut with tension. "Brother Reynold, why did you not bring my daughter home to me?"

"Father—"

The earl cut Katherine short with a shake of his head. "No, child, I wish to hear this from Brother Reynold."

Reynold glanced at Katherine, who lowered her head and slowly brought up one arm to be cradled by the other. Loving father or no, the man didn't respect his daughter.

"I wanted to bring her home, my lord, but she refused to give me her true name. She insisted the kidnapper would look for her there."

"So you brought her here."

"This is where she bade me go."

"And your journey was safe and uneventful."

This was harder than Reynold had expected, to lie to one who could easily be Reynold's liege lord. But protecting Katherine was more important. He had already hurt her enough.

"The kidnapper pursued us, and once we were set upon by thieves," Reynold said.

The earl's keen eyes assessed him. "And you alone, a monk, defended Katherine."

Reynold nodded. "I have only been a novice these past eight months, my lord."

Lord Durham frowned. "But when your brother first talked about marriage years ago, wasn't there a younger brother destined for the monastery? I didn't think it was you."

"My brother, Edmund, died eight months ago, and I took his place."

The earl's brows shot up. Before he could respond, they were distracted as another procession came through the gatehouse.

"Lord Durham," Reynold said, "is this more of your retinue?"

"No, Brother. 'Tis a family member of yours, whom we met upon the road. Your sister, Lady Margery."

As Reynold smiled and walked away, Katherine felt a surge of panic begin to overtake her. Surely her father must see the guilt and deception in her eyes. He did not deserve such a poor daughter.

She blinked back tears as his arm came around her shoulder. Together they watched brother and sister reunited. Reynold reached up to help his sister dismount from her dappled mare, and she fell into his arms with a fierce hug. Holding hands, both dark-haired and tall, they spoke softly together for a moment, then walked towards Katherine's family.

Katherine straightened, thankful at last for James's gift of clothing. Reynold's sister possessed an undeniable elegance in her cream-colored gown, laced at the bodice and draped in beribboned folds down the long lines of her body. A maiden still, she wore her dark curls uncovered, caught at the back of her neck with a ribbon. She gave a fluid curtsy as Reynold introduced her.

"Lady Katherine Berkeley, may I present my sister, Margery Welles."

Holding her father's arm, Katherine sank into a deep curtsy, then breathed a sigh of relief as Margery smiled at her.

"Lady Katherine, it is good to finally meet James's betrothed. I have been waiting many years for him to marry."

"As have I, my lady."

"Let us not 'my lady' each other to death. I am simply Margery, so you must be Katherine."

Katherine smiled and thought perhaps she had found a friend. But as her father spoke to Margery, self-doubt and despair gnawed at her heart. What if Margery knew what kind of a woman she was, how Katherine had pitted Margery's brothers against one another?

And her surname, "Welles," was that also Reynold's name? My lord, she'd had—relations—with the man and didn't even know his full name.

Katherine's throat tightened and she felt unworthy of them all.

Chapter 18

Reynold escorted his sister inside, followed by the earl and Katherine. Margery sent him an occasional slanting glance but he ignored it, wondering what she must have heard from Lord Durham, as well as their brother.

"Would you care for wine, Margery?" he asked, leading her to a cushioned chair before the hearth.

"Ale, I think." She grinned.

Reynold shrugged in amusement and brought her a tankard. "No dainty goblet for you, baby."

"Now, now, Reynold, our childhood is long past." She glanced at Katherine and Lord Durham speaking together a few feet away. "I understand you rescued the child from a harrowing experience."

"The 'child' is two years your senior, and a betrothed woman."

"Unlike myself?" Margery gave him an impish smile.

Reynold grinned and shook his head. "Had James sent you a message?"

"No. A few weeks past, he insisted I come for a long stay, while King Richard and Henry Tudor play their games across the countryside."

"Hardly games."

"Forgive my impertinence, Reynold, but I am nigh sick to death of this endless feuding."

Reynold's gaze shifted to Katherine, and he felt his tension ease just looking at her. "Then Katherine's father told you everything?"

"I'm sure not quite everything. All I know is someone abducted her, imprisoned her at St. Anthony's, then you helped her escape and brought her here."

"You have the basic facts."

"Ah, but there must be more."

Margery studied him so intently that Reynold wondered what she could see in his face. He made a concerted effort to ignore Katherine.

"I still cannot adjust myself to the sight of you in those robes, Reynold. They would have suited Edmund, but you—"

Reynold tensed and drained his ale.

"I'm sorry," Margery said softly. "I forget that some things wound even you. Is it so very difficult?"

He tried to smile at her. "I have adjusted to my new life. It is not as bad as I imagined it would be."

She rolled her eyes. "But bad enough, I am certain. I'll never understand why you did this. Edmund's death wasn't really your fault."

Reynold sent her a sharp glance. "I can't discuss this, Margery. Not now."

She leaned forward and touched his arm. "Then tell me why our brother has finally accepted his wedding. Did he see Katherine and realize what a fool he'd been?"

Reynold nodded, watching Katherine against his better judgment. Her long golden hair tumbled down her back, and in his mind he could remember the shine of her curls by firelight, as they erotically hid her breasts from his hungry gaze.

"Reynold?"

He glanced quickly at his sister.

"Perhaps James's motive was not so much love as finances."

He shrugged and eyed her beneath lowered brows.

"Don't give me that evil-eyed look," she said playfully. "We both know how James lives his life."

"You underestimate Katherine."

Margery began to respond, then sank back in her chair and gazed thoughtfully at Katherine. Reynold wished he'd kept his mouth shut. Margery was a shrewd girl—too intelligent for her own good. And now she watched Katherine with great speculation.

Reynold sighed. He was tired of constantly guarding his words and thoughts. He knew he gazed at Katherine far too often. The anxiety of endlessly wondering who would notice his preoccupation proved to be too much. He felt a sudden need to escape. Excusing himself to Margery, he avoided Katherine and her father and headed outdoors.

Although the cool, sunny day was refreshing, the inner ward itself did not give him peace. Everywhere people bowed to him, from serving girls down to the lowest scullery boy. No one smiled; good-natured conversations died away with one glimpse of his black robe. He was an outcast. He wondered how much James had told everyone about Edmund's death.

More depressed than ever, Reynold veered towards the stables which formed the foundation for the barracks built above. Amidst the smell of hay and horses, he finally relaxed. He patted nuzzling equine noses, and brushed out glossy coats while the stableboys gave him wide berth.

A familiar whinny made him hesitate.

"Thunder?" he whispered.

There, in the last stall, was the final possession he had given up before entering the monastery— his stallion. Thunder's nostrils flared and he tossed his black head as Reynold advanced.

Memories washed over him as Reynold buried his face in the horse's neck. Days spent in the saddle, where only Thunder's bravery and companionship kept Reynold going. Hours spent practicing the art of war until horse and master each dripped sweat, yet moved as one.

He stepped back and looked over the animal. He had never known if James had sold Thunder or not, and had asked no promises of his brother. But obviously Thunder was well cared for. James knew value when he saw it, Reynold thought wryly.

As he began saddling his horse, one of the lurking stableboys called from the shadows, "Brother, not that 'orse. 'E throws all but the master."

Reynold smiled. "I was his master for many a year, lad."

He led the horse outside. Soldiers leaned out the barracks windows above him, laughing good-naturedly and pointing. Reynold hitched his habit a bit higher and mounted Thunder. The laughter died down behind him as he rode out of the inner ward, dodging people and carts and animals in a temporary bid for freedom.

For an hour, he concentrated on nothing but moving with the animal. Wild thoughts of escaping to tournaments or mercenary work in France flitted through Reynold's mind. He knew it all for naught. He couldn't desert Katherine. She may belong to his brother, but still he could not leave. Though she did not know it, her mission was not yet complete.

Ahead of a bank of dark clouds, Reynold returned to the castle, hot and tired, but content. He knew what had to be done.

In the tiltyard, he came upon the knights and their squires preparing for war. He reined in Thunder, watching the men riding with lances lowered to snare metal rings. He laughed aloud when the spinning quintain knocked a swordsman to the ground.

"I'm sure you could teach us all a thing or two,

Brother," said a voice behind him. "But then, you don't swordfight any more, do you."

Reynold turned in the saddle and saw James, dusty, sweaty, and coldly triumphant atop his charger as a boar was dragged through the castle gates.

Reynold smiled stiffly, unable to forget he would soon be the loser in the most important battle with his brother. "A fine thing it is that I swore no vows, James. Who else would have kept your betrothed safe? But then, I am sure I have grown quite stiff in the last few months."

"Not if your seat in that saddle is any indication," he said, a reluctant smile turning up one corner of his mouth. "I saw you flying through the fields but a few minutes ago." James shook his head ruefully. "God's teeth! One of my men crossed himself. Thought it was death all in black headed for the castle."

Reynold shrugged and turned back to watch the soldiers. "Your bride's parents have arrived."

James rode up beside him, but not too close. "I saw the earl's banner." He paused. "Brother, care to make a wager? Or is that against your vows?"

Reynold's horse danced away from James. Maybe the beast was smarter than its master, he thought, not for the first time.

"I have no money, James."

"Ah yes, gave it all to Margery, didn't you."

Reynold remained silent. He knew they had gained the attention of the knights and their men, who no longer even pretended to practice.

"Very well, then," James continued, raising his voice. "Perhaps we shall merely wager our respective pride against the outcome. Let us practice together—for old time's sake, of course, dear brother."

The day grew colder, and Reynold's heart with it. He remembered another day, raising his sword against another brother. Bile rose in his throat, and he knew his face went white. He almost shouted to the ward, *I killed my brother! Do you not understand?*

But there was James, the smirk dying from his face, waiting to finish what he had begun with his fists eight months before. Would he only be happy when Reynold was dead, too?

Then he spied Katherine and her father, arm in arm, and he understood. Although James had promised to say nothing to Katherine about Edmund's death, Reynold knew it would come soon, and he was powerless to stop it. And above all, lurked the newest, secret sin against his brother. If Reynold's humiliation would help James, then Reynold owed him.

Reynold said with a distant voice, "I trust we shall use blunt swords."

James actually laughed, his blue eyes flashing. "As if we would ever want to hurt each other. Would you care to change your habit? I'm sure the armorer has a spare tunic."

When Reynold emerged from the armory in a sleeveless leather jerkin, he saw Katherine and her father standing with James. Katherine's face reddened, and she looked anywhere but at him.

The Earl of Durham, on the other hand, was obviously enjoying himself. He was tall and barrel-chested, no stranger to combat. "My future son claims you were the strongest knight in all England. Does he merely exaggerate, Brother Reynold?"

Reynold slanted a glance at his brother, not understanding the game. "My brother has a kind tongue, my lord, even when it runs away with him. James, shall we finish this quickly?"

James handed him a dulled sword. Together they moved into the center of the tiltyard. Dust swirled around them from the earth below as Reynold took up his stance opposite his brother. James wore a smile which Reynold couldn't quite interpret. What did he hope to gain from this?

He felt the heaviness of the sword in his hand, and was amazed at how unfamiliar its grip was after only a few months. He never thought he'd hold one again—had sworn to himself that he wouldn't. And here he was, facing off against his last brother. His heart pounded in his ears, blocking out the cheering crowd.

Then James's sword flashed down in a ray of the sun, and Reynold tried to forget his years of training. He fought defensively, allowing James to play to the crowd. Sweat dripped from his brow, his stomach was in knots. All he could see was Edmund's face across two swords, Edmund's clumsy parries. He was trying so hard not to be sick that he wasn't paying close enough attention to his match with James. Almost without realizing it, his body remembered its training, became one with the rhythm of the deadly dance. It was only when James tried a particularly deft move, and seemed so surprised when Reynold easily deflected it, that Reynold saw what was happening.

He was unable to give less of himself in combat, was barely restraining himself from forcing James back, from disarming his own brother. And all it would take was one prick of his sword . . .

Reynold stumbled back in horror, his sword falling from his hands. The crowd gasped as James pressed his advantage, only inches from Reynold's throat. And for one instant, Reynold almost wished James would kill him, because nothing would ever let him forget Edmund's last moments of life. And then he heard Katherine scream.

He whirled towards her, saw her white, tear-drenched face, and couldn't bear for her to know what kind of man he truly was.

Katherine, sick to her stomach, watched in shock as Reynold fled the tiltyard.

Her father patted her white-knuckled hand. "Katherine, do not worry yourself so. James is fine. They are merely grown boys playing. Ah, but Brother Reynold is wasted in the monastery. When a man can fight like that . . ."

Katherine was not reassured by his words. Even she could tell that James had not Reynold's talent. She closed her eyes as every moment of the sword-fight flashed through her mind. Reynold had been magnificent. Hands that had caressed her swung

the sword in a dance of flashing sunlight and
deadly turns. The muscular body that had lain at
her mercy moved with strength and agility. She
had no doubt that had he chosen to, he could have
killed his brother, even with a blunted sword.

But then something had happened. Reynold had
given up, allowed his brother to best him. The look
in his eyes sent panicked chills through her blood.
What so haunted him, drove him into the monastery?

Katherine's heart ached for him. His misery felt
like a physical part of her. She had to force herself
to remember the misery he had inflicted on her.

"Father," she said. "I promised I'd spend time
with Mother. Please excuse me."

James waved as if to call her over, but she ignored him. He seemed to take too much pleasure
in his brother's misery. As she turned away, the
skies finally released a light summer rain, cool and
drenching. She knew she should go inside, but she
found herself hesitating, searching the inner ward.
And it wasn't until she saw Reynold, disappearing
towards the back of the castle, that she knew she
had been looking for him. Her feet traced his path
although she angrily told them not to. When she
rounded the corner and couldn't find him, she insisted to herself that she return to the castle.

But instead she went inside the overgrown
lady's garden. The rain fell softly, almost hissing
as it splattered across leaves and flowers. Kather-

ine followed the weedy path back towards the wall, where vines hung over trellises, forming a secluded walkway. Ducking her head, she entered the tunnel, and came face to face with Reynold.

Chapter 19

~~~~~~∽∽∽~~~~~~

Reynold's wavy hair was plastered to his
head, rain fell in streaks down his anguished face. They stared at each other for endless
moments.

"Leave me!" he finally said, his voice hoarse.

She stepped closer. "Reynold, what is happening? Why did you throw down your weapon?"

"James bested me," he whispered, slumping
down on a bench against the ivy-covered wall.

"Do not lie to me. I know what I saw. Your
face—"

He squeezed his eyes shut, and the rain dripped
down his cheeks like tears.

Katherine came closer, telling herself to leave,
but unable to comply. Reynold was hurt, he was
aching inside, and she couldn't just leave him like
this. Hesitantly, she spread her damp skirts and
sat down beside him.

When he said nothing, she finally whispered,
"Tell me. Tell me everything, Reynold. Why did
you go into the monastery?"

He sighed, and then the painful words began to tumble out. "My brother, Edmund, was destined from birth for the monastery. He was sickly as a child, pale, skinny. There was nothing he liked better than burying his face in a book. I—I did not understand him."

There was bewilderment in his voice, and such self-hatred that Katherine longed to hold his hand, but she could not.

"He embarrassed me," Reynold continued softly. "How could I, this worthy knight, have such a wretched brother? He could not even defend himself."

"Oh Reynold," she whispered, and this time she slid her fingers over his, where they clenched his thighs.

"When I could take it no longer, I challenged him to learn to swordfight. I goaded him, I bullied him. And in the end, Edmund gave in." He gave a ragged sigh. "When I lifted my sword to James, all I could see was Edmund's white face, his concentration, his pathetic efforts to please me. I—I tried so hard to be easy on him, to instruct him. But he was not like my other training partners. He did not know when to get out of the way."

Katherine encircled his shoulders with her arms, tears spilling from her own eyes, mixing with the rain. She almost didn't want to hear the rest, but she knew Reynold couldn't stop now.

"My sword caught him on the shoulder. It was but a scratch. My God, we *laughed* about it that night. He was proud of himself, and I was arrogantly sure I had done my knightly duty. But by the next day, the wound was inflamed and he had a fever. And the day after that—''

His voice broke, and he buried his face in his hands. Katherine was on her knees on the bench, arms as far about him as they would go. His shoulders shook, and she held him, soothed him.

"It wasn't your fault, Reynold. Surely you must see that."

He wrenched from her embrace and stood, whirling until he leaned over her. "I killed my own brother! I was embarrassed by him. I forced him—''

"In your own way, you tried to help him. Even a monk must know how to defend himself. But his death was an accident!"

"It took five days, and as I sobbed at his bedside, he forgave me over and over again." Reynold shuddered. "But I never forgave myself. And neither did James."

Reynold closed his eyes, but he could not block the sight of Edmund's pain-ravaged face.

"Reynold, Edmund had the right of it. He would not want you to suffer like this. James's opinion doesn't matter—only your own does. You *must* forgive yourself."

As he looked into her earnest face, so serious, so anguished for him, Reynold felt something wrench inside himself.

"But I cannot! I cannot just . . . let his memory go."

She clasped his hands. "If you forgive yourself,

you'll be able to remember the precious times you spent with your brother, not his death. You will go back to the monastery at peace with yourself."

Reynold looked at Katherine in amazement, wondering where the timid, naive girl he first met had gone. Bolstered by her serene gaze, he felt the ache in his heart begin to ease. He had told her everything about him, and she had not run, had not looked upon him with either contempt or fear.

Very slowly, he lifted her hands to his lips and held them there. She tasted of sweet rain and perfumed skin. She trembled, and finally broke away.

"I must go," she whispered. And then she ran.

Reynold couldn't move. He stared after Katherine in shock. Everything he had believed about himself was lying in shattered pieces. Just telling her about Edmund had dissolved away the heaviness that had clung to his heart. Images of his brother flashed through his mind, but he no longer saw his face contorted in the agonies of death. He remembered Edmund as a youngster, wheezing for breath through another one of his attacks, but insisting Reynold read to him long into the night. The bloodlust of practice and battle receded only with Edmund. He realized those moments were some of the most peaceful in his life. Edmund never took Reynold's goading seriously, always thought the best of everything Reynold said. He had taught Reynold that the weak were not to be pitied, that they had strengths of their own, secrets they could share.

Without knowing it, Reynold had absorbed Edmund's lessons in peace, in helping others. Without Edmund's subtle guidance, he never would have been able to help Katherine the way she needed him to. In his old life, he would have done everything for her, because of course he would have thought her a weak woman, incapable of doing things that needed strength. Through Edmund's example he had learned that some people have a different kind of strength.

Reynold released a shuddering sigh and bent his face into his hands. Everything had changed, including what he thought should become of his life.

As the sun began to set, Katherine watched with a heavy heart as James conversed easily with her father. She could not stop herself from wondering how they would look at her if they knew of her weakness, her sin. And what they would do to Reynold made her too ill to think of.

She turned to watch Reynold, who smiled and talked with his sister. He appeared more comfortable with Margery than he was with James, although that seemed natural, given that he and Margery had the same father. He was more relaxed, peaceful. Didn't Reynold feel as awkward and guilty as she did? Or did talking about Edmund finally relieve his soul?

Katherine's mother entered the great hall just as the servants were setting up trestle tables for the evening meal. The inevitable coldness filled Katherine's heart whenever she looked at the countess. She remembered her mother's angry accusations when Katherine had confessed the attack by her priest. Dazed and hurt by her mother's disbelief, aching from the pain of her broken arm, Katherine had listened stoically to the sermon, then realized she had to bury the attack inside her. Why should her father believe her if her mother didn't?

Now that she was older, Katherine realized she should have gone to her father. He was protective of her, and distrustful of her mother's confidantes. But that priest was long since gone, and there was no point in opening old wounds. Besides, how could she complain that one monk had attempted to rape her, while she allowed and encouraged the embrace of another? She could not bear the thought of her father's contempt.

Holding her weak arm, trying not to trip through the rushes, Katherine approached James's table and sat beside him. Her parents, her mother's priest Brother Adams, Reynold, and Margery joined them. Margery took her seat on the other side of James, leaving Reynold no choice but to sit in the empty chair beside Katherine. She tried not to look at him, though her fingers shook as she sipped her wine. Margery smiled at her and she smiled back.

"The message you sent was well timed, James," Lord Durham said as he split a loaf of bread. "I was already preparing for a journey south to His Highness."

"How is King Richard taking the news of the Tudor's landing?"

Katherine stiffened.

"He is relieved that the culmination is at hand. He has lived with Henry's shadow over him for far too long."

"So you think our king will be victorious?" James asked.

"How can he not? Henry is no warrior. He needs others for that. King Richard can fight his own battles."

"He is a wise man to request your counsel, my lord," James said. "But perhaps you can spare us a few days for your daughter's wedding."

There were gasps of pleasure from the dinner guests, but Katherine's hearing seemed to fade away. Marriage to James. She always thought she'd have time to prepare—yet she'd had five years and suddenly it wasn't enough. She couldn't lift her gaze from the table. James's hands were folded loosely before him, as if he were at ease with his own power to change all their lives. On her other side, Reynold's strong, rough hands were clenched in fists. Katherine remembered his manipulations, the pain she had suffered when she'd first seen the two brothers side by side. Though she understood him so much better, Reynold would have to solve his own problems.

"I have sent a messenger to King Richard," James was saying, "to ask for a special license to marry during this time of impending war. By tomorrow Katherine and I will be man and wife."

His hands enfolded hers, and Katherine tried to smile up into his face. The room retreated and there was only James, arrogant, confident of his desirability. She tried to imagine this man in her bed, doing the things Reynold had done to her. Her dinner seemed to creep back up her throat.

"Katherine," her mother said, and Katherine tore her gaze away from her betrothed. "James had told us to bring your wedding finery, but I had no idea we would be so . . . rushed."

Katherine felt her face drain of blood at the disapproving condemnation in her mother's expression. The countess actually thought that there was an unsavory reason for James's haste. She lowered her eyelids to hide the surge of anger that rose within her. Katherine had a sudden wild urge to stand up and confess all her sins, every last one, in such detail that her mother would run screaming from her presence forever.

"Now, Maud," Lord Durham said, "war may soon be upon us. You would deny your daughter an early chance at happiness just for propriety?"

Lady Durham ignored her husband and leaned to whisper in her monk's ear. Katherine's insides crawled with revulsion. She felt Reynold's light touch on her leg and drew a deep breath to control herself. He always seemed to know what she was feeling and how best to comfort her. It was difficult to remain angry with him, although she needed her anger to keep other, more frightening feelings at bay. Since he had told her about Edmund, her defenses seemed to be slowly unraveling.

James smiled. "I admit to my share of wedding nerves these past years. But now that I have had the chance to know your daughter better, I think myself a fool. I would have enjoyed her grace and companionship these many years. You cannot fault a man for realizing his errors and correcting them."

Katherine's father nodded with pleased good humor.

"If you have no objections," James continued, "I would have our priest, Father Carstairs, perform the ceremony. My brother would be my first choice, but he is yet a novice, and I find I cannot wait for his final vows."

Katherine felt a giggle welling up inside her, hysterical and struggling to be free. She brought her napkin to her mouth and pretended to cough. Her eyes watered as the laughter seemed to go on and on inside, reverberating through her soul.

Her mother stood up with icy grace. "If the wedding ceremony shall be performed tomorrow, Katherine and I have much to prepare. Come, Katherine."

Lady Durham's room was already furnished with her personal possessions and bed, unloaded earlier by servants. Her mother's things had not changed during Katherine's lifetime. No rug to sinfully warm the feet, wooden stools without the comfort of cushions, thin bed curtains that let in a draft to remind the occupant not to become too comfortable.

Katherine sat in her customary seat beside the roaring fire, wondering for the hundredth time if the licking flames were to remind her of eternal damnation. It was already too late, she thought with a mental sigh.

Her mother indicated a worn trunk beneath a shuttered window. "I brought your garments, and the sinful amount of cloth promised you in your marriage contract."

"Thank you, Mother," Katherine murmured, lowering her gaze in resignation.

"The bed linens you wove have been brought into the castle. From the appearance of the family apartments, you will be doing much weaving. It occupies the mind, as you well know."

"Yes, Mother."

"Do you have any questions, Katherine?"

"Mother?" She raised her face in confusion. Her mother looked away.

"About marriage."

Katherine stared in stupefaction. "I—well, nay."

Lady Durham seemed to shrink a bit as she let out her breath. "You are fortunate James is kind to you. With your—affliction—I was worried you would only be able to attract old men or those interested in your fortune."

"Which is exactly what happened," Katherine said, forgetting herself in her bitterness.

Her mother looked sharply at her. "All men expect a good dowry. Only a vain, sinful woman believes she is the main inducement to marriage."

"Yes, Mother."

"I feel blessed that you have never had reason to be vain."

Katherine looked away.

"Do you need to see the gown for your wedding? I must have it pressed."

"I remember well what it looks like." She had spent months designing and sewing her own creation with loving detail. She was beginning to think no man deserved it.

"Goodnight, Katherine."

She looked back at her mother, who was holding a dark bedrobe. On the eve of Katherine's wedding, the woman was still able to be coldly dispassionate. Katherine felt a piece of her heart die.

"Goodnight, Mother."

Katherine lay in bed, eyes wide, staring unseeing at the ceiling. A sliver of moonlight penetrated her open shutters, but the fireplace was dark and silent. With a heavy sigh, she rolled onto her stomach. It was no use trying to sleep. Tomorrow was the day she'd spent her entire girlhood dreaming about. She should count herself lucky that James was a young man, and attractive. He treated her courteously even when no one was about. He was not miserly with his money—although that was the reason he obviously needed her dowry. Katherine would live well. But would she be happy?

Although she struggled against it, Reynold's face, dark with shadows, swam before her closed eyes. She shivered in wonder at the emotions that arose to squeeze her throat. Restlessly, she moved her legs against the sheets. Although his face once inspired fear, now his narrowed eyes and stern lips spoke of passion held tightly under control, always simmering, waiting to burst forth and submerge her in wave upon wave of desire too long hidden.

Katherine groaned and wrapped her arms around the pillow. Her wedding day loomed, yet all she could think of was her soon-to-be brother by marriage. She would be happy with James's devotion if she had never met Reynold. She would also probably be dead.

She squeezed her eyes shut and a single tear fell from her lashes. She could not change the past. She must bury her guilt and live a pure life to atone for her sins. She should confess—but no. She could not tell James's priest, who would know her voice. She could only confide in God.

Katherine slipped from the bed and knelt down on the stone floor. She folded her hands and bowed her head, prepared to promise her Lord anything if He would ease her conscience.

The door suddenly opened and Katherine's head jerked up in shock. Reynold squeezed his large body through the smallest opening possible, then quietly shut the door behind him. He leaned back against the portal and simply looked at her.

Katherine could only gape at him, feeling as if words would never pass her stunned lips again. Then panic set in. With a gasp, she gathered the skirt of her bedclothes around her and jumped to her feet. She pointed wildly at the door while backing away.

"G-get out!" she cried in a voice barely above a whisper, her body shaking. She stumbled backwards against her trunk of clothes, and fell hard into a sitting position atop the lid. Reynold seemed to rise above her, like a seductive demon in his black robes.

Chapter 20

Katherine tried to rally the revulsion she once felt upon seeing Reynold. But now excitement and danger throbbed through her veins, her breathing came in gasps, and her hands shook. She twisted them into her skirts.

"Reynold, this is the eve of my wedding!" Her voice cracked once and she cleared her throat. "If my parents discover you here—"

"Dress quickly, and no one need know."

"Dress—"

He sank to his knees before her. Katherine pushed backward as his face neared hers, and almost fell off the trunk, but he caught her arms.

"Release me!"

He did as she asked, but still he loomed too near.

"Reynold, what insanity prompted you to risk exposure?"

"Not insanity, my lady. I feared for your peace of mind should you find out that my brother does

247

not believe your story of the traitors to King Richard."

Katherine's wariness faded slightly. "But—I was there when he sent his men to warn the king. He promised—"

"He only made his promise to soothe you, Katherine. He does not believe a mere woman could have useful information for the king."

"He thinks I have lied?" she demanded, attempting to stand.

Reynold pushed her hips onto the trunk, and Katherine was too upset to protest.

"He does not believe you a liar. He just thinks the information would be easily discovered by the king without your help."

"But how could a man, even a king, believe his own friends would turn against him?"

He put a finger to her lips and the shock jolted through Katherine's body. She knocked his hand away and looked anywhere but into his face.

"I agree with you," he said. "It is still vital that we take your message to the king."

"Reynold, you will do this for me?" she asked, searching his face.

"I cannot do it alone."

"Surely, one of your sister's men—"

"I need you, Katherine."

His hoarse voice made her shiver and she hugged her arms across her chest. The crescent moon faded away as a cloud came between it and the earth. Reynold's dark face grew murkier, and she could no longer tell if he was staring at her with those intense, strange-colored eyes.

"Tomorrow I marry your brother," she answered flatly, willing him to accept that and leave.

"I am not talking about that! You are the dead queen's cousin. Do you think King Richard will believe me, a monk from a ruinous monastery, or his own relative?"

"Reynold, you must convince him! I cannot—"

"You can," he said, dragging her to her feet and squeezing her wrists when she tried to flee. "I will not let your cause die. I will not allow you to hate yourself some day because you were too cowardly to finish the mission you started."

"Cowardly!" She strained against his grip until her arms ached, then kicked him in the shin. Reynold grunted and pulled her against his body.

She fought the lure of his muscles enveloping her, tempting her to shut out the world and think only of sweet desire. "I will not disappoint our families, Reynold! I must marry tomorrow and you shall go to the king."

"Not without you." With one hand he held her face still. "I saw your kidnapper tonight."

Katherine drew a ragged breath of alarm, then struggled harder.

"Do you not understand?" Reynold continued. "He will not rest until you are silenced, whether you stay here or not."

"James will protect me," she whispered.

"James is a strong man, but sometimes a fool. He does not see the threat."

"I shall make him see! We'll have that man arrested while you search out the king."

"What if the kidnapper finds you first?"

Katherine shook her head wildly.

"Foolish hopes, my sweet. You are coming with me."

Although she kicked and fought, Reynold dragged her towards the door, then bent to pick up his magic sack. He dropped her to the bed, where he emptied his sack of its contents.

"Your gown, my lady."

Katherine turned her face away. "I thought they had burned it."

"I saved it for you. Now get dressed."

"I will not! The next gown I wear will be for my marriage to James."

Reynold cursed softly, then turned her facedown onto the bed. "Then I shall dress you myself."

Katherine gasped. He skimmed her legs with his fingers as he lifted her nightclothes, suspending time for a heart-stopping moment. She could feel herself falling under the spell his hands wove, succumbing to the magic of desire.

She arched away from him and whispered, "I'll do it myself! I swear!"

He instantly moved away. Katherine pushed herself off the bed with the wariness of an animal. She felt trapped, afraid of her own longings for this man. But she wouldn't go with him. She'd lull him into security, then flee at the first opportunity.

With dismay, Katherine realized her enemy the moon had shown himself again. How would she dress? As she hesitated, Reynold lifted the robes over his head and dropped them to the floor. He stood naked before her, obviously unashamed of his desire for her. Katherine's mouth dropped open and she stood frozen, staring at him. She felt torn apart by her own sinful desires, and frightened that he might seduce her the night before her wedding.

Instead he turned away and donned his braies and tunic. The breath left Katherine's lungs as she sank back against the bed, burying her face in the rough wool of her disguise. Thank God she did not have to choose between fighting him or relinquishing herself. The sinful part of her sighed in disappointment, and she buried it quickly. Turning her back, Katherine dropped her nightclothes and donned the smock and sleeveless gown.

When Reynold appeared beside her to fill his sack, Katherine shrank away from him.

"Do not fear me," he whispered. His fingers stilled and he bowed his head. "I could not bear it."

Katherine almost confessed that it was herself she feared, the traitorous part of her that even now longed to spread herself on the bed and invite him inside her. *Run*, a voice urged within. Reynold turned towards the door before she could make her weak limbs move.

"Come, Katherine."

She followed, holding onto the knowledge that she would flee—where? To her parents, who would look at her peasant clothes as proof of her sin? To James, who would know of her betrayal?

Reynold took her hand and led her into the quiet
hall. Katherine held back, gazing wildly at all the
closed doors, afraid to run, afraid to be alone with
him.

Reynold felt Katherine's hesitation, saw her look
down the deserted hallway. If she screamed now—
he bent and tossed her over his shoulder. He heard
a squeak as the air was forced from Katherine's
lungs, but she thankfully made no other sound.
She was not foolish enough to wish to be caught
in such a compromising situation.

She began to pound on his back and claw with
her nails. Reynold bore it, chuckling softly to himself. She was beautiful and brave, if only she
would believe it. When her feet kicked at his groin,
Reynold stopped smiling and held those lethal
weapons in a firm grip.

As he descended the stairs into the great hall,
Reynold swatted Katherine's backside to warn her.
She responded by smacking his as hard as she
could. All around them on the floor lay their families' retainers, servants and soldiers. To avoid
picking through sleeping bodies, Reynold veered
sharply into the first corridor.

The darkness swallowed them quickly. He tried
to think of nothing but Katherine's weight on his
shoulder and the smoky odor of torches that had
burned all the previous day. He could not dwell
on how his brother would view this. Would he let
Reynold explain why Katherine had to talk to the
king? Or would James realize what had happened
between his brother and his betrothed?

Reynold hesitated then, his steps slowing. Would Katherine's parents think she had gone willingly with him? Perhaps he should leave a message of explanation. He imagined them all preparing for a wedding and finding no bride. He admitted to himself that he felt little guilt for delaying Katherine's marriage. He did not want to watch, did not want to pretend it could be him standing beside her at the church door.

He picked up his pace, following the corridor by feel alone. When he hesitated at a turn, he heard the unmistakable sound of footsteps approaching them quickly. Katherine gasped and clutched his tunic. He knew how frightened she was to be caught like this by her parents. Holding his breath, Reynold tried to listen above his heartbeat. If only it were a guard, or a kitchen boy or—

"Reynold!"

The whisper of a woman's voice floated down the dark corridor. Katherine stiffened. He suddenly recognized the voice.

"Margery?"

Katherine's body seemed to wilt as Reynold peered into the darkness. He first smelled the scent of his sister's perfume a moment before she stopped before him.

"I heard you upstairs, Reynold. What is going on?"

He reached out to touch her, just as Margery did the same. Their hands met and clasped tightly. Katherine jerked on his shoulder, then moaned.

"Reynold!" Margery said with a gasp. "Are you carrying . . . a woman?"

" 'Tis Katherine. Follow me outside and I will explain everything."

Reynold took Margery's hand and began to pull before she asked any more questions. He hoped no one else saw them. He'd have much explaining to do—a monk carrying one woman and dragging another. His hand finally encountered an iron door. He wasted a precious moment searching his pouch for the keys he had earlier pilfered from James. He pulled them out from beneath Katherine's legs and earned himself a quick kick.

"Reynold?" Margery whispered.

"Shhh!" He found the key, forced the lock, and stepped outside. He descended the narrow stairs built into the wall beside the overgrown lady's garden, which was barely visible in the sliver of moonlight. He turned to face his sister, hoping the shadow of the trees sheltered them from any passing guards.

Margery ignored him as she bent down to see Katherine's face. "Are you all right?"

"Tell him I'm about to become ill all over his stockings."

Reynold swung her to her feet, only to watch her stagger and fall to her knees with a pitiful groan.

"Katherine!" he whispered, reaching to help her stand.

She slapped his hands away and held her stomach. "I need a moment to breathe. Margery, please, this isn't what it appears."

"I will make the explanations," Reynold said. "My sister will believe us."

"He kidnapped me!" Katherine cried, then covered her mouth and stared over her shoulder into the shadows.

Margery's hands landed on her hips as she faced Reynold. "Brother, dear, you had better have an interesting explanation for this."

"Of course I do." He told her all about the traitors and James's disbelief. "I cannot allow Katherine to feel guilty if King Richard is not warned. He will not believe me, but a relative of his dead wife—"

"I am to be married in a few hours!" Katherine said, climbing unsteadily to her feet. "What will James think?"

Reynold folded his arms across his chest. "Margery can explain everything."

"Explain what?" Margery countered. "What this looks like, or what you say it is?"

"It is one and the same," Katherine said. "A kidnapping. Your brother forced me from my bed, dressed me in this hateful gown—"

"Dressed you?" Margery interrupted, a smile quirking her lips.

"Forced me to dress! And when I tried to resist, he carried me like a sack of grain." She staggered again and clutched her stomach. "I doubt I'll be capable of eating for days."

Reynold ignored her. "Margery, meeting you is

much better than leaving a message. You can explain to James that I am not stealing his bride."

"Aren't you?"

Reynold refused to think about that just yet. "We cannot waste a moment. Even now, Henry Tudor may be preparing for battle."

Margery rested her chin in her hand, head down, her tapping toe softly rustling her gown. Reynold tried to wait patiently, but when Katherine took a step backwards, he grasped her arm and brought her closer.

"Going somewhere, my lady?"

Before Katherine could answer, Margery nodded. "I'll do it. I'll explain why you have taken her, and that Katherine is unwilling. Katherine, this will protect you, but Reynold—James will not be pleased."

"I shall risk it. What can he do—send me to a monastery?" Reynold asked.

Margery touched his arm. "Be careful, brother. Perhaps you act too soon in this matter."

Reynold stepped away and without warning, swung Katherine over his shoulder. She moaned and halfheartedly slapped at his backside. "I am sorry, Katherine. If we are discovered, this will protect you."

"How do you mean to escape?" Margery asked.

Reynold shrugged. "I shall distract the guards as best I am able."

"Didn't James ever tell you about the door he cut into the curtain wall?"

"A door?" Reynold demanded, aghast. "He

breached his own defenses so foolishly?"

"No one has besieged us in two hundred years, Reynold."

"But if a war befalls us—"

Margery laughed softly. "He regrets it now. Yet he was intrigued with having an escape route if unwelcome company came to call."

"Just tell me where the fool cut his own walls and we shall leave."

She pointed past the lady's garden, where the land sloped downward. "In the opposite corner to the dungeon. I've heard you're familiar with that area."

He looked askance at his sister. "I have James's ring of keys. When we are through, I shall leave them beside the door. If James tries to follow us, delay him as long as you can. Tell him the kidnapper is still here—he is a red-haired stranger lurking about. He has a propensity to wiggle his tongue between his missing teeth. You should easily recognize him. Do your best to make James see that I will protect Katherine with my life."

Margery placed a kiss upon his cheek. "Good luck, my brother. Lady Katherine, forgive his methods, if you can."

Katherine grumbled something into his back as Reynold strode forward. He halted at the rattle of a sword leaving its scabbard.

Chapter 21

〜◦〇◦〜

Reynold stood frozen, wondering how he would fight with Katherine on his shoulder. If he set her down, would she flee to escape detection?

"Yonder ghost!" cried the cracked voice of a man barely grown. "I swear by all that's holy I do not fear you!"

Reynold clutched Katherine's legs to his chest and hesitated. Suddenly, Margery darted out in front of him.

"Kind soldier," she called, moving through the shadows like a white-clad spirit.

Reynold heard a strangled gasp.

"Nay, I live," she insisted. "Do you not recognize me? I am Margery, sister to your lord."

"Milady—"

"Have you seen it, kind soldier? My puppy has flown from me and I'm quite distressed. Please, help me find the poor lost thing."

"But milady—"

Their voices dwindled away and Reynold chuckled as he trudged down the sloping ground while balancing Katherine. When he found the rusted door, partially covered in ivy, he shook his head in disgust at his brother's stupidity.

"This will take but a moment, Katherine," he whispered, trying each big iron key on the ring.

Her grumble was faint, and her body hung limply.

When he finally found the key, it took most of his strength to turn it. Once outside on the narrow bank of the cliff, he tossed the keys back inside and closed the door as quietly as possible. He immediately swung Katherine down and caught her as she collapsed.

"Katherine?" He patted her cheek and breathed a sigh of relief as her lashes fluttered. She took in a lungful of air and coughed. "I think compromising you would be better than robbing you of breath."

She shook her head. "I'd rather die," she choked out.

Reynold arched a brow. "I'm flattered."

"It's still not too late. You can take me back, Reynold, and I will tell no one."

Shaking his head, he put a supporting arm around her waist. "You will thank me for this, Katherine."

With an inelegant snort, she pushed away from him and stumbled over her skirt. Reynold caught her arm.

" 'Tis a long slide to the river. Hug the castle wall as we walk."

Katherine stared down into the valley. When she and Reynold had been trapped in the dungeon, the scenery was eerily beautiful and tempting. Now it only seemed dangerous. She followed Reynold, fool that he was. She bit her lip and studied the uneven ground. Perhaps he would lead her close to the gatehouse where she could call for help. Yet she was the true fool. How could she betray Reynold?

He didn't give her a choice. When they left the dangerous edge of the sloping river, he immediately pulled her into the darkness of the forest. The trees seemed a towering menace by night, no longer a playful respite from the sun.

"We will travel by forest path as much as possible," Reynold whispered over his shoulder. "The roads are more treacherous than ever as men prepare for war."

"Is it truly so near?" she asked, forgetting her anger for a moment.

"Katherine, we are close to Nottingham Castle and the king. Scurriers say Henry Tudor has feinted towards London, but he knows the king stands between him and the city. They will meet soon, and it will not be far from here. We must hurry."

As she tripped over a tree root and clutched Reynold's arm more tightly, Katherine felt a reluctant sense of purpose. The king deserved to know who he could count on. She did not care for Reynold's methods, and she wouldn't soon forgive him for what her parents would put her through.

They found a woodcutter's path soon enough and the footing proved easier. Yet the darkness of night pressed in on her, and the trees seemed to lean over.

"Should we not conserve our strength and sleep?" Katherine asked.

"You wish your betrothed to find us so easily?" Reynold kept his back turned and his voice cold.

"Perhaps I do. Then he would know how much this means to me."

Reynold's grip on her hand tightened.

"Where are your robes, Brother Reynold?" The words escaped her lips unthinkingly, but she did not regret them. The anger seemed to build inside her moment by moment, choking her with bitterness. "If you had worn them, perhaps your brother would not wonder at your motives when next we meet."

Reynold suddenly whirled toward her and brought their bodies together in a crushing embrace. The air escaped her lips in a rush, and her breasts rose and fell against the hard wall of his chest. She moaned softly at the vivid memories etched into her mind and skin.

His mouth but an inch from hers, he whispered, "If I wore those robes, my sweet, our kiss would seem too sinful."

Before she could frame a response, his mouth took hers in sweet possession, demanding and arousing. Her body responded without her mind's permission, her arms about his neck, one thigh sliding between his. She had missed his touch, missed the way his body could arouse such passion in hers. The knowledge that she could easily allow him to take her here on the forest floor finally brought her senses back. Pushing at his shoulders, she turned her head away.

"No, Reynold, please!"

He pressed his mouth to her cheek, her hair. "I cannot go back to the monastery, my sweet. That life is not for me."

"Your vows!" she cried, aghast.

"You knew I was a novice, Katherine. My final vows had not been spoken. And now I see the wait had a purpose."

"But Reynold, your family—what will they say?" A sick flash of guilt twisted her insides. Yet hadn't she seen this coming, hadn't she herself helped Reynold deal with Edmund's death?

Reynold captured Katherine's face in his hands, and looked into her wild, frightened eyes. He knew she was not ready to face what he meant to do. She still clung to her denials.

"I will solve everything," he said.

"But James will—"

Reynold covered her mouth with his hand. "Do not speak his name, my sweet. My brother will learn he cannot have everything he wants."

She shook away his hand. "Where will you go, Reynold? You will be so alone if your family disowns you."

"Not alone, Katherine," was all he would tell

her. He tried to kiss her again, but she resisted.

"You are being foolish to court such disaster," she said. "Your brother might insist your lands remain part of Margery's dowry."

"I will talk to James later. For now all that matters is warning the king."

James awoke at dawn to the blast of horns and the clatter of men in armor. He pulled on his clothes and met up with Margery in the hall, her hair wild about her shoulders and back, her face white.

"James, what is it?"

"If Katherine doesn't awaken, do not disturb her. This might be nothing—or it could be a summons from the king."

"It is about to begin then?"

He nodded and swept on by her. As he descended the stairs, the hall opened up before him. Katherine's father, Lord Durham, awaited him before the hearth. James recognized the dust-covered man beside him. Sir Arthur Watley, normally a cheerful man, presented only a grim countenance.

"My lord Bolton, His Majesty requests the presence of you and your retainers. Henry Tudor will soon be upon us."

The hall had gone quiet as servants and soldiers alike stood still. James sighed and looked to Katherine's father. "My lord, you, too, are summoned?"

Theobald Berkeley's joviality had disappeared. Though older, the knight who had fought so long ago with King Edward IV had obviously not forgotten his skills.

"James, I have sent out messages to my knights to join us at Leicester. The rest of my men can be ready within the hour." His forced smile looked more like a grimace. "My daughter will not be pleased that the wedding must be delayed. She has waited long for this day."

James shrugged. "You have raised her well. She will understand. After I have called my knights in from their outlying manors, we can be mounted by noon. If you prefer not to wait . . ."

"I can spare a few hours," the earl said. "Perhaps you wish the marriage to take place this morning?"

James thought about leaving a bride without a wedding night—then remembered he would be taking Katherine's money to battle, where new weapons were sorely needed. He felt a little sick at the necessity of her dowry. "Perhaps your idea is best for Katherine. Let me speak to my sergeant-at-arms, then I'll go to her."

Durham squinted as he gazed up the staircase. "Can't imagine what's keeping the girl, with all this commotion. She's usually an early riser."

"Much has happened to Katherine in the last week. She needs her rest."

After speaking to Galway, James turned to see Margery descending the stairs in a hurried manner quite unlike her usual cool grace. When she looked up and saw them all watching her, she dropped her skirts and smoothed them, crossing the rush-covered floor sedately.

"James, will you be leaving soon?"

"Lord Durham and I depart with the sun's zenith."

As James watched her pale face, something deep inside him stirred with uneasiness. "Break your fast, Margery. We might be needing your help. I will awaken Katherine and tell the poor girl we must leave."

Margery seemed to hesitate, but she merely bowed her head in submission. That in itself alerted James that something was wrong. He took the stairs two at a time and followed the corridor to Katherine's room. When she didn't answer his knock, he opened the door softly.

"Katherine, my dear? I'm sorry to awaken you but—" He broke off and squinted into the gloom. "Katherine?"

She was gone. He found her nightdress on the floor and her bed made up. Had she attended early mass with her mother? James pulled the door shut behind him, listening with satisfaction as the slam echoed through the bare corridor.

"Margery!" he bellowed.

She appeared at the top of the stairs before he could take a step. "Have you helped Katherine in some scheme? Don't you two foolish females realize we are at war?"

Margery's mouth opened, but she didn't seem to know which question to answer first.

"Is Katherine nervous about the wedding?

Surely she realizes I will do whatever..." His voice trailed off as Margery's face flushed red.

James swore. "Where is my brother when he is needed? Surely the horn should have dragged him from his knees."

"He could not have heard the horn," Margery said in a soft voice, her fingers absently toying with her girdle. "He has gone to do his part for King Richard."

"God's teeth! Margery, what the devil are you talking about? Richard has enough priests."

"He did not go as a monk, but as a loyal subject. You would not believe Katherine's message was important, but they do."

"They—" James closed his eyes in sudden understanding. "Katherine went, too."

"She did not go willingly, James," Margery said, reaching out to touch his hand.

He pulled away.

"Reynold knew she was related by blood to the king, who would be more likely to believe her than a stranger. I swear Katherine did not want to upset you or her parents."

"Reynold abducted my betrothed?" James said, still in disbelief.

"He merely—borrowed her. They'll be back as soon as their mission is complete. Reynold was also worried because he saw the kidnapper about. He said for you to alert the watch."

James eyed her coldly. "You knew they were leaving and did not tell me."

"Reynold is my brother, too! I could not betray his confidences."

"So you betrayed mine instead."

"James—"

"You must not speak of this to the earl."

Margery gasped. "You want us to lie to Katherine's father? Why must we?"

"Suffice it to say, Katherine does not want him to know the true reason she was originally kidnapped."

"But—"

"Not now, Margery. We are protecting Lord Durham. Leave the matter to me."

When James broke the news to Katherine's parents, stunned silence greeted him. Then Lord Durham surged to his feet.

"Have my horse saddled."

The countess came to stand beside her husband. "What can your brother be thinking, to take Katherine on the day of her wedding? And he, so recently confined to a monastery. Perhaps his mind is not right."

James gritted his teeth. "I will deal with my brother. I think he felt he was protecting Katherine from her kidnapper. When I discover why he did not trust me—" He broke off. "They cannot be far. I will go after them. It is unsafe for Katherine to be unprotected in so dangerous a time."

"Reynold is protecting her," Margery said.

"Enough! Lord Durham, my men and I will meet you in the king's camp. It should not take long for me to find my errant brother. Galway can track a squirrel through the forest."

The earl clenched his fists. "I will demand an explanation from him. Why should he take her from a fortified castle—"

"My brother does not think as you and I, my lord. But he is an honorable man." James had to grind out the words to placate Durham, but his own suspicions clouded his mind. "I have yet to have a full explanation for how this kidnapper escaped my men. They had best find him now, or they shall feel my wrath."

And they were not the only ones who would feel his anger.

Reynold and Katherine reached Nottingham Castle at dusk, only to discover from travelers that the king had departed for Leicester. Out on the road once more, Katherine looked back over her shoulder at the dark castle perched high up on its rock. The wind whistled about them, blowing away the last of the day's warmth. She shivered.

"Can we not shelter at the castle?"

"That has been our pattern, so we will change it. We do not want your kidnapper to find us too easily."

"Perhaps James caught him."

"We cannot assume so. The kidnapper seems to take our capture as his personal mission. Come, Katherine, the woods are warm tonight." His voice deepened as he spoke, ending on a husky note.

He took her arm and drew her forward, though

Katherine followed most reluctantly. She longed for the castle with its protection and crowds. But Reynold led her away, into the dark of the forest, and they would sleep alone.

Chapter 22

❧∽◯◯∽❧

Although the woods were dark and Reynold's grip on her arm was disconcerting, Katherine's exhaustion overtook everything else. Her feet felt leaden, and she stumbled over every branch and rock. How long had she walked today? Had their silent journey really begun last night? When Reynold stopped, Katherine's eyelids fluttered closed. Even his presence didn't bother her. If only she could sleep.

As Reynold turned to ask Katherine where she'd like to camp, he saw her eyes close and her body sway. He caught her up into his arms and she didn't resist, merely dropped her head against his shoulder and slept. Reynold smiled. He had pushed her too hard, rarely letting her rest. She hadn't complained, only glared at him occasionally with that anger she used as a shield. He knew she feared being alone with him, that she still did not understand that her love would never be for James. He was exhilarated that he could affect her as much as she did him.

270

The waning moon occasionally peered through the tree tops as Reynold placed his burden on the warm ground. From his sack he removed two blankets and set her on one. He lay down beside her and covered them with the second blanket. She sighed and snuggled against him.

Reynold knew he should sleep. Dawn would soon arrive, and with it another hard march. But in the shadowy darkness, Katherine's face was so intriguing. He touched her soft hairline which ended at a point on her forehead, leading his fingers down to her pale brows. He smoothed each gently, then smiled as she wrinkled her nose. He wished he could see her eyes, as dark, dark blue as a summer sky at dusk. If only he could look into her face for the rest of his life.

With a sigh, he dropped his head to his arm and continued to study Katherine. He could not take her back to James, whatever she may think. Reynold could not bear to see her married off to a man who did not care about her. Oh, he didn't doubt that James might grow fond of her. But that was a paltry emotion compared to love. And Reynold loved Katherine. She had brought him out of the darkness, taught him to love, made him see that his life was his own.

He cupped her soft cheek with his hand and kissed her forehead. If only he could make her see that God had thrown them together, but it was up to them to find a way to make it last.

*   *   *

At dawn, her scream woke him. Reynold's eyes flashed open and he rolled just in time to escape the knife descending towards his head. He pushed Katherine aside as he leapt to his feet, using one arm to shield himself from another blow. A quick stab of pain made him grimace. He arched away from the knife, whirling to face his opponent head on. The kidnapper grinned, showing the gaping hole where his front teeth should be.

"Reynold, take care!" Katherine cried from behind him.

"Stay back!" he commanded, hoping for once she'd listen.

Reynold kept an eye on the knife in his opponent's hand. "You should not have returned," he said with as much nonchalance as he could muster.

The red-haired man wheezed a laugh through the hole between his teeth. "I ain't quittin' 'til the job's done. And I never, ever lose. I ain't after ye, yer lordship. Ye could just leave."

Reynold watched the twisting knife glitter in the fading moonlight. "The lady's problems are mine. Whom do you serve?"

The man slashed forward with his knife. Reynold grabbed the wrist with both hands and forced it upwards. Chest to chest they struggled for possession of the weapon. The kidnapper's free hand clawed at Reynold's face, and he kneed the man in the stomach. The knife slipped free.

Just as Reynold took hold of it in triumph, he felt a sharp stab of pain inflame his thigh, and looked into the satisfied face of his attacker. Somewhat amazed, he stumbled backward and the leg gave out beneath him. He went down hearing Katherine scream, and watched the second knife weave in his face. Flames seemed to lick along his leg, dulling his senses. Why didn't the knife finish its work? Was that thunder he heard?

"They're coming for me!" Katherine cried.

The knife wavered and retreated. Reynold sank back on his elbows, shaking his head in bemusement. Didn't she hear the storm coming?

Katherine stood protectively over Reynold, afraid to imagine his injuries. The thundering of horses' hooves grew loud enough to shake the ground. The kidnapper hesitated but a moment, cursed, and melted into the black forest. Katherine fell to her knees.

"Reynold?" she yelled above the sounds of horses and men in armor. She had not realized how close to the highway they slept, but now she was grateful.

He groaned softly, and rolled his head towards her knees. Katherine felt tears sting her eyes, and her chest ached as if she had been the one injured.

"Oh, Reynold, can you hear me?"

His eyes remained closed, his face pale white in the early morning light.

"I'm going for help. I shall return in a moment!"

As she pushed through the forest undergrowth, the first big drops of rain fell through the leaves. By the time she reached the highway, her wool peasant's gown was dripping. She pushed by the last bush then gasped and jumped backward as a towering stallion bore down on her. The road was filled, four or five deep, with horses and their armored riders, many carrying shields and banners. This was no leisurely nobleman's entourage riding from one manor to another. An army of soldiers was on the move. The battle between King Richard and Henry Tudor must be near.

Katherine hesitated over the most painful decision she'd ever faced. Should she put the king before Reynold? If she needed to, she could quickly bind his wounds, and leave him in a nearby village until she returned.

Yet a moment more, and her choice was easily made. She could not leave him to a stranger's care. The army streaming by would no more believe her story than her own betrothed had.

She needed medical supplies. In desperation, she waved her arms and screamed for help. It was futile. She had seen firsthand how a knight could treat a noble enemy with courtesy, while spitting on peasant women and children. The rain fell and she was splashed with mud from the horses. Katherine brushed streaming water from her face and tried not to panic. How could she possibly take care of Reynold alone? And now he might be bleeding to death. She was such a fool!

Katherine turned and pushed her way back into the forest, before the marching infantry could come upon her. Panic and despair sent her racing through the underbrush, heedless of the branches that snapped in her face with stinging wetness. Oh

God, what if he'd died while she was gone? What if the kidnapper had come back?

She stumbled out into the clearing, then fell over his body hidden in the grass. He groaned, and she cried out in relief.

"Reynold, I'm here," she said soothingly, feeling the ground steady beneath them as the army rode farther away. "I'll help you."

Katherine quickly examined the scratches on his face and the small wound in his arm, which had already stopped bleeding. She ran her hands down his hips and thighs, then gasped and brought her palm away, wet with blood. A puddle of it soaked into the ground.

For a moment, Katherine felt weak with helplessness. Her basket of herbs lay far away in Durham. She closed her eyes and prayed for strength. Reynold would die if left in her meager care.

The forest was deathly quiet but for Reynold's harsh breathing. Katherine stole a glance at his dear face, contorted in pain. How could she sit here in self-pity and let him die?

With a sudden grim determination, she pushed his tunic up to his hips. She unfastened the points of his stockings from his belt and carefully pulled the wool away from the gash in his leg. Blood oozed a slow river down his thigh into the grass. Katherine sat back and let the rain wash away as much as possible. Reynold flinched, and she placed her hands firmly on his body.

"Don't move," she whispered. "I'll take care of you."

He settled back into a deep sleep with the trust of a babe. Katherine hoped she was worthy of it. She grasped Reynold's magic sack and rummaged through it until she found some rags. She exposed them to the rain, then began to scrub his wound gently. His leg stiffened but he made no sound. Her stomach quivered with queasiness when she was forced to pick a few bits of wool out of the wound. The blood continued to flow and she knew she must wrap his thigh tightly. She had known so many people who grew feverish and died over much less serious a wound than this. She suddenly remembered Reynold's brother and shivered.

She folded the last rag and held it to Reynold's injured thigh. She used her own stockings to tie it in place, then sat back and lifted her face to the pouring rain.

The moisture ran between her parted lips and down her tongue. She sipped at it gratefully for strength, then she opened her eyes and looked down at Reynold. He had not moved.

Katherine leaned over him and shielded his face from the rain. With gentle fingers she wiped the wetness from his skin. He was so white and still. She held back tears as she remembered his dear face pressed to her breast, and his ready smile, which always lifted her spirits. It was very easy to forget she should be angry with his deceptions.

His dark lashes fluttered, and Katherine held her breath. His violet eyes seemed dazed until they focused on her.

"Katherine?" Though hoarse and weak, his voice sounded lucid.

"Yes, Reynold?"

His eyes narrowed. "The ground is wet."

" 'Tis raining. We need to find shelter, but you know the area better than I. Do you remember where we are?"

He frowned. "South of Nottingham Castle. But you must leave. He will come back."

"Soldiers on the way to the battle frightened him off. We'll leave together." She covered his lips when he would have protested. "Is there shelter nearby?"

He grimaced in what Katherine thought was pain. She touched her fingers to his cheek to soothe him, and received a glare in return.

"Do not touch me like that, Katherine, unless you mean it."

She pulled her hand away.

He said, "There is a . . . small village farther down this path. The last time I was here, the village was slowly dying, but there might be shelter, and someone who can help us."

Katherine stared doubtfully at his leg, with its bulky bandage. "Can you walk? Perhaps I should go for help alone."

"No." He sat up slowly. "If the battle is near, it will be too dangerous. Can you help me up?"

Katherine took his arm, but was unprepared for his weight. When he pulled, she fell on top of him and they bumped heads.

"I'm sorry," she murmured, gripping him once again.

Reynold sighed. "Are you ready?"

She nodded, then grunted and lifted until he swayed on his feet. His arm swung around her shoulders and she staggered, then steadied herself. "I'm ready."

Reynold tested his weight on the injured leg, then nodded tightly. "It aches, but I can move it. The damage must be less than it appears."

"Thank goodness," she said, striving for a natural voice.

Reynold smiled and lifted her chin. "I promise 'tis not far."

Katherine closed her eyes at the sweetness of his touch and the warm ache that filled her chest. She could not let herself be affected like this. She had already committed great sins against her betrothed. Would she be able to live with what she'd done? Would these haunting memories ever leave her?

Katherine turned her head away and began to walk slowly while Reynold stepped and hopped. Finally they found a pace that suited them both, and they moved through the dripping forest in silence but for their heavy breathing.

After an hour of exertion, steam was rising from Katherine's wet gown. Her breath came in gasps. Reynold grunted occasionally as he limped. She looked down at his wounded thigh and gasped. Fresh blood had seeped through the bandage.

"Reynold, your leg," she said, guiding him toward the base of a towering oak tree.

He allowed her to ease him to the damp earth. "Katherine, we cannot delay."

"I'll just take a moment to tighten your bandage."

He sighed loudly and crossed his arms over his chest. Katherine hid a smile.

"You're not a good patient, sir."

"The pain does not do wondrous things for my temper. I am beginning to wish I had never brought you on this ridiculous mission. We will not reach the king in time."

Katherine glanced beneath the bandage and grimaced. She tightened the stocking holding it in place. "You were right to bring me, Reynold, loathe though I am to admit it. I would have forever blamed myself for not trying."

She finished her task and looked up into his face. His intense, hooded gaze caught hers and held.

"Are you perhaps glad I took you for other reasons?" he asked softly.

Katherine watched his lips as he spoke, and remembered their softness and the sweet torture they could evoke. Already James's face seemed to be drifting from her memory. No, she could not allow this. Katherine bent her head and removed her hands from his warm leg.

"There is only one reason we are together here," she said.

"Katherine, we have no need to lie to ourselves."

She stood up. "I will not discuss this. You will take me to the king, and then I must return."

Even as she spoke the harsh words, her throat closed up and she could feel tears stinging her eyes. Why must he make their family duties so difficult?

Reynold struggled to his feet in silence. Katherine felt panic begin to creep up on her again as she saw how white his face had become.

"Reynold?"

He shook his head. "Let us hurry, Katherine. I fear I will not last much longer."

Katherine slid beneath his arm and began to pray.

Chapter 23

⌒◯◯⌒

As the trees began to thin, the rain fell in harder sheets that obscured Katherine's sight. Her back ached from the strain of bearing Reynold's weight. He had stopped speaking, as if he needed all his energy just to limp forward in ever-clumsier strides. She tried to keep her panicked thoughts from darting into the future, but to little avail. What would she do if Reynold proved too weak to continue?

Then Katherine felt the man beside her flinch. His courage and suffering pierced her heart. He chased away so many of her doubts about the decisions she'd made. If she'd gone home in the beginning, she never would have grown close to Reynold, never would have known what it was like to be desired for the woman she was, not her dowry.

She also never would have broken her betrothal vow, but that was something she would have to live with. No, she could not regret the decisions that had brought her here. Reynold was hurt defending her, and she owed him more than she could ever repay.

They came out of the forest onto a hillside that sloped away in rolling waves of farmland. Off into the gray distance, she could see a ribbon of road she was sure must be the highway. For now she resolutely turned away, hoping no one would see them. But tomorrow, when Reynold was better, that road would lead to the end of their mission.

Ahead of them she saw a cluster of small houses and a larger stone building that must be a church. Katherine tried to pick up her pace, but Reynold shook his head.

"I am not sure we shall find help here, Katherine. Do you not see the fallow fields? The local lord must be converting his land to pasture for sheep. See them grazing there on the hillside?"

Katherine saw a huge, shifting white coverlet that seemed to blanket several hillsides. "I don't understand why you think we'll not find help."

"The village has no farm land left. What family can survive that?"

Katherine looked into his grim face. "We must try, Reynold. Won't there be someone here to guard the sheep? Perhaps the church—"

"Perhaps . . ." he murmured, closing his eyes and bending her shoulders with his weight. "I shall need to rest soon, my sweet."

"We must get you out of the rain. The church will not turn us away."

*   *   *

Reynold felt only deep sadness when they stood in the overgrown and neglected village green. Barns and sheds sagged against one another. Wooden houses with thatched roofs stood open to vandals and thieves alike. The thin wail of a child made him shiver.

Katherine sighed. "How could the lord of the manor allow this?"

"Sheep are easy to maintain, and so much more profitable. It is the way of the future, Katherine."

"Surely the priest has not left the poor shepherds alone."

"We shall see."

Reynold did his best to hold most of his own weight. He could feel the trembling in Katherine's frail shoulders, but it pleased him that she seemed to use her weak arm without thinking about it. He was so proud of the courage she had shown, although he knew she feared for their future. He wanted to tell her he would always take care of her, that he loved her, but those were words she would not welcome. Especially not now, when he knew she might have to go on without him. They were too near their goal and he was slowing her pace.

The water continued to drip from Reynold's hair into his face. His wool tunic seemed to give off steam. Was Katherine as hot as he felt? When had the day grown so warm? He leaned his head against hers, his mouth against her wet hair. He didn't feel as if his voice would be strong enough for her to hear.

"The church," he murmured.

Katherine glanced quickly towards him, bumping her nose into his chin. He knew she was worried, and he wanted to tell her not to be. The wound was not mortal. But words would not pass his lips. He settled for a brief kiss to her brow as she dragged him forward.

The church was a squat building made of stone, with the cross of Jesus on its roof. Its carved wooden doors were faded and gouged.

Reynold cleared his throat to whisper, "I wonder how many young couples stood in this doorway to be married."

Katherine would not look at him. She grasped the door handle, gave it a tug, and the door creaked open. Together they limped into the gloomy interior. The open floor where parishioners usually stood was covered in layers of dirt. Broken shutters hung from parchment-covered windows. At the far wall, a tattered cloth covered a stone altar.

Reynold tilted forward, and the floor seemed to rush up to his knees. Katherine cried out and stumbled down with him.

"Reynold, let me put down a blanket to cover the filth."

He managed to keep his balance, then allowed her to help him onto his back. He groaned and closed his eyes.

"Does it hurt badly?" she asked in a soft voice, her slim hand resting on his chest.

He shook his head, although the fire in his leg

threatened to consume him. He looked up into her sweet face. "We have done this before, have we not? Only then, my lack of wounds led to a wondrous night."

"Shhh," she said, as her face reddened. He felt her cool fingers probing the wound, heard her gasp.

"I will not bleed to death, my sweet," he whispered. "Bind the wound again and come talk with me."

He endured her ministrations, then opened his eyes when she sat beside his shoulders. He smiled up at her white face.

"You are not going to cry, are you, Katherine?"

She stiffened and glared at him.

"Are you so sorry to be with me rather than at the church doors with James?"

"Must we speak of that?"

"Would you not today be a truly married woman?"

She remained silent.

"Do you love him?"

"I trust my father's choice. I will grow to love him."

"That sounds like stubbornness rather than true feeling."

"Why do you speak of this, Reynold?" she demanded, her eyes bright with unshed tears. "We both will do our duties to our families."

"I will not."

" 'Tis wishfulness talking," she admonished, but he saw how quickly she looked away.

Reynold's voice sounded hoarse to his own ears. "Since I have met you, my sweet, I realized I was not meant for the lonely life of a monastery. Edmund would not want me to be miserable. I can do more good for my family in other ways."

"You are feverish."

"Only because of my love for you."

Reynold caught her hand before she could move away. "Do you not see that what we feel for each other is real?"

"It is only our wishes that make it seem so." A tear escaped her lashes and her lips trembled.

He struggled up onto his elbows. "Is it my wishes that make me burn for the sight of you? Am I mad to remember the passionate hours you spent in my arms? Katherine, I thought I would melt into the ground when our families separated us and you played prospective bride with my brother!"

"I am his prospective bride!" she whispered as loudly as she dared, stealing a glance at the forbidding altar. "How can you speak of our sins in a holy church?"

"It would only be a sin for you to marry a man you do not love. James will make you miserable. Damn it, Katherine, our love is a gift from God that we should seize before it is too late!"

Reynold knew he had gone too far when she pushed away from him and began to delve into his sack. Her shoulders shook.

"Katherine, look at me."

"You need nourishment. Close your mouth until you can fill it with food."

He sighed and lay back on the hard ground. "Will you always fight me?"

"Yes!" she whispered, her suddenly fierce gaze locking with his. "I will fight this hell-concocted corruption of my soul. Although I have sinned, I will do as my father ordered me. I will complete the vows I have sworn."

"And be miserable the rest of your life," he answered darkly.

"Then that is God's punishment, which I so richly deserve!"

"God does not wish us suffering, my sweet," he murmured, reaching to touch her soft cheek.

She ducked away. "My life has been nothing but! And you are his worst torture yet." She gasped in what sounded like a sob. "Reynold, what have I done to deserve such as this? When I was ready to do His will, why did the Lord allow me this brief sight of happiness? I feel I am being laughed at from all sides!"

Reynold sat up as quickly as he could, wanting to offer his comfort. Katherine didn't move, just knelt forlornly in the dirt, watching her tears drip to her knees. The room wavered and Reynold fell back.

Her hands soothed his cheeks and forehead as she whispered sweet words. He wanted to tell her he was not some child so easily mollified, but her touch was a cool and gentle balm against the heat burning him.

"My children," said a sudden, cold voice. "Mass ended many an hour ago."

Reynold relaxed. It was but the priest come to inspect his visitors. Yet Katherine's startled reaction suggested the exact opposite. She froze and held her breath. Her face drained of color and her lips moved without sound. When he would have spoken, she covered his mouth with trembling fingers.

"Answer me!" the imperious voice demanded.

Reynold lifted his head to peer around Katherine and saw only a bald priest in a tattered black cassock. His shoulders were hunched and he leaned on a carved stick, but his age was not so very advanced. Surely he would understand.

Katherine shook her head slightly in warning, then licked her lips. Turning her head, she peered at the priest through a lock of her hair. Reynold felt the prick of her nails in his arm.

"Father," she said, her voice hoarse and unnatural, "forgive us, but there is a storm outside. Thieves set upon us and my husband was injured. He needs shelter."

The priest moved forward warily. Reynold noticed that he barely leaned on the walking stick. "What do you want of me? As you can see from the plight of the village, I have nothing to give you."

"We ask for nothing from you."

Reynold glanced quickly at his "wife," for he thought her words disrespectful from such a modest young woman.

"Then we understand each other," said the priest, nodding his bald head.

He leaned over Reynold, a dark shadow in the gloom.

"What happened to you, my son?"

"I have been stabbed, Father," he answered.

"Clean up when you're through."

Reynold frowned, then became more uneasy as he watched the old priest studying Katherine's bent head. She barely seemed to be breathing as if she felt his scrutiny.

"You, woman, did you once live in the village?"

Katherine tried most desperately to control the frantic pounding of her heart. He was standing over her, the monk whose cruel voice still haunted her nightmares. Her hand stole up to cover her mouth before she could moan aloud in terror.

Seven years before, he had stood above her, a dark figure of evil, who would molest a twelve-year-old girl and swear her to secrecy lest she die from a bolt of God's lightning. In her fright she had told, but no one had believed her hysterical cries. Eventually she learned he had been sent away.

Now he was here, far from the corridors of power where he had longed to be. And if he found out who she was, he would kill her.

Chapter 24

"**D**id you hear me, girl?" the priest demanded. "What is your name?"

Reynold looked baffled by her behavior, but Katherine could not explain.

She licked her dry lips and kept her eyes downcast. "Father, I have never traveled through this village before. You must be mistaken."

When the priest remained silent, Katherine busied herself with Reynold's leg. As she rewrapped his wound, she wished desperately for medicine, but she could ask no favors of her childhood tormentor. When Reynold clasped her arm to get her attention, she narrowed her eyes and gave a barely perceptible shake of her head. He was so weak that he closed his eyes and slipped from consciousness. Biting her lip, she leaned over him and felt his forehead.

"If he does not live," the priest said, "I have not the men nor money to bury him."

"He will live," Katherine replied fiercely, glaring at the man. She saw her mistake immediately.

The priest frowned and stared at her. She held her breath, unable to look away from those black, hate-filled eyes. They suddenly narrowed and Katherine gasped as he gripped her arm with a cruel hand.

"Lady Katherine, you have aged well," he said, his voice a reptilian hiss.

She shuddered. "Release me at once," she said, with the hollow echo of authority in her voice.

His grin was slow and smooth, stretching the wrinkled skin of his face. His eyes danced with sudden merriment.

"I never thought to see you again, my lady. The parish does not provide me adequate funds for travel. How kind of you to come to me instead."

Katherine leaned protectively over Reynold. "Stop this foolish pretense at politeness."

"Why, my lady, I am ever polite," he said, genially spreading his hands wide. He glanced down at Reynold's still face and a flicker of distaste glittered in his eyes. "This poorly dressed man is your husband?"

Katherine knew she was not a very good liar, so she skirted the question. "We have been traveling, and did not wish to attract attention."

"Traveling while a war is about to begin? With no retainers or guards?" The priest's eyebrows rose towards his bald head.

"My husband insisted."

He clucked his tongue. "How foolish of him. Yet how fortunate that you came upon my humble little church." He looked up at the smoke-darkened timbers of the roof. "I have not the amenities you are used to, 'tis certain. I have no amenities at all, thanks to your father."

Katherine's stomach tightened with dread as the priest's voice seemed to rise with each word. She clutched Reynold's hand and wished to God that he would awaken.

"My father did nothing to you."

"Oh, but he did, my lady Katherine."

He suddenly grabbed a handful of her hair, yanked back her head, and forced her gaze to meet his. Katherine cried out and clawed at his hands.

"I told you not to tell anyone, didn't I?"

When she couldn't answer, he shook her head violently.

"Didn't I?"

"I was frightened!" she cried, feeling tears well from her eyes as strands of her hair tore from her scalp. "But it did not matter. My mother didn't believe me."

"Perhaps you thought not, but your father chose to punish me regardless."

"Punish?" She gasped as the priest pulled her head so far back she thought her neck would snap. The revelation that her father knew and had believed her made her feel relief that lasted but a moment.

The priest sneered. "I, though nobly born, was banished to this peasant parish, with no hope of advancement, no need for my special skills and great intellect. I have been made to work in the fields!"

"There were not enough young girls for you?" Katherine spoke before thinking.

His fist struck the side of her face, and she fell hard to the dirt floor. She braced herself on her hands, trembling, trying to gather the strength to kill him. She knew one of them would have to die. There was no doubt in her mind that he deserved it.

The priest grabbed the back of her gown, hauling her to her feet with a power she didn't think him capable of. He pulled her backwards against his body, his arm like a snake about her waist. She vividly remembered everything about him, the harsh projections of his hip bones, the wiry strength of his muscles. Time seemed to slip away from her as she heard his harsh breathing at her ear, felt his hands grope her breasts. She was a child again, terrified and alone.

"That's it," he murmured in her ear, "do not fight me, young miss."

Katherine remembered those words, relived her fright and confusion. His hands made her feel dirty, and she had vowed never to feel that way again.

She jabbed her elbow into his stomach and the priest grunted. He caught her flailing wrists with one hand, and with the other ripped the neckline of her gown. Katherine screamed until her voice went hoarse. She kicked at his legs and flung her body from side to side, anything to avoid the loathsome feel of his callused, boney hand on her bare flesh.

He threw her hard to the floor, knocking the air from her lungs and bruising her ribs. Panting, she reached for Reynold's boot only inches from her fingers. The priest gripped her ankle and dragged her backwards. Katherine's panic erupted in a sob, as tears blurred her vision.

"Reynold!" she screamed, but he lay like one dead. Was he gone from her, leaving her all alone to face a madman? She felt the priest tearing at her skirts, grasping at her bare legs. Katherine twisted and flailed in his grip, her face scraping the rough floor. With a sob she kicked up behind her. The priest gave a high-pitched shriek and fell back. He rolled on the floor, clutching between his legs, invoking curses that burned her ears.

Her bruised chest heaving, Katherine crawled towards Reynold and grabbed the eating knife from his belt. She scrambled to her feet and backed away from the priest, holding the knife before her in a shaky fist. The room seemed to shiver between the tangled strands of hair in her eyes. The priest had ceased to groan. His face dripping sweat, he pushed himself to his feet and stepped around Reynold's body. He lifted the walking stick up menacingly.

"You should not have done that, my lady," he said. His bleached face cracked in a hideous grin.

The stick weaved in tiny circles. Katherine's tired eyes followed. She shoved the knife towards him and he backed up a step.

"Stay away from me!" she cried. "I'll kill you, I swear it!"

He laughed in a low, hypnotic voice. "No, my dear, your memory is playing tricks upon you. I did nothing you did not want me to do."

"You lie! I was but twelve years old!" The blade lowered an inch. "You betrayed everything I believed in."

"My hands upon you felt right," he said soothingly.

The walking stick glittered in the sudden flash of lightning.

Tears dripped from her eyes. "God help me," she murmured forlornly.

"Only I can help you, Katherine." He laughed in triumph and raised his weapon.

As the walking stick whistled down to strike her, Katherine's soul rebelled. She flung up an arm, barely deflecting the blow. The pain burned, but it seemed like it was happening to another person. She raised the knife high above the priest's chest, saw his momentary look of terror. Yes, now he knows the fear!

Before Katherine could attack, the priest stiffened and let out a shriek. He fell forward, his body striking hers, knocking them both to the ground.

She screamed and sobbed, twisting beneath his weight. "Never! Never! Never!"

"Katherine!"

Reynold's beloved voice sounded so far away. She went still, her chest struggling for air, her nose filled with the fetid stench of the priest.

"He's dead," Reynold said.

She felt the heavy weight of the corpse being lifted from her. Rolling to her side, she clutched her hands over her bare chest and sobbed. Her bruised ribs ached. She gasped Reynold's name and he lifted her up, surrounding her with his warmth and tenderness.

"I am here, my sweet," he murmured into her hair.

"I—I thought you were dead," she managed to say, her voice hoarse from screaming.

"I shall never leave you," he said fiercely, hugging her until she groaned. "Forgive my clumsiness—"

"No, hold me tightly, Reynold." She buried her face in his rough tunic.

"He is the reason you broke your arm?" he asked a few minutes later.

She nodded and burrowed closer. "Oh, Reynold, your leg."

"Hush, my sweet, it is better. I will not die from so paltry a wound. Tell me what he did to you."

Katherine blotted her tears against Reynold's chest and took a deep, shuddering breath. She wished she could forget that the priest was lying dead on the floor. "Let us leave this place first."

"Katherine, the storm yet rages. And we cannot leave the body like this for all to see. Tell me everything."

She expected the telling to be difficult, but it all suddenly rushed from her like a river when the damn is broken. How she'd trusted the monk who advised her mother, how naive she'd been to think that he wanted to be her friend. She'd been so alone, with a mother who would not send her away to be taught a noble wife's duties, yet ignored the teaching herself.

"I trusted him," she whispered. She glanced once more at the body and shuddered.

Reynold kissed her brow and the corner of her eye.

"He lured me into his room, and I was so foolish—"

"Cease," Reynold ordered quietly. "You were a young sweet girl, who knew not the dark side of life."

"He—he tried to kiss me first, and I thought—I thought he just wanted affection, but didn't understand—" Katherine swallowed, wishing her words were coherent. "Then he put his tongue in my mouth and—"

She looked up into his face, with those dark brows which hid such generosity and goodness. "It was not that way when I kissed you. He pinched me, and put his hands . . . he pulled up my skirt—" Shivering, she leaned against Reynold's chest once more.

Through their silence, the rain beat a steady pulse on the leaky roof. The wind blew gusts of rain past the tattered parchment at the windows. And still Reynold held her, absorbing her sorrow.

He spoke gruffly. "Did he—"

"No. I kicked him and ran. That's when I stumbled and broke the fall with my arm. I almost welcomed the blinding pain. I didn't have to think anymore, I could just . . . let go."

"Why did your father banish the priest instead of having him executed?"

She looked up into his eyes, feeling for the first time that her heart would someday recover. "But don't you see, I never knew my father did anything. I only told my mother, and she didn't believe me."

"What?" Reynold lifted his head to look into her face, clearly aghast.

Katherine frowned and carefully smoothed his tunic where she had grasped it. "This changes so many things. Perhaps my mother believed me, but did not know what to do. Or perhaps she told my father, and he believed me." She gave a ragged sigh. "I can't tell you what it felt like to think my parents didn't care . . . especially my father. I feel so much better, Reynold."

Then she remembered the body on the floor. "We've killed a priest," she whispered. "What shall we do?"

James Markham jumped away from the window just in time. Rain had long since plastered the hair on his head, and seeped down beneath his armor to wet his padded fustian. He leaned back against the rough wall and tried to pretend he hadn't seen what he thought he had. But his mind, though dazed, could not deny what had occurred.

He shook his head in bemusement. He almost wished Galway was not so proficient at following a trail. James had been thankful to find Katherine and Reynold alive, after all the blood he'd seen in the clearing. By the time he had followed the trail of blood to the church, the mad priest was stalking Katherine, spitting words James couldn't hear over the storm. Just as James was about to leap through the window to Katherine's rescue, Reynold had risen as if from the dead. If only it had ended there.

James angrily closed his eyes, but the picture was burned in his brain. He could still see Katherine falling into Reynold's arms, his face bending to hers, his lips kissing her cheeks, her tears. James had turned away before his worst fears could be played out.

He pushed himself away from the wall. He didn't have time for this, he thought grimly. His men waited nearby, prepared for battle. Forcing his anger aside, James vowed he would deal with Reynold and Katherine later.

Chapter 25

Katherine spent the rest of the stormy day, sitting within Reynold's arms, staring at the stone altar, behind which they'd hidden the priest's body. Her gaze was drawn to it continuously, although Reynold tried to distract her with stories of his childhood. Part of her was merely relieved, as if a great weight no longer bowed her head. But another part mourned her childhood and recent years, when she hid her true self. She had never trusted anyone—after all, no one would believe her if they knew the truth.

Reynold knew. He knew and accepted, and perhaps even loved her in spite of it all. Katherine sighed and tucked her head beneath his chin. If only love were all that mattered.

She looked down at herself and surveyed the damage done to her gown and smock. Both were ripped almost to her waist.

"I cannot travel like this," she said, pointing to her chest.

Reynold looked down, then quickly up again. He cleared his throat. "I have some thin cord we can use to mend your garments. It will be visible, but it will cover you."

He handed her a knife and string from his sack, then gave her directions while obviously trying not to stare. Katherine fumbled with the knife, afraid she'd cut herself in her attempt to prick new holes to lace up the dress. With a sigh, Reynold finally took the knife away.

They brushed heads as they both bent over her loose bodice. Reynold's hands seemed to shake as he tore new holes, but Katherine made no mention of it. She breathed in air warmed by his body, touched by his scent. When he began to thread the cord, his knuckles brushed the slope of her breast, and her skin burst into tingling awareness. They broke apart hastily. With clumsy fingers, Katherine finished the lacing herself.

"Reynold," she whispered, glancing uneasily at the altar, "let us leave here."

"When lightning no longer singes the trees, we will leave. But first I must take care of your tormentor."

She grasped his arm as he rose. "But the lightning—"

"Precisely the reason no one will be about. I shall drag the body farther into the forest, where it will look like thieves fell upon him."

"I'll help you." She stood up and ignored his look of disbelief.

"Katherine—"

"You are still weak. Show me what to do."

He stared into her eyes a moment, then finally relented. "Behind the altar is the door to the priest's garden. Peer outside for any villagers. But do not let yourself be seen!"

The last of Katherine's fears began to vanish. She was cleaning up the carnage from some of the worst moments of her life, and it felt right. She even took the priest's arm and pulled when she worried over Reynold's injuries.

In the dark, the forest crackled with the energy of the storm, but she refused to allow herself to be cowed. That part of her life was over. She would be brave and do her duty by James, to keep peace between their families. She would be strong enough—she had to be.

Reynold insisted they remain in the church until just before dawn. Though Katherine longed to be on her way to the king, she knew the storm would only hinder them. And still she worried over Reynold's leg. Sleep would give him time to heal. His fever was gone, the bleeding stopped. She intended that he have as much rest as he needed—which meant no fisticuffs. Surely if the kidnapper were following them, he would have caught up by now.

Reynold drew her against him and sat stiffly, as if he dreaded her touch. Katherine allowed herself to relax in his embrace and sleep, until the grayness before dawn, when he woke her. They left before the few remaining villagers could come to mass.

They traveled between hills and crossed many a flowing stream before making camp that night near water. Reynold's face was white with strain, but no fresh blood stained his bandage. In silence, they ate the last of the twice-baked bread and dried beef Reynold had brought from Bolton Castle.

The setting sun glinted off the nearby stream with a hazy golden glow. Katherine sighed. It would be wonderful to scrub away the last of her recent ordeal.

"Reynold—"

"Yes, you should bathe," he said, smiling at her surprised reaction. "Your mind is not hard to read when you gaze so longingly at the water."

"Do you still have soap?"

Nodding, he delved into his magic sack and came up with a tiny, soft lump of soap wrapped in cloth. "I have been meaning to look at the scrape on your face and make sure it is clean."

She touched her right cheek and winced. "I had forgotten. When he knocked me to the ground . . ." Her throat tightened, swallowing up her words.

"Do not speak of it," he said gently.

After getting a rag from his sack, Reynold took her hand and led her to the stream. Together they knelt on the bank, where he dipped the cloth in cool water and dabbed at her cheek. Katherine sucked in her breath and looked up into his face. He frowned as he concentrated, his gentle fingers caressing her with the rag. Katherine let go of the last of her anger at his deceptions and tried to find peace. Amazing as it seemed, he must truly love her, and she ached for his pain.

The cloth dripped water down her face and neck, trickling between her breasts. Licking her suddenly dry lips, she loosened the laces. She saw Reynold's gaze drop to her chest. His fingers stilled on her face. His eyes searched hers for a moment, then glanced at her lips.

The slow curl of heat began its insidious crawl below her stomach, winding its way through her body until she felt overwarm and languorous.

His hands framed her face and slid into her hair. "Katherine," he whispered, then lowered his lips to hers.

With kisses, he caressed her mouth, her cheeks, her forehead, her hair. Katherine leaned into him, her hands on his shoulders, their bodies lightly brushing together. Every sense was aware of him, his mind, his heart, his warm body. He was everything she wanted, but could never keep.

His open mouth captured hers once again. As their tongues met and stroked, she moaned and clasped him tightly to her. His thighs rode between hers and she rubbed herself against him, feeling the roughness of linen across her breasts, and his hard loins between her legs. She was mad with longing for him; nothing and no one else mattered but the feel of his big hands on her body.

Reynold loosened the laces at her neck and reached a hand inside the torn material to cup one breast. He lifted it in gentle hands, teasing the peak while exploring her lips with his. Katherine revelled in the feel of his body worshiping hers, showing with his hands and lips how he desired her.

Pulling her harder against his hips, Reynold kissed her neck and the hollow of her throat. Katherine's head dropped back, giving him access to any part of her he wanted. He pulled the gown off her shoulder and pressed kisses to her collarbone and the curve of her breast.

His lifted his head. "What is this?" he asked, staring at her breasts.

As if in a dream, she allowed him to lift her body toward the last glow of the sunset. Purple bruises dotted her skin.

"He hurt you." Reynold's trembling fingers traced the marks.

She shook her head. "It doesn't matter. Just kiss me, Reynold."

"Oh, my lady," he whispered, and the sorrow in his voice shattered Katherine's heart. Tears stung her eyes and she leaned against him, inhaling the scent that was only Reynold, feeling his warmth and strength surrounding her, protecting her.

He separated their bodies, and before Katherine could even think about what she must do, he lifted the tunic over his head, and discarded his braies. She caught her breath, marveling at how the beautiful lines of his body moved her. Every scar was a piece of his history, every muscle a testament to his dedication. She did not speak, but merely smiled as he gently removed her clothes. When she tried to come into his arms, he held her back.

"Wait, my lady," he murmured.

At her low groan of frustration, Reynold looked up at her with sparkling eyes. Still on his knees, he picked up the discarded rag beside them and leaned over the water. Katherine watched the workings of muscle in his arm and side, and could not resist running her hand down his body.

He straightened and paused, his eyes closed, as she traced the muscles of his chest and stomach. Reynold caught her fingers.

"Not so soon," he said, and picked up his soap.

"What are you—"

"Shhh."

He soaped the cloth and Katherine felt an excited, anxious shiver run through her body. She was unprepared for the first touch of the wet cloth on her breast; she shuddered with a maddening need for more.

"Let me cleanse you, my lady," he murmured, rubbing the cloth slowly, mesmerizingly over her breasts. The material grew warm with his movements, and slid over the soapy wetness of her skin. "Forget everything but you and me. I will wash your past and your hurts away."

Katherine gave a ragged sigh and closed her eyes. Reynold lifted her and eased her back onto his tunic. She surrendered to his warmth, to his sweetness. As the last bright light of day vanished, the trees formed a fresh green canopy over them, and the water murmured in her ear. She lay still and Reynold washed her.

Every movement of the wet cloth against her skin brought her flesh to tingling life and awareness. He lingered at her breasts until she moaned her need of him. Still he tormented her, wiping soap and moisture down her body, following the line of one leg as he encircled it with his hands and massaged downwards. He soaped each foot, lingered at her ankles, then slid the cloth up the inside of her leg.

Katherine shivered with desire. She pressed her hand to her mouth, throwing her head back, arching off the ground. He could not possibly dare to—

He released her legs and began to soap one arm.

Katherine's tense body sagged back to the ground in disappointment. She heard Reynold's soft chuckle, but even that faded away as he soaped her fingers and forearm, circled her elbow, and slid up to her shoulders. His wet, soapy hands massaged her breasts, and she shook so hard that she stuttered over her words.

"R-Reynold, please," she cried, reaching up for him. He eluded her hands and leaned over her to wet the cloth in the river. She lifted her head and licked his nipple. He groaned and sat back.

"Not yet, my sweet Katherine," he said hoarsely as he dragged the cloth from her breasts down her abdomen. "I am not nearly done with you."

As the water dripped down her body, she moved restlessly, eyes half-closed, watching Reynold. He parted her legs, and then as he gazed into her eyes, he slid the cloth down between her thighs. Katherine sucked in her breath, then cried out as a wave of savage desire rolled through her body. He caressed the deepest, pleasure-sensitive part of her, until she shuddered and covered her face.

When his hands left her body, Katherine opened her eyes in a panic. He was suddenly there, covering her, his hard body imprinting itself on her flesh. She wrapped her legs and arms about him as with one thrust he filled her completely. Katherine convulsed into a release of desire so intense, she could only hold him and shake.

And then he began to move, and she could no longer tell where the first burst of passion ended and a new one began. She only knew that every touch of him was like fire in her blood, painful and sweet, and she could never, never have enough.

Reynold lifted his shoulders up and looked down into Katherine's face. As he slid deeper and deeper into her, she cried out, rolling her head back and forth, and arching her body up to meet every thrust of his. He did not want to lose this image of her, even as the darkness grew ever stronger and their surroundings faded. She was all he would ever want, and she was slipping away. He moved slower, striving to delay the stunning release that would only bring reality back to them again.

When he finally could control his passion no longer, he poured himself into her, shuddering, dropping down to pillow in the softness of her body. Katherine clutched his shoulders, and with a moan, joined him in sweet pleasure.

As their breathing eased, and their racing hearts slowed, Reynold rolled off Katherine and sat up. She slid her hand up his thigh, but he stopped her and got to his feet. He had been so determined that he would not leave their lovemaking with a feeling of melancholy, but the sadness pulled him down. If only he could make her see how pure and good their love was, if only . . .

As he stood at the edge of the water, looking out into the darkness, she came up behind him and pressed against his back. Her breasts teased him, and instead of rejoicing at her passion, he felt only more depressed.

"Katherine, do not—"

And then she pushed. Reynold tottered on the river bank off-balance, and fell in face-first. He came up sputtering water, to hear her laughing! With a growl he caught her wrist and pulled. She gave a merry scream and fell on top of him, and they both went under.

For the first time in a long while, Reynold felt hope blossoming again in his heart. He chased her along the river's edge, caught her up and tossed her into the depths. They frolicked like children, then made wild love again beside a fire that lit Katherine's body with a golden glow. She fell asleep in his arms.

He cradled her against his chest and whispered, "I love you," over and over into her ear, praying that somewhere deep inside she would hear and understand.

Chapter 26

Before the sun rose, Reynold awoke and lay still, savoring the feel of Katherine's naked body entwined with his beneath the blanket. In the grayness of early morning, the birds began calling to one another, and the forest rustled to life. The peace and enchantment of such a day renewed Reynold's determination. This would not be the last morning he awoke with Katherine at his side.

He turned his head and nibbled at her ear. She murmured in her sleep and batted at him as if he were a bothersome insect. Grinning, he pressed kisses to her ear and down her cheek. She shrugged her shoulders and slapped at the side of her head, only to freeze when her hand encountered his jaw.

Reynold could not help but laugh as she felt his face for a moment. He turned and pressed a kiss into her palm.

With a smothered gasp, she bolted upright and looked wildly at the surrounding forest. She turned and stared down at him. The blanket slid off her breasts to pool about her waist.

Reynold groaned. "Fair maiden, do not tempt me."

She did not even notice his state. "We have slept the morning away!"

"The sun has yet to rise," he protested.

"We must leave at once." She got to her knees and the blanket slid off Reynold and dropped to the ground. She stared wide-eyed at what his body obviously wanted to accomplish the first thing in the morning.

"Reynold, you're still naked!" she cried in alarm.

He laughed. "So are you, my lady. Perhaps we should take advantage of such good fortune and—"

"Not now!"

She scrambled to her feet and Reynold was treated to a wondrous view of her backside as she bent to retrieve her garments. He groaned and threw his arms wide.

"Reynold, do not linger," she said from beneath the folds of the smock dropping over her head. "The king yet depends on us."

He sat up. "Wherever did you throw my tunic in the heat of passion?"

Her cheeks blushed, but she didn't cease dressing. "By the bank of the river—I think."

He enjoyed her discomposure with his nakedness. "Are you positive we must leave at this moment?"

"Reynold!" Katherine watched in alarm as he rose to his feet, his body intimidatingly large, familiar though it was. He limped by her, tossing a grin over one shoulder. She bit her lip and stepped back, not trusting herself where he was concerned.

He bent to pick up his tunic. Katherine caught her breath. He paused, looking out over the water, and promptly dropped the garment to stretch. Her wide eyes couldn't take in enough of him. The first rays of the rising sun touched his muscled back, caressing it as she longed to. Hours of lovemaking had not tempered her passion for him.

Reynold took two awkward steps and dove into the river.

Katherine ran to the edge, hands on her hips, the spell broken. "Get out of there! We must hurry."

He got to his feet, waist-deep in water, slicking his wet hair back. "Throw me the soap."

She stamped her foot in outrage. "But last night we—I mean you and the water and..." Her words trailed off in confusion. She could scarce contemplate let alone express what they had done.

Reynold held out his hand for the soap. "Katherine, I smell like you. The people we meet today shall give us strange looks, but if that does not bother you—"

Aghast, she looked down at her body and let out a little scream. With a wriggle, she drew the gown and smock over her head and tossed them aside. She picked up the discarded soap and ran into the water.

Reynold waded near, his big body sending ripples in her direction. "Katherine, what a wonderful idea."

She held out her hands threateningly. "Stay back, or I shall throw the soap as far as I can—and I will use my good arm!"

He looked suitably chastised as Katherine soaped her body in haste. He made no attempt to do anything but watch her with glittering eyes. She hurried, knowing the longer she lingered, the more precarious her situation. Reynold looked to be having trouble breathing, not a good sign.

There was only one last place to wash, and she was too mortified to finish, with Reynold's glowering gaze heating her body. She rubbed her hands in the soap then tossed it high in the air in his direction. Startled, he reached to catch it, and while he was distracted, Katherine finished her bath. With a smile of satisfaction, she rinsed off and rose from the water.

Reynold gave her a thundering frown that would have, at one time, scared her into speechless cowering. She stuck out her tongue and flounced from the water, hips swaying.

With a roar he splashed after her. Katherine shrieked and raced for her garments, holding them before her like a shield.

"We must go!" she pleaded, standing dripping wet and naked. "Please, Reynold, no more games."

He lumbered to a halt, his glistening chest heaving, his obvious passion threatening to wipe every-

thing else but him from her mind. She must not
be swayed.

"Please," she repeated, and sighed with relief as
he nodded.

"Dress yourself," he said hoarsely, and turned
his back on her.

After Katherine securely wrapped Reynold's
thigh, they spent the day trudging down the highway with a weary line of travelers, all either dis-
placed by the impending war or following it.
Beggars trailed along beside the crowd, chanting
for handouts.

After dark, they reached the bridge into Leicester, but the gates on the far side were closed for
the night. Katherine was almost thankful they had
to sleep amidst a crowd. She could not spend a
night alone with Reynold at a comfortable inn.

At dawn, a horn sounded the opening of the
gates. Katherine and Reynold packed their blankets into his magic sack, then joined their fellow
travelers crossing the bridge and entering Leicester.

She searched the high walls of the town for the
king's banner. Disappointment made her shoulders sag.

Reynold drew her hand under his arm. "He has
gone already, my sweet. Let me take you to an
inn."

"But—"

He led her across a muddy pit in the center of
the road. "Katherine, I need information. The men

will not talk to you. And I will appear suspicious if I bring my wife with me on such a mission."

It was on the tip of her tongue to say she was not his wife, but she let it pass. It sounded like such a wonderful dream. To be the wife of someone like Reynold, a man who would cherish her for herself and not her money. She thought upon James's image with loathing.

The houses crowded in on one another, seeming to lean over the streets in dangerous abandon. The streets grew filthier, and pigs rutted with delight. Katherine lifted her skirts as if they were made of the finest silk rather than coarse wool.

"I am sorry," Reynold said, in an angry, formal voice. "We cannot afford a good meal, and as for staying the night—"

"Do not explain, Reynold," she said gently.

He crossed his arms over his chest and scowled. "We do not need rooms, as we will be following our king."

"You have hardly slept," he murmured, looking down on her with renewed warmth.

She blushed. "Neither have you. After we discover where the king has gone, we shall rest your leg then continue our journey."

The common room of the Goat Inn rocked with bawdy laughter. The smell of unwashed bodies and greasy smoke brought a wave of queasiness upon her. Reynold hesitated in the doorway. Katherine swallowed a gulp of air, lifted her chin, and prepared to push her way inside. Instead, Reynold caught her arm and drew her back into the heat of day.

"You shall come with me," he said, turning to march the way they had come.

"But I thought you said—"

"I cannot leave you alone in such a place. Surely the market will have food to eat and pretty things for you to look at while I search for information."

"Will you buy me silks, Reynold?" she teased, glancing at him from beneath her lashes.

He rolled his eyes. "You learn too quickly, my lady." His gaze softened and he caressed her cheek. "Would that I could give you the world, Katherine."

His wistfulness touched something within her, and she smiled sadly. "You have given me much, Reynold, do you but know it."

A peculiar expression crossed his features and he frowned down at her body. "Do you speak of a child, Katherine? So soon?"

She gasped in shock and stepped away from his hands. "Reynold, do not say such things! I could never—my father would—oh!"

Katherine turned her back and strode away, slogging through mud. The nerve of him, bringing up such a sensitive subject, when he knew what it would do to their families should they conceive a child together. Though a tiny part of Katherine wondered if it were perhaps too late for recriminations, the rest of her refused to dwell on it. Just in time she came to her senses and jumped clear as a horse and rider thundered down the street. If Reynold dared to lecture her—

Instead he gazed after the horse. "A soldier in armor, Katherine. Perhaps the king has returned."

The market was in an uproar when they emerged from an alley. Foot soldiers in leather jerkins bartered for cheese and bread. Armored knights laughed over the quality of wines, but bought them anyway.

" 'Tis not the king's men," Reynold whispered into her ear. "Katherine, I shall return in but a moment. Search out the nearest meat pie." He placed a coin in her hand and melted into the crowd behind her.

Katherine watched the people ebb and flow around her, ignored the occasional leer, and tried to discover what felt different. She knew she was perceived as no great lady now, and no one called for her to spend her coins. Yet she stood here alone in a crowded market and was not afraid. She did not search the ground for hidden obstacles to trip her feet, nor did she absently clutch her arm. Where had she gained such confidence?

It came to her with a warm glow she could not suppress. Reynold. Her partner in a hopeless mission, her support when things seemed bleak. With him behind her, she felt safe enough to seek her own strength.

Before she could think further on so wondrous a thought, a squire in red and white livery caught her eye as he bartered with a farmer over vegetables. There was something about his manner which—

And then it hit Katherine with the coldness of a fall into a winter pond. That boy was squire to one of her father's vassals. He was often teased for his tight-fisted ways with his master's coin. Now red-faced, he leaned towards the farmer to press his point.

Katherine ducked behind a tented stall but could not seem to catch her breath. The army must be her father's, on their way to join the king. She groaned and covered her eyes. Why hadn't she thought to better conceal herself?

A sudden scream and the crash of a wooden stall brought Katherine out of hiding in time to see Reynold bearing down on her at a dead run, three mounted men giving chase as they wove between stalls and pigs and people.

"Run!" Reynold shouted, motioning her down an alley.

"Katherine!" cried a voice from farther away.

She froze at the sight of her father, towering on his warhorse above the stalls. Although he was yet two aisles away, Katherine had no doubt he would neatly divide the market in pursuit of her.

Reynold dragged at her arm but she shook him off. "It is too late," she murmured, as she turned to face her father. "Let me speak with him, Reynold. Perhaps we need his help after all."

"Katherine," he said in a low voice, "forgive me, but we still do not know if your father is one of the traitors."

"I have to believe in him, Reynold. If not, my life has been a lie."

He said nothing more.

Horses surrounded them, hooves pawing, manes tossing, eyes rolling wildly with the excitement. The knights began to dismount and Reynold stepped in front of her.

Katherine pushed him aside. " 'Tis all right. My father's men will not hurt me."

But she had forgotten what they all believed of Reynold, that he had stolen her from the home of her betrothed. Two armored men grabbed him by each arm and dragged him from her side. Reynold stumbled heavily in their grip.

Outrage and fear warred within Katherine. They were handling Reynold like a criminal. "Hold!" she commanded in the harshest voice she could muster.

The soldiers obeyed her at once then looked up to her father, tall and imposing on his horse. The Earl of Durham lifted the helmet from his head. His cheeks were ruddy, his hair plastered to his scalp with sweat. Yet he stared at her as if she were his foot soldier and not his daughter. Never had Katherine experienced his great anger, but she refused to allow her father to frighten away her determination.

"Father, we have much to discuss. You and I need privacy, and Reynold needs to rest. He was wounded while protecting me."

Her father's expression did not change, but at the tilt of his head, the soldiers reluctantly released their captive. Reynold swayed, and for a moment, Katherine thought she would have to hold him up, regardless of her father's cold stare. But Reynold righted himself and limped forward.

"Hold, monk," the earl said in a dangerous voice.

Katherine realized her father no longer stared at her face, but at her body. She looked down and saw flashes of skin between the loose laces and torn garments. Her father's face went white, and his horse pranced in agitation beneath him. He grasped the hilt of his sword.

"Father!" she cried, running to touch his boot. " 'Tis not how it looks. I was attacked and Reynold saved me. He is an honorable man."

Reynold lifted an impassive face to the earl. "And I am no longer a monk, my lord. I have given up the calling. I will not return to the monastery."

Katherine winced at Reynold's timing. She never thought her father could look angrier, but he succeeded so successfully that her heart faltered. She could not let Reynold bear the brunt of his wrath.

"Father, take us to your quarters," she said, drawing the earl's attention from Reynold.

Lord Durham tightened his grip on the reins. His warhorse danced and tossed its head, towering over her. "I do not have time for this, daughter. My men will break their fast, then we pursue the king."

"We deserve your time, Father. 'Tis about the king."

"Do you know where he has gone?" Reynold asked.

Katherine winced as her father gritted his teeth. "We will speak in private, Brother."

Their gazes clashed as she held her breath. Reynold finally took her arm. Lord Durham spurred his horse forward. Before Katherine could object, she was lifted onto her father's lap.

"Rolf," he said to his nearest man, "take the monk up behind you."

The room Katherine's father had procured was on the second floor of a respectable inn. A large curtained bed took up one corner, and rugs instead of straw covered the floor. Chairs surrounded a bare trestle table.

To avoid her father's suspicious stare, Katherine wandered to the window and pushed open the shutters. A fountain bubbling with water occupied the center of a shaded garden. She sighed, wishing she could feel as peaceful as the garden looked.

"Katherine," the earl said, and she turned to face him. "You shall remain here until I return. 'Tis not safe on the road—" he nodded sarcastically at Reynold, "—as you have pointed out."

"Reynold but protected me."

"You would not have needed protection had you remained within James's walls. But you did not have a choice in this matter."

His unconcealed hostility focused on Reynold, who straightened as if he faced his own military commander.

"Lord Durham, although I regret my actions, I deemed them necessary."

The earl threw up his hands. "Christ's blood, what is going on here?" he demanded.

She took a deep breath, then came forward and touched her father's arm. "Those men did not kidnap me for ransom. I knew too much. The lady Eleanor—"

His face flushed.

"—overheard some of your friends plotting to betray King Richard and side with Henry Tudor."

He went white, then after giving Reynold a quick glare, turned his full attention back to Katherine. "Why did you not speak to me? All of this over a simple misunderstanding?"

"No, Father, I speak the truth," she said gently. "The new maidservant overheard Eleanor and me. I think she betrayed us to the traitors."

"Katherine, 'tis too harsh a word!"

"They could have had me killed, but they did not. Unfortunately, they chose to hide me near a monk who could not ignore a crime."

She smiled at Reynold, then realized her mistake when the earl scowled.

"Father," she continued quickly, "do you understand why I could not return home? The kidnappers would have been waiting for me. Besides, your life was in danger! What if people thought you were involved?"

His shoulders bent lower, and for a terrible moment, he looked truly old. "My daughter, you risked your life over my foolish reputation?"

"Don't say you are unimportant, Father! You mean everything to me." Her voice caught and she bit her lip. "Please forgive Reynold his actions of the previous days. He knew how important it was for me to finish what I started. You never expected anything of me. For once I wanted to do something . . . worthy of you."

Reynold could take no more. He hated the fact that Katherine thought herself unworthy of her parents' love. He wanted to take out his anger on Lord Durham's face. How dare he let her think no one believed her story of the monk's attack.

Reynold took a step forward, his fists clenched. But the earl suddenly enveloped his daughter in a hug so tight Reynold could hear the breath leave her lungs.

"Katherine, my dear child, you have nothing to prove to me. You are a good daughter," he whispered in a choked voice. "I wish your mother and I had been better parents."

Katherine burst into tears.

"There now, child," the earl said gruffly, holding her away from him. "We have work to do. You mustn't get yourself upset."

Still crying, she turned and buried her face in Reynold's tunic. Keeping his arms to his sides, Reynold looked from Katherine's blond head into the shocked face of her father.

Chapter 27

"Katherine," Reynold said. "Perhaps you should tell your father the names of the traitors." For one insane moment, he thought maybe she would confess her feelings and free them of this horrible silence.

She stiffened and immediately stepped away from him. Reynold gritted his teeth.

"Father, I—"

"Just tell me the names, child," Lord Durham said, his voice unemotional.

Reynold knew the man was no fool. Yet he was thankful for Katherine's sake that her father was not going to pursue what he'd just seen. Reynold didn't think she was ready to face the truth.

Quietly, Katherine recited the three names which had caused her so much trouble. "The Earl of Northumberland, Lord Stanley, and the Duke of Suffolk."

At each name, her father flinched as if struck. When she was finished, the earl closed his eyes and bowed his head. Suddenly he slammed his fist hard onto the table, sending it crashing to the floor. If he was acting, he was performing well.

"My friends," he whispered in an agonized voice, then whirled away with a clatter of armor to gaze out the window. "You overheard them, Katherine?"

"No, sir, the lady Eleanor did. Then I was kidnapped, so I knew she must have heard the truth of it."

"You told all of this to James, but not to me?"

Katherine took a step closer to Lord Durham's forbidding back.

"Father, I had hoped he would take care of it. And I did not know you would soon be arriving."

"Did James send a message to King Richard?"

"He did, my lord," Reynold replied. "But he told me it was merely a ruse to pacify your daughter. The men had no true intentions of approaching the king. I could not let this go. Katherine would never forgive herself if—"

Lord Durham turned and scowled at Reynold. "And you know my daughter's mind so well?"

Reynold didn't dare look away. "We have spent many days in conversation. At first, Lady Katherine refused to trust me—why should she? She was frightened of the man who was following us."

"The kidnapper?" the earl asked, his grizzled face reddening.

Katherine slipped her hand into his arm. "Time and again Reynold protected me. Do not judge him harshly. I, too, was angry when he stole me from his brother's castle. Yet the battle approaches, and I don't think Reynold and I can succeed alone. Will you help us?"

Lord Durham patted his daughter's hand. "I will take your message, child."

"But what if the king thinks—"

"I will convince him of my innocence. And I will tell him of my daughter's bravery."

Katherine felt tears sting her eyes. She had always known she was right, that her father had no part in this treason. He clapped his hands loudly and his squire poked his head into the room. Owen Fielding, the son of a neighboring baron, had been fostering with the Berkeleys for many a year. The young man had been following Katherine around for as long as she could remember.

"Bring us dinner, Fielding. Then seek out our master armorer for Welles, here. He shall accompany us to the king. We have much to discuss," he added, glancing at Reynold from beneath bushy brows.

Katherine stood aside while a flurry of servants set silver plates on spotless tablecloths. Towels and utensils and even rare glass goblets from home soon followed. She ate the morning meal with Reynold and her father, trying to decide where her feelings lay.

On one hand, she was relieved that her father knew the truth, that he believed her and would take her warning to the king. Yet—she sighed and chewed her bread slowly. Her father and Reynold were busy discussing the route to the king's camp at the Bradshaws, and she was alone with her thoughts. In a sense the men had already left her. Her part in her last great adventure was over.

Katherine dutifully smiled at Owen who served her fish soup, but her thoughts were anything but happy. Resigned, aye, that would be the best word. Perhaps she should disguise herself, follow the men to the king? But what good would that do? Her father could take her message more quickly. Her presence would be useless.

She might as well get used to that. When she married James, she would be his newest castle decoration, another servant to keep his household running smoothly and his bed warmed at night. But would he love her? Would he share his day and his thoughts with her? Could he be at all like his brother?

Katherine suddenly met Reynold's gaze and tears stung her eyes. He was leaving her. No longer would he warm her at night, or make her laugh by day. He had insisted he would not return to the monastery. But what would James do to him? Would he use his brother in his own army, where Katherine would have to sit at the same table with him every day? She couldn't imagine this ache in her chest ever dissipating with time. She tore her gaze from Reynold's and bent her head over the soup. All the danger, all the excitement, everything she felt for Reynold—she had to put it behind her.

Through each course of food, Katherine could only manage a few bites. She knew the men needed their strength, for the battle might be joined when they arrived. She wanted to speak to Reynold, to thank him for his help and his comfort, but her father controlled the conversation. Then the Berkeley armorer arrived, and he and the earl walked around Reynold as if he were a horse about to be bought at auction. The armorer ran his hands across Reynold's arms and chest, hemmed and hawed, then admitted he might have a suit of armor to fit.

"But don't expect comfort, boy," he said ominously.

Caught up in the fever for battle, they left Katherine alone, without even a wave of farewell. Her gaze took in the comfortable room, suddenly so confining. How long would they keep her here? What if something dreadful happened and they didn't return?

Katherine straightened her shoulders and angrily forced away the terror of helplessness. She refused to fall back to being a little girl who needed constant protection. Should the worst befall her, she would survive. Hadn't she proved she was capable of that?

Her father's squire silently returned and began to clear the table. Katherine remembered him as a frightened boy, barely nine, come to train under the Earl of Durham. Now he was taller than she, almost a man at sixteen. Hadn't she taught him to dance? Would he face his first battle today? Fondly, she touched his arm.

"Owen, can you tell me where my father has gone?"

"To the stables behind the inn, my lady," he said, sparing her a glance as he hurried through his task.

"Thank you, Owen. Fare well today and make me proud."

He looked up at her, his face red, his eyes searching hers. "I'll defend your father's life with my own, Lady Katherine, if God wills."

"God's will is for you to return safe and whole." Katherine remembered Owen's love of the tournament, his belief in a knight's chivalry, something so many noblemen had forgotten. She looked down at her peasant gown and sighed. "If I had a token to give you, I would."

He shook his head and smiled. "Lady Katherine, save your tokens for your future husband. I am pleased to take your good wishes into battle and perhaps—" He caught one of her hands in his and pressed his lips to her fingers. "—a kiss, my lady, for luck."

And then he was gone. How many men would be killed today? Would her father arrive in time to stop the carnage? Could Reynold, for all his strength and skill, be pierced by a crossbow's dart or the clever thrust of a sword?

Before she could think what she meant to do, Katherine ran out the door and down the stairs, through the common room. She reached the street and came to a halt.

Owen had said the stables were in the rear. She

fled to the far side of the inn and skidded to a halt. Her father's army sprawled before her, a mass of men laughing, spitting, checking their weapons, adjusting their clothing. She could see the foot soldiers, the common men from her father's villages, each with a long-handled pike so deadly to a knight's horse. The longbowmen in their leather jerkins carried bows taller than themselves. Huge chargers danced and snorted and tossed their heads when the heavy knights mounted. The sun dazzled her eyes as it reflected off their polished armor and wove through the silks of their banners.

How would she find her father?

A bearded archer swung an arm around her waist and pressed his face into her hair. "Come to wish us a safe journey, lass?"

A voice hissed, " 'Tis Lady Katherine."

Around them silence spread like ripples in a pond. The archer stiffened, then released her, his eyes wide in terror. "My lady—" he began, but Katherine interrupted him.

"Good sir, I wish you and all your comrades a safe journey. Have you seen my father?"

He nodded swiftly. "Let me escort you to the stables, my lady."

She took his arm as if he were a noble come to court her. She heard gruff voices whispering her identity as masses of soldiers gave way before her. They bowed their heads and she gave them her best smile, though her lips trembled with suppressed tears. She inwardly berated herself for worrying about the end to her grand adventure, when all these brave men might die.

At the stable, she turned and waved to her father's army. They cheered and called her name. Laughing, she blew kisses from her fingertips then turned and stepped into the stables.

The air was immediately cooler, the light dim after the brilliant sunshine. Soon enough her eyes adjusted and she saw her father, Reynold, and the armorer surrounded by pieces of scattered armor. Reynold had changed into a loose shirt and hose. Katherine was so used to seeing him as either a monk or a peasant, that he seemed like a different person. When Owen came running in to take his place with the armorer, Lord Durham stood back to watch as the breastplate and backplate were buckled to Reynold's torso.

He was preparing to go to war, and Katherine might never see him again. Their gazes suddenly met and locked. She could no more look away than she could will herself to stop breathing. The squire and the armorer attached the gorget to protect his neck, buckled on the pauldron and vambrace to cover his arms. Katherine watched Reynold being transformed before her and she was frightened, frightened of what the armor had to protect him from. He had not been able to train in the last eight months. Would his strength give out?

His amethyst gaze bore into hers as the men buckled padded plates around his legs and locked his feet into the sabatons, the steel boots. The armorer handed Reynold a helmet and gauntlets, then swiftly began to pack away his supplies. Katherine couldn't move, locked in Reynold's heated gaze as if he physically clasped her to him.

She distantly heard her father say, "Welles, come along," as he walked outside, followed by his armorer. He did not see her in the shadows. She was alone with Reynold, her knight, her protector. She was drawn towards him, and with one arm he pulled her against the jointed plates on his chest.

"Reynold," she whispered, dropping her head back, willing him to kiss her no matter who might see.

His mouth took hers with the rough kiss of a soldier who might not return. Katherine parted her lips and met his tongue with her own, moaning softly into his mouth. She clasped his warm head to her, feeling the damp hair at his neck, knowing she could never touch him again. When Reynold returned, she would go to his brother.

Tears started in her eyes and she gentled the kiss, hoping he could drink somehow of her strength. *Please, God, bring him home safe*, she thought, squeezing her eyes tightly shut in prayer.

"You are crying?" Reynold asked against her lips.

Katherine shrugged, inhaling his breath, her forehead touching his. She wanted to beg him to come back to her, but instead whispered, "You will be careful?"

"You know I am," he replied, then gazed at her with deadly earnestness. "I am frightened for you,

Katherine. I don't wish to leave you alone. What if this is the plan, to lure me away and leave you unprotected—"

"Shhh," she whispered, covering his lips with her fingers. "I will be fine. I'm sure my father is leaving men to guard me."

"But what if Lord Durham—"

"No more doubts," she insisted fiercely. "My father would never hurt me. I'm trusting you to protect him as you have me."

"I will do my best," he said, then looked over her shoulder. "He is ready, Katherine."

She sighed. She could tell that he had begun to think of other things, to prepare himself for the coming battle. She wanted to kiss him once more, but he released her just before her father approached.

"Welles, Fielding is holding your horse," he said, giving Reynold a stern look.

Katherine watched helplessly as Reynold nodded to her. He picked up his shield, emblazoned with a crimson lion, and left the stables. The sunlight shone about him and reflected off his armor, until with squinted eyes she could only see him as a stranger bathed in light.

"Katherine."

She turned to look into her father's well-worn face. Her heart gave a pang as she realized he was older and slower than Reynold, but might still be fighting this day.

He hesitated over his words, then sighed. "Katherine, you will remain here, with Fielding to guard you until we return. I only wish I could spare more."

"But Father, you need all the men you can—"

"You are just as important to me as the king is," he said gruffly, and Katherine's eyes began to sting again. Her father seemed to search her face and see directly into her soul. "We have things to discuss when I return, daughter."

Katherine's skin chilled even in the summer heat. She had shown too many of her feelings. She bowed her head. "I will do as you wish, Father."

He patted her shoulders awkwardly, then bent to pick up his helmet and gauntlets. "Go to your room, Katherine. It is dangerous for you to stand here with the common people and watch us leave."

She gave him a dutiful smile and waved as he mounted his charger. He wheeled the horse towards the front of his small army and suddenly he was no longer old, but a warrior protecting his king.

A horse trotted up beside her, then nuzzled at her shoulder. Katherine turned and wrapped her arms as far around the animal as she could, shutting out the suffocating heat of the day and the sounds of the army departing.

Reynold leaned down from the horse to caress her arm. "Good-bye, my sweet Katherine," he whispered.

She stepped back, shielding her eyes to see him against the bright sky. "Oh, Reynold, I have no token to give you!" She knew it was a foolish thought, a faraway memory from the tournaments of her youth.

"I carry you in my heart." He kicked at the horse's sides and trotted away from her.

Had she imagined those soft words? She ran a few steps after him, then slowed to a stop as he joined the other mounted knights. Her heart hung in her chest like a heavy weight, threatening to choke her. She put a hand to her eyes to stop the tears, but there was no time to mourn. The townspeople caught her up in a wave of humanity that surged towards the streets as they cheered and waved good-bye.

"My lady!" came a distant voice from behind her. She didn't want to listen. She wanted to follow the army's departure until the last glint of armor disappeared over the West Bridge.

"Lady Katherine," the voice insisted, and she finally recognized Owen Fielding.

With a sigh, she turned and went against the mob, shoving friendly hands away. Before the inn, they met in the last remnants of the crowd.

Wearing a thundering frown which distorted the fine lines of his face, Owen gripped her elbow without his usual courtesy. "I'm to watch you," he said sullenly, pulling her towards the entrance. " 'Tisn't safe for you out here."

Katherine dragged her heels. "Owen, I wish you didn't have to stay. Who will guard my father's back?"

"He's got that monk now, doesn't he," the boy said with barely disguised jealousy. "And from what his lordship told me, he's got a thing or two to say to that man."

Chapter 28

The torturous sun neared its zenith, and Reynold thought he would faint. For three hours he had been roasting in padded armor, feeling as cooked as a Christmas goose. He told himself it was only a few miles to the king's camp at Sutton Cheney, but that did not guarantee respite. For all he knew, the battle could be joined, and he would have to fight instead of rest and quench his thirst.

Eight months in a monastery had made him forget the weight of armor and the stifling heat of combat. If only he were wearing his own suit, which bent where he bent, and moved soundlessly with each adjustment of muscle and bone. Once again he put a finger in the gorget at his neck and wished his strength were enough to bend metal. The armor had chafed a raw spot in his neck, and who knew how many other places.

Suddenly Reynold tensed and squinted down the long column of walking and mounted men. The horse beneath him snorted and tossed its head at Reynold's abrupt change of mood. Was that Katherine's father, leaving the front of his army and riding toward the rear? Perhaps the man was merely inspecting his men, or coming to confer with his knights on battle strategy. But with a resigned feeling of dread, Reynold knew the earl was coming for him. He couldn't shake a feeling of foreboding, that all his plans to protect Katherine were for naught. And when he had seen, too late, that Durham had left only one boy to protect Katherine, as if there were no threat, no kidnapper, he could only think the worst about the earl. For now, he had no choice but to follow him carefully into battle, and see where his loyalties lay.

He sighed and wished it were all over, his confrontation with Durham, the anger, the man's insistence that he never see Katherine again. He did not wish to disobey her father, yet he could not imagine Katherine's bright smile banished from his life. Reynold still felt confident that he could convince Katherine they belonged together. He knew he was being selfish, but for once he refused to back down before his family's wishes.

He met the steady gaze of the old earl as the man swung his horse to trot alongside his. "My lord," Reynold said, nodding warily. " 'Tis a fine army you have mustered."

"Good people all," Lord Durham answered.

For a few minutes, Reynold listened to the steady clop of the horses' hooves, and the occasional boisterous laughs of the surrounding knights. The gorget cut into his throat until he couldn't breathe, couldn't swallow, could only wait in dread. What did the earl suspect? Was he waiting for Reynold to confess all? He would wait forever if he expected Reynold to implicate Katherine in anything unholy.

"Brother Reynold—"

"My lord," Reynold interrupted. "In the haste of these times, you may have forgotten that I said I am no longer one of the brethren. If you do not wish to use my Christian name, you may use Viscount Welles."

Reynold held his breath, watching the earl's face. He thought perhaps the old man respected strength more than anything. He breathed a silent sigh of relief when the earl cocked a bushy eyebrow and gave him a thin smile.

"I had forgotten you and your brother had different sires. Yet you gave it all up for the monastery?"

Reynold hesitated. "Eight months ago, I thought it for the best. My younger brother died because of an accident while training with me. In my guilt, I took his place at the monastery."

"What made you regret your decision?"

How he longed to say "your daughter," but that would have been foolish. "I have come to believe that my brother, Edmund, would not have wanted me in the church out of guilt. I can do more good with my life by overseeing my land and being of service to the king."

The earl was silent, his piercing eyes squinting

towards the head of his army. "What land do you possess, Welles?"

"I have eight manors scattered throughout Lancashire, and a small castle which was my father's home."

"Who has controlled them these last eight months?"

"Officially, James, but Margery has done most of the work." Reynold hesitated, scratching beneath the armor at his healing thigh. "My lord, I do feel a great debt to my sister. Though she might have had all of my wealth had I remained in the monastery, she still did not wish that life for me. I am going to offer her two of my manors and their lands to add to her dowry."

The earl nodded. "Is she betrothed?"

Reynold grinned. "She and James cannot come to agreement just yet."

"She is well into marriageable age."

"I think James is loathe to force our sister, my lord, seeing as how he himself has still avoided marriage."

The earl glanced at him sharply, and Reynold regretted his foolish tongue.

"Do you think your brother was forced?" the earl asked dryly.

"No, my lord. Yet I think James does not understand the good life he could have."

"And you, the younger brother, are gifted with such wisdom?"

"Eight months can seem a lifetime, my lord, and now I think I see more clearly than James does."

The earl leaned toward Reynold and narrowed his eyes. "And what does your clear vision see about my daughter that Lord Bolton does not?"

Reynold inclined his head. "Your scurrier comes at a gallop, my lord. Perhaps there is news from King Richard."

A corner of Lord Durham's mouth turned up, but he spared Reynold further conversation. Reynold closed his eyes in relief when the earl turned away. But what the boy had to say shook all selfish thoughts from his mind.

Katherine stood at the window, looking down into the inn's expansive garden. She felt dead to the world, all purpose in her life gone. There was nothing left for her to do but submit to James. She chafed under such restrictions, and her mind fought for different solutions, but there were none.

Two bowls suddenly clattered together behind her. Owen attacked the dinner dishes as if they fought against him. He was silent, not his usual pleasant self since her father ordered him to remain behind.

Katherine sighed. "Owen, perhaps the servants could prepare me a bath—if it wouldn't be much trouble."

"Of course, my lady, anything you wish."

Over her shoulder, she watched as the red-faced squire struggled to balance a tray and avoid her eyes at the same time.

"Do you blame me for your assignment, Owen?"

His head lifted with a start. "No, my lady. I—merely regret I was chosen to assist you."

"Am I that difficult?" she teased.

His lips quirked reluctantly. "Never, Lady Katherine. I'll return in a—"

He gasped and the tray crashed to the floor, spilling soup and dishes everywhere. Katherine whirled around and saw the loathsome face of her kidnapper as he rose into the windowsill.

She started to scream, but he lunged at her and she scrambled backward. The man tumbled into the room and lurched to his feet. Katherine knew she'd never make it to the door. Frantically she searched about her for a weapon. She was suddenly shoved hard to one side by Owen, who faced the much larger man with merely his eating knife.

"Go, my lady," Owen said in a strained voice as he and the kidnapper crouched and faced one another.

But the man's black eyes focused on her intently, and Katherine knew he would kill Owen to follow her. His smile revealed a gaping hole through which his tongue protruded. She remained trapped in her corner of the room, the bed between her and the fight.

The kidnapper laughed and feinted forward with his fist. Owen jerked backwards, his face reddening.

"Boy, move or I'll hurt ye."

Owen raised his knife. "Stand back! Leave Lady

Katherine be! Take me for ransom if you must. My father—"

"Owen!" Katherine cried. " 'Tis too dangerous."

The man chortled, then knocked aside Owen's knife. Katherine watched it skitter beneath the bed, then raised her gaze in horror as the kidnapper advanced. Owen retreated as slowly as possible, retrieving a dirty dish from the table and tossing it. The man ducked, then lunged forward and up, grabbing Owen by the neck like an unwanted puppy. With a vicious shake, he tossed Owen against the wall. The boy crumpled to the floor and remained still.

"Now, my lady," he mocked, "ye've got no monk, nothin' but a boy. I was a patient man— followed ye, I did. I did me best to keep ye safe, but what did it get me? Ye're still free. People are laughin' at me, they are. Can't 'ave that. Ye need to be taught a lesson before we see my master."

"You won't tell me the coward's name?" she demanded, hearing a high-pitched crack in her voice.

"Plenty o' time," he crooned, taking a step forward. "No monk, no father, just you and—"

Katherine turned towards the door, and when the kidnapper stepped that way, she rolled across the bed. She landed hard on her stomach on the floor, then stuck her arm beneath the bed, searching for Owen's knife. A quick painful slice across her finger told her she'd found it. Just as she rolled onto her back with the weapon, the kidnapper, with a triumphant cry, dropped on top of her, and the knife sank deep into his chest.

Katherine gasped in agony from the hilt of the knife bruising her ribs, and the weight of his body. Frantically she shoved and squirmed, tears running down her face. The man's head bobbed lifelessly next to her own, his sweat smearing her cheek, his blood soaking into her gown. She gasped in one more lungful of foul air, then heaved with all her might. His body sagged to one side, away from the bed.

Trapped by the furniture, Katherine dug her heels into the floor and pushed herself upward, out from under his body. His shoulder and arm dug painfully into her chest, but at last she was free of him. The blood smell rose from her own clothing. She crawled a few feet away and retched on the carpet.

Katherine sat back on her heels, swaying with the pounding in her head and the nausea. She looked over her shoulder at the body and shuddered. He had to be dead. There was too much blood soaking her to the skin.

Her heart grew deathly cold. It could easily be her blood, her death. And she had never told Reynold she loved him. The pressure in Katherine's chest erupted in a harsh sob, and she covered her mouth. He could be dying right now, the man who had taught her about courage and strength. He had believed in her, no matter her weak arm or her foolish ignorance. He had made her feel protected and cherished, but never less than an equal. He had loved her. And what had she done for him?

Katherine had let Reynold think he wasn't good enough for her. Tears burned a path down her cheeks. She could have spoken to her father, explained about her love for Reynold. Instead she had worried about her honor and pride, and let a good man possibly ride to his death thinking himself unworthy of her love.

Each sob was ripped from Katherine's lungs like torture, but she welcomed the pain. She deserved it. The only way to atone for what she had done was to go to Reynold, to beg his forgiveness and confess her love. If it wasn't too late. She sniffed back her last tears, trying to rediscover the determination Reynold had shown her she possessed. She would let nothing stand in her way. Her future was with Reynold. Wonderful nights in his arms stretched before her endlessly—all she had to do was make it happen.

She crawled to Owen, and gently turned him over. He groaned and his forehead wrinkled in pain. His swollen brow oozed a trickle of blood.

"Owen?" She patted his face. "Can you hear me?"

He blinked, then squinted up at her. "Katherine, what—"

Before she could reassure him, he shoved hard against her arms and tried to get up.

"That man—"

"He's dead," she said, fighting back another wave of nausea.

Owen stiffened in her arms, then slowly allowed himself to sag back against her. "Dead?"

"I killed him."

Owen's eyes opened wide. "You, my lady?" Then his gaze took in the scarlet stain across her chest. "You're hurt!" he cried, flinging himself from her arms to hover over her. "Shall I fetch— but no, you could bleed to death. Perhaps if I see the wound—" His face reddened. "I mean—oh, my lady, tell me what to do."

She took his fluttering hand. " 'Tis his blood, Owen. Please help me to my feet."

When he grasped her other hand, Katherine instantly remembered the wound she had received in her mad search for the knife. "Perhaps I will need your services after all."

Katherine sat in her chair while Owen cleaned and bandaged the shallow cut across her fingers. She couldn't help but watch the corpse, as if the man might still begin to move. He was not the only one searching for her. What of the kidnapper's master? Would he come himself, or send a new man, one whose face she wouldn't recognize, one who could openly approach her on the street, and she wouldn't know to run. She must warn Reynold in case he became the next target.

She looked down at her wool gown in distaste. "I can't wear this, Owen. And I have no other garments."

He frowned. "Your father left me coins, but to use them all on clothing would be foolhardy. Perhaps we could ask one of the maids—"

"We can stay here and pretend to be respectable, but they won't believe us."

"You're the earl's daughter!"

"You and I know that, but do I look it? For all they know, I am a woman you—"

"My lady!" Owen cried, blushing to the roots of his hair. "You should not know of such things."

"I have seen too much," she said, her shoulders bowing. "I wish I could say that I am the same, but I'm not."

"You have changed, my lady," Owen murmured, patting her wounded hand as he released it. "Your arm seems to pain you no more."

Katherine smiled. "Reynold taught me not to think about it, and sometimes I actually forget it was broken."

They looked at each other for a moment, and Katherine wondered what she was supposed to do. What would Reynold do? A wave of longing rushed through her, and she closed her eyes. What was he doing now? Riding to fight Henry Tudor, or perhaps engaged in battle already. She shivered. Please, God, let her not be too late.

"Call up the innkeeper, Owen. We must explain this death."

"But Lady Katherine, you just said they will not believe the truth."

"Yet we must attempt the telling. I will not run away in secret. Go ahead."

While Owen was gone, Katherine remained in her chair, her gaze fixed on the dead man. For so many weeks he had been the source of her terror, and now he was gone. She longed to bathe the stains of his death from her body. But not now, not until he was removed.

Owen opened the door and ushered the innkeeper in. The man was blustery and jovial, clearly a source of amusement in his public rooms. He grinned obligingly at her, and then his face slowly paled.

"Girl, your dress—" He saw the body. "God's blood," he whispered. "What 'appened?"

Katherine rose to her feet. "I am Lady Katherine Berkeley, daughter of the Earl of Durham, who purchased these rooms. That man—" she pointed to the body, "climbed in through the window and attacked me."

"Are ye badly injured?" he asked, gaping at her chest.

Katherine blushed at the scrutiny. "This is his blood. I had to stab him as he came down . . . atop me." She choked out the last words, then clasped her shaking hands together.

The innkeeper gazed around himself at the disheveled bed and the broken dishware. "Ye say ye're Lady Katherine?"

She lifted her chin. "I am."

"Beggin' yer pardon, little lady, but ye might just be apin' your betters. 'Tis not for me to decide. I'll send for the sheriff. Ye could be a whore who killed for a purse."

"Why would I call you then?"

But the innkeeper wouldn't listen to her protests. He turned and left the room, looking back once at the body with a shake of his head.

Katherine and Owen gazed at one another grimly.

"Surely he doesn't think that I would deliberately . . ." Katherine's voice trailed off.

"I will saddle my horse in case we must flee, my lady. Unless you wish to visit the gaol?"

She shuddered.

"Where shall we go?" Owen asked.

"To my father, of course." And Reynold, she added silently.

Owen bowed and edged toward the door, only leaving when Katherine insisted. Once again she sat alone with the corpse, waiting for a man to pronounce judgment upon her. As the minutes sped by, she began to doze, her head dropping to her chest. It had been many nights since she'd slept in peace. She was startled awake by the innkeeper's voice.

"There she sleeps like a innocent, my lord sheriff, like a man's death don't weigh 'eavy on her soul."

Katherine rose slowly to her feet, trying to recapture the dignity her garments did not inspire. She allowed the sheriff, a thin, sallow man, to gaze at her critically, while trying not to show how her heart pounded.

She finally turned to the innkeeper. "Sir, if I were guilty, would I not have fled by now?"

The sheriff scratched his bristled chin. "She talks like an earl's daughter."

"Gentlemen, forgive my state of dress. I was kidnapped from my home by that man, and was only recently reunited with my father. I have not had time to send for my own garments."

The sheriff reluctantly removed his cloth cap. "Ye may be who ye say ye are, milady, but I must wait for the earl to tell the truth of yer story. Come with me, if ye will."

Katherine didn't move. "I wish to remain here until my father returns."

"I can't allow that, miss."

"Lady Katherine," she said.

"If that be yer name, then ye 'ave nothin' to fear, do ye, milady? Come along now."

Katherine avoided his arm and descended the stairs into the common room unassisted. The friendly voices grew quiet and all movement ceased as straining eyes took in her blood-stained gown and her escort. She felt very far away, nothing at all like herself. They were about to imprison her. Once more she would be put into a dark pit, this time without Reynold's comfort. She would survive it—she must. When her father and Reynold returned, if they returned—

Katherine found it suddenly hard to breathe past the lump in her throat. They could be dying only miles away. She lifted her chin and looked with disdain at all the healthy men who ogled her.

"Your king fights for his life nearby!" she cried out, her voice piercing the heavy silence. "Why do you men yet remain?"

Heads lowered, shoulders hunched forward, and every gaze dropped from hers. She saw the shrugs, heard the muttering.

"You should be ashamed," she said in her most withering voice.

The sheriff gave her a gentle push from behind and she stumbled through the door. Thank goodness the sheriff had allowed her to leave first, for there was Owen, ablaze in her father's colors, as he kicked the horse's flanks and shot forward. With a gasp, she caught his hand and managed to find the stirrup as he lifted her off the ground. The peasant skirt wouldn't give enough for her to ride astride, so she perched on the horse's rump and clutched Owen's waist.

The sheriff shouted from behind her, but she put him from her mind. She was free, with the wind in her hair, and a horse carrying her away from Leicester. The distance grew ever smaller between her and Reynold. She would tell him of her love, and together they would deal with James.

Chapter 29

⟁⟁⟁

The scurriers, Lord Durham's advance men, brought the news to the earl's army. While their mounts steamed and trembled below them, the men gasped that King Richard was dead.

The pain in Reynold's chest had little to do with the king who had ruled so briefly. The kingdom would go on as always—but would Katherine? He dreaded having to inform her that her mission had failed. And still doubts whispered inside his head, that the earl's army had almost reached the king— but not quite. Was that deliberate? Reynold looked up as Lord Durham spoke to his soldiers.

"You're sure as to the events you witnessed, Crosby?"

The man bobbed his head as he gulped down water. "I saw with my own eyes how His Majesty the king and a few retainers charged that traitor's line. Why, the king took down many a man before he was overwhelmed. My lord, he wore his crown plain for all to see. I saw the sun flashing off it from hundreds of yards back."

Katherine's father nodded his head almost absently. "Yes, he would never hide his identity, nor shield himself behind his men."

"Aye, my lord. Only such a one as Henry Tudor could do that, no fighter he."

Reynold watched the small army as the news was passed outward. Wave upon wave of soldiers stood with their heads bowed.

"My lord," the scurrier continued, "the new king is headed this way, for Leicester is my guess. They're but a few miles behind me."

The earl sighed. "We shall not meet them on the road, lest in their bloodlust they attack unwisely. We shall await them in Leicester."

When a few men grumbled nearby, Lord Durham's temper finally snapped.

"Do you wish to have homes to return to?" he shouted. "Do you wish your wives and daughters flung from their houses by men to whom you did not even raise swords? The battle is over! We have lost. All we can do is go on with our lives."

Reynold had never heard an army move forward so silently. But once again, dark thoughts overtook his mind. It seemed too easy that the king was dead, without the Earl of Durham shedding one drop of blood.

The farther they rode, the more Katherine felt dread winding around her heart like rotting ivy. Something was wrong. The air hung still and oppressive, the countryside was motionless. Her father's army had recently passed this way, yet something deep inside told Katherine that much more was going on. Was the battle joined? Would she find Reynold fighting for his life? She shuddered and huddled closer to Owen's back. The squire sat straight so that she could lean against him.

"Are you tired, my lady?" he asked over his shoulder. "It won't be much farther now. In fact, do you see that dust cloud over the edge of the hill? It must be your father's army. They have yet to reach the field of battle."

"We hope," Katherine added darkly.

Owen's prediction proved true. As they topped the hill, the Durham army sprawled before them, curling in a long line down the winding dirt road.

"Owen, shouldn't they be heading away from us?"

The boy didn't answer, but his hands clutched hers at his waist. After a moment, he kicked his heels into the horse and they galloped down the green hillside directly for the army. Shouts of recognition reached her ears, and Katherine waved. But her eyes were busily searching the men.

The soldiers looked no worse for wear, besides being drenched in sweat and dusty from the road. Perhaps Henry Tudor had veered in another direction, and there would be no battle this day. She saw her father's banner at the rear of the army, and nearby Reynold's dark head. Her relief was so overwhelming she felt light-headed. Now she could tell him what was in her heart. She waved and Reynold lifted a hand.

Owen guided the horse into the midst of the knights, who called good-natured jests that Katherine barely heard. She and Owen rode up between the warhorses of her father and Reynold. She smiled at Reynold, almost bursting with the need to tell him of her love, to ask his forgiveness. He attempted to frown at her, but his lips wouldn't quite obey him.

Her father had no such problems. He swept the helmet from his head and glowered at her. "Katherine, you have disobeyed me! Whyever would you put your life at such risk?"

"Her kidnapper attacked us," Owen said.

Katherine felt the stiffness that held his back rigid, and she silently blessed his attempt to help her.

Reynold's horse danced a step as he fought to bring the beast even closer. His face had gone pale and hard with anger. "I knew this was going to happen. Are you hurt?"

Katherine longed to take his hand as he reached for her, then thought better of it. His gaze suddenly dropped and his eyes went wide at her bandaged hand and stained gown.

"Is that blood?"

She opened her mouth, but her father's stern, "Katherine!" brought her gaze to him.

Owen said, "My lady but defended herself, and killed the villain as he attacked her."

Her father's mouth sagged open. "You killed the man, Katherine?"

She tried to remain dignified as she nodded.

Turning to Reynold, she saw his worried eyes, then the slow, proud smile he bestowed on her. She sighed with happiness. He was all she ever wanted, her dark knight, her love. But she could not leave her wits in the clouds.

"We cannot relax our vigilance, Father. The man seemed most desperate to punish me for eluding him again and again. Perhaps his master feels the same."

When her father gave a heavy sigh, Katherine's happiness began to dissolve away. He looked tired. She could not stop herself from thinking that he was too old for this.

"My child, perhaps you are no longer in danger."

A chill went through Katherine. What could he mean? She opened her mouth to protest, then subsided and looked about her once more. She had forgotten that the army was headed for Leicester, no battle having been fought. Reynold's dark brows were lowered in a frown, and he looked at her in great sympathy.

"What has gone wrong?" she asked.

"We were too late, Katherine," Reynold said. He reached for her hand and she took it, squeezing tightly. "King Richard died on the battlefield ere we reached him. I am sorry."

Katherine felt as if the horse reared under her, as if the whole world had turned upside down. While she had frolicked with Reynold, or laid abed an extra hour, the king had died. Her throat seemed to close until even a sob would surely burst her chest. A man had died because knowledge she possessed hadn't reached him in time.

"Katherine, we are not sure what happened," Reynold said, as if reading her mind. "Do not blame yourself. The king foolishly trusted the wrong people."

The dam seemed to burst and she found herself sobbing against Owen's back. Her heart ached for the men she might have been able to save. Suddenly she found herself plucked from the horse's back and into strong arms encased in metal. She pressed her face into Reynold's hard chest and cried for all that she should have accomplished.

"Thank you, Owen," the earl said quietly. "I will tell your father of your bravery. Take your place with the other squires."

Katherine's sobs soon melted into shudders. She knew she should sit up and stop betraying her feelings for Reynold. She was beyond caring, it seemed. She only wanted his arms around her, to smell him and taste him, and never let him go.

"I love you," she whispered.

He stiffened, and responded in a hoarse, quiet voice. "What did you say?"

"None of this was your fault," she went on, hiccupping on a sob. "You were valiant in my defense."

"No, the first part. Repeat it."

Katherine nestled closer, and raised her head until her lips could touch the skin above his gorget. "I love you."

He squeezed her tightly, then seemed to shudder. "I thought you would never—admit—" He paused and cleared his throat. "—especially with the king—"

"I know," she interrupted, swaying with the motion of his body on the horse. "I feel horrible that I did not succeed with my message. But Reynold," she looked up into his beautiful eyes, "I would have felt worse if I'd done nothing at all, or if you had not kept me going when I would have given up."

They stared into each other's eyes for a moment, then Katherine's gaze dropped to his lips.

Reynold whispered, "I want to kiss you."

"Please."

He arched one eyebrow. "Do you care nothing for your father's reaction?"

She sighed. "You are right. I must respect his wishes."

"And marry James?"

"I have a small influence with Father. Persuasion will be necessary to change his mind." Her smile vanished and she gazed deeply into his eyes. "Do you really want me, Reynold? I might not bring anything to our marriage."

"Just yourself, my love. It is enough."

His voice was a low rumble in his chest, soothing and comforting. Yet she could not allow herself to be so relaxed. She must still confront her father.

Sighing, Katherine turned her face away from the sun and allowed the slow rhythm of the horse to lull her towards sleep. Relaxed as she could only be in Reynold's arms, she blinked her heavy eyelids once, twice, then caught sight of her father's rigid profile. Sleep deserted her.

"Is something wrong, my sweet?" Reynold asked, his lips grazing her ear.

Though she shook her head, she could not stop staring at her father. He did not insist on carrying her himself, nor was he blind. Why did he keep quiet? The earl always held strong opinions, and seldom kept them to himself.

"Father?"

He did not answer, and she waited a moment before calling to him again. He finally turned his head and she saw his expressionless face.

"I need to talk to you about James," she said, ignoring the way Reynold's arms tightened.

"We will not discuss him now." The earl turned back to gaze over his army.

"But, Father—"

"Katherine, do you not see what is about to happen when the new king reaches Leicester? He is but a few miles behind us."

"I did not know," she said.

"After I see King Henry, and discover if I may keep the lands that have been in our family for centuries—"

His voice thickened and she could not stop the tear that fell to her cheek.

"Then we will discuss your future, Katherine."

"Yes, Father." She turned her head away and gripped Reynold's hand.

*   *   *

As they approached the walls of Leicester and the stone bridge into the city, Katherine could hear the church bells peeling. News of King Henry had already gone before them.

She sighed and let Reynold's arms comfort her. Everyone was battle weary. The crown had changed hands so many times in recent memory that the power of loyalty was dulled. And perhaps her father would suffer for his.

The earl called his knights around him, and Katherine and Reynold remained close enough to hear his words.

"I shall send my sergeant-at-arms to guide our soldiers around to the northern side of the city, where they will camp outside the walls. We must all swear our fealty to the new king. If things do not go well, I will send a message to the soldiers to leave for home, where perhaps a new earl will soon reside."

The squires and knights fell in behind the earl, who raised an arm in salute as his foot soldiers filed past. Katherine had never been so proud of her father, as he tried his best to protect his people.

A half hour later, as the last of the villagers went by, Katherine slumped back against Reynold in exhaustion. She had never before realized how difficult it was to remain dignified and proud when all she wanted to do was cry. Would her father be punished for his loyalty to the last king?

When the earl, Katherine, Reynold, and the band of knights crossed the stone bridge and entered the city, milling crowds surged towards the road, then fell back when they recognized the earl's banner. People were obviously awaiting the new king. Her father's knights drew up in front of the inn, where the innkeeper gaped up at Katherine.

"Will you please fetch the sheriff, sir?" she called down, then smiled when the man pushed a poor lad to obey. She looked up at Reynold. "They probably think you captured me, foul murderer that I am."

At her father's questioning stare, her smile died. "Did I not mention that I had to escape the sheriff?"

Lord Durham rolled his eyes, and Reynold's body shook with mirth. He dismounted and helped Katherine to the ground. His hands lingered at her waist.

"I hate to let you go," Reynold murmured into her ear. "I am afraid my good fortune cannot last and you will be taken from me."

"Only by force, my love," she whispered, leaning against him briefly. "Only by force."

After explanations were made to the sheriff, Katherine preceded her father and Reynold up to their room on the second floor. Thankfully, the corpse was gone. Shattered goblets and dishes still littered the floor. Reynold stepped over the mess and frowned at the bloodstain by the bed.

Katherine said, "We can't wait for Owen to return from stabling the horses, Father. I'll send for a maidservant."

Owen returned soon after the carpet was replaced and the room straightened. Katherine gladly offered to help the squire remove the men's armor. She pushed Owen towards Reynold and saw to her father.

He harrumphed, then remained silent beneath her quick fingers. After a few minutes, when she had loosened his breast and back plates, he glanced down at her.

"Where have you learned so much, child?"

"I have always watched Owen or the other squires aid you, Father."

"I am not speaking of my armor." He nodded to Owen, who left the room.

Katherine pursed her lips and pretended to concentrate on her task. How to answer such a question from one's own father? Should she just confess that she had fallen in love with a man who had taught her she could rely on herself, that she could trust her own judgment?

But doing so would admit that her father had not taught her these things, that somehow he had failed her. No, she thought, it was much more complicated than that. Her life might have turned out fine if not for that evil monk, her mother's disbelief, and so many other things which she had allowed to influence her life. But no more.

She was saved from answering by shouts down below. After pulling a tunic over his shirt and hose, Reynold flung open the shutters overlooking the street.

"My lord, perhaps you should see this."

The earl, Reynold, and Katherine gathered at the window and gazed down upon the crowd. They had begun to chant, "Tudor," over and over, until Katherine wanted to shut her ears. She bitterly remembered how just this morning they had cheered the Durham army.

Reynold pointed down the street, towards the West Bridge. "They have come."

Trumpets preceded the new king's army, and banners bearing the red dragon of the Tudors waved in the breeze. The king saluted in triumph, wearing the royal crown upon his fair head.

Katherine felt ill. The man had less claim to the throne than King Richard's niece, daughter of the old king. But nothing could be done now. She had tried everything and failed. She must now live peacefully under a new king. Would he forgive her father?

Knights and soldiers, some bloodied and limping, marched down the streets, accepting cheers and flowers from the shouting crowd. Though Katherine felt obliged to watch every minute of it, she soon wished she had not. Were her eyes playing tricks on her?

A familiar banner unfurled in the wind. James's banner, James's men, and finally . . . James himself.

Chapter 30

⌒◯◯⌒

Through a buzzing haze, Katherine heard the earl's hoarse oath, and Reynold's simple, "My God."

She had swallowed every lie, every pretense James had used, when all along he had been a traitor. Her chest was tight with repressed sobs, but there were no more tears inside her. Instead she looked full at Reynold, and wished she could absorb his pain and leave him free of it. His face was cold and remote, a warrior confronting betrayal, not just a fellow soldier's, but his brother's. He must hurt much worse than she did.

"Reynold," she said softly.

He raised his hand, then turned and stalked away. "Do not speak of it now."

When she would have followed him, the earl restrained her. "Leave him to think in peace, my child. Come watch and remember King Richard's murderers."

As she shook with anger and betrayal, Katherine

was thankful for her father's supporting arm, for as James reached the inn, his gaze seemed drawn upward. He saw them standing in the window, and the smile slowly dissolved from his face, replaced by a grim frown. His horse trotted past, pushed by the soldiers and the crowd, but James's gaze held Katherine's until a bend in the road took him from sight.

Katherine sagged away from the window, but her father held her upright. She clutched the window frame, feeling remote and numb. Then across the bridge, at the rear of the army, came a horse carrying a naked corpse across its back. A young boy hunched over the horse's neck, wearing torn clothing in the king's colors. Katherine grew hot and her stomach heaved. It was the king's body, and his head rhythmically bounced against the bridge's stone walls. As the crowd below jeered, she dropped to her knees and heaved up what little her stomach had carried.

"Katherine?" Reynold lifted her from the floor, gathering her close.

She gave a wan smile and sighed. "If that is what battle brings, I never want to be near one again."

"You shall not, my lady. I will protect you," he said, feeling that his overwhelming love for her could easily consume everything in his life.

Katherine tried to protest as Reynold lay her down on the bed, but he touched her lips with the tips of his fingers.

"You have seen and done too much today. Rest."

"But James—"

"He will be coming soon, if I know him." A spasm of pain twisted his stomach. "Did I ever know him?"

Reynold wet a towel and sat down on the edge of the bed. Gently, he wiped Katherine's face. He knew the earl stood silent, watchful, but it was too late to think about propriety. The old man had better understand that Reynold would not meekly walk away from his love for Katherine.

The knock at the door took no one by surprise. Katherine gently pushed Reynold's hand aside, and slid her legs over the edge of the bed. The door rattled again and Reynold stepped forward.

"No," she said. "I must do it."

Katherine took a deep breath, and flung the door wide. She truly didn't know what she would feel on first sight of her betrothed. James stood unmoving in the doorway, wearing a black doublet and hose, with embroidery at the neck his only bow to fashion. He had a beaver hat tucked under one elbow.

Katherine stared at him, trying to remember how once he'd dominated her girlhood dreams. She had known nothing about him, only that he would be the man she'd marry. He had always been a stranger.

"You had me kidnapped." She didn't know where those words came from; they just seemed to well up out of her bitterness. Everything suddenly made sense.

James sighed. "May I come in?"

After he entered, Katherine made an exaggerated show of looking into the hall. "My lord, are there no men to do your bidding?"

James set his hat on the table before finally meeting her gaze. "If you'd let me explain—"

Katherine was pushed aside as Reynold launched himself at his brother. Her father pulled her away as the two men crashed to the floor.

Reynold rolled and easily subdued James beneath him. "She could have died because of you!" He slammed his brother's head into the floor.

When Katherine would have stopped them, her father held her back. "They must deal with this," he said.

James fiercely struggled against Reynold's grip. He arched his back in an attempt to throw his brother off. "I didn't know! I tried to keep her safe when the others would have killed her. I deliberately sent her to your monastery, in case things went wrong!"

"Think, you fool! What kind of man did you entrust her to? A man who would imprison her in a dank undercroft—"

"He was not supposed to—"

"A man who would follow us across the country, terrorizing your betrothed, until she finally had to defend her life! Look at the bloodstains on her gown!"

Grabbing James's head, Reynold forced the man to look at Katherine.

"He almost killed her today. Luckily she killed him. Is that how you treat the lady you would marry?"

James sagged slowly, the fight draining from his body. "You do what you will, Reynold. But I swear to you I did not know his true character."

Reynold released his brother's head and sat up, still pinning James to the floor with his body. The weariness on Reynold's face almost broke Katherine's heart.

"You lied to me—you lied to all of us," Reynold said, his voice hoarse, his eyes bleak. "She came to you for help and you pretended—"

"Won't you see reason? I thought I was protecting her."

"Your protection was never worth much." Reynold got to his feet and gave his brother a look of distaste. "All you ever cared for were your clothes and the appearance of your great hall. Oh yes, you wanted to protect Katherine—you were protecting her money."

James slowly stood up and faced the three of them. "You believe I am that callous?"

Reynold crossed his arms over his chest. "What do I know of you, James? We were raised by different families, and I can see what kind of honor they instilled in you. You could not even tell us your true allegiance."

James slammed a hand on the table and Katherine jumped.

"Damn your eyes, Reynold! You sat in the monastery and knew nothing of how the country was changing, how people talked. Anarchy was coming. They didn't believe Richard any more."

"And that enabled you to betray him?" The earl spoke for the first time. "You are not the man I dealt with honorably."

"My lord—" James began.

"I will fight this contract I have with you." His voice sounded tired but determined. "I will not allow you to take my daughter, after what you have done to her. If I have to bribe the pope himself—"

"It will not be necessary, my lord," James said. He took his beaver hat in his hands. "I could not force Katherine to marry. I would not want . . . that."

When he met Katherine's gaze, his face was impassive, yet his eyes seemed to burn with remorse. She found she could not speak the cruel words she had intended.

"I will not marry you, James," she said. "I could never trust you and I don't love you."

He lowered his head. "We never had the chance to love."

"And that is your fault as well. I waited five long years for you, and you never came."

"I was a fool."

She barely heard the words.

"And now you love my brother." James lifted his head. "Perhaps that is as it was meant to be."

Katherine hesitated, dreading her father's reaction. She relaxed when she felt him pat her hand. "Reynold has been willing to sacrifice his life for me. He appreciates my strengths." *And inspired me to conquer my weaknesses,* she thought.

She found herself staring into Reynold's eyes, hardly daring to imagine they could have a future together. "He believes in me."

The earl released Katherine and faced James with his hands on his hips. "You will take the dowry."

All eyes turned to him in astonishment.

"I will not," James said in a harsh voice.

"I do not wish to see you at some future date making demands of my daughter, perhaps threatening her."

Katherine had never seen such a cold, proud look come over James's face. She suddenly saw him as he could be, and it saddened her.

"I refuse to be so dishonored," James said.

Her father leaned into James's face. "You will take the money in exchange for agreeing to break the betrothal. I must tell the priests something. And then, when you spend that money, you will remember what you did to earn it."

James straightened, his face grim. "I will never spend it." He opened the door, then paused and turned to look at Katherine. "I'm sorry for what my stupidity did to you. If you need my signature, I'll be with the king."

When he left, silence hung heavy in the room. Katherine was too stunned to move, could barely draw a deep breath. She was no longer betrothed.

Her soul filled with hope as she looked at Reynold. When had this love for him grown to encompass her mind and heart? He was everything to her. Only he could fulfill all her dreams. Only he could laugh with her, love her, father her children.

Reynold stepped before the earl. "I know we still have tragedy yet to face, my lord, but I can wait no longer to speak. I wish to marry your daughter."

The earl rocked back on his heels, fists on his hips. "Why does this not surprise me?"

Relief weakened Katherine's knees and brought tears to her eyes. She would not have to disobey her father. She ran to hug him, whispering tearfully, "You have made me so happy."

The earl patted her back, then released her. "Welles, until I have spoken to King Henry, I can make no promises."

"Your blessing is enough for us. Allow me to accompany you, sir."

The earl smiled. "I'd like that."

Katherine took Reynold by the arm and looked up into his beloved face, free of guilt for the first time. She stretched up for his kiss. His mouth was warm and sweet, even chaste.

"For one's future wife," he murmured against her lips.

"I'll expect more, much more," she said. He embraced her and she felt as if she'd come home.

Epilogue

February 1486

"**Y**ou are very lucky I am not big with child," Katherine said to Reynold as she smiled at the wedding guests filling her father's hall.

Reynold raised his goblet to the knights calling out a bawdy toast of good health. "And why is that, my sweet?"

"Because tonight would not be half so enjoyable. I would be fat."

Reynold leaned into her face and gave her a leer. "I have waited six months for tonight. Be you fat or thin, I would ravish you. I did not fall in love with your belly."

Katherine giggled then attempted a smile for her mother, who wore gray instead of black, perhaps to celebrate the nuptials.

"I am trying to follow your advice, Reynold, but it is so difficult to converse with my mother."

"She is here, is she not, instead of cloistered in a chapel praying for my soul." Reynold sighed. "My having fallen from the holiness of monastic life does not endear me to her."

Katherine leaned into him. His brilliant blue doublet smelled of leather and man. "Can we leave now? I fear if I do not taste your lips soon . . ."

Reynold closed his eyes and whispered her name hoarsely. "Katherine. I promised your father a long feast. He has remained near to home since being pardoned by the king. I think he deserves a celebration in honor of his only child."

Katherine ran her fingers lovingly across his smooth jaw. "We are married, my lord viscount," she said dreamily, then, "Viscount! The audacity of you to hold such a thing from me."

Reynold grinned. "You withheld your name, I withheld mine. Remember, I never thought I would use my father's title again. But for you, I would be growing old in a ruined monastery."

She smiled. "I did save you, didn't I?"

"Too many times to count. But do not think you know everything about me. I still have a few mysteries you could unearth. Speaking of mysteries . . ." He attempted to peer down the bodice of her red brocade gown. "Is that an animal blocking my view?"

Katherine caught her breath, unable to take her eyes off his lips. "Ermine trim."

"It must be removed," he whispered, his breath on her cheek, his fingers stealing under her veil to touch her hair. "No more mysteries. 'Tis time to celebrate."

He swept her up in his embrace and Katherine laughed aloud as the crowd cheered. She put her arms around her husband and never looked back.

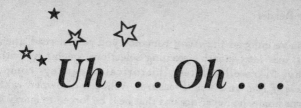

Dear Reader,

If you've enjoyed the Avon romance you've just read, then don't miss next month's exciting selections, beginning with Cathy Maxwell's latest historical Regency romp, *Because of You*, an Avon Treasure. When a disowned rake returns home, he never dreams that he'll be forced to marry a vicar's innocent daughter. And he never expected to feel the passion that soon flares between them.

A stolen kiss with a prim and proper debutante proves the undoing of a masterful duke in Sabrina Jeffries' *The Forbidden Lord*, an Avon Romance. This sparkling, powerful Regency-set historical is unforgettable.

Do you love stories set in the wild west? I sure do, and there's nothing like a sexy cowboy to pique my interest. In Maureen McKade's Avon Romance *Untamed Heart*, a local lawman decides to clean up town...and that includes shutting down a sassy saloon owner's establishment. Can this unlikely couple find true love?

And if you're looking for a delightful romance, then don't miss Sue Civil-Brown's utterly delicious *Chasing Rainbow*. Opposites attract when a globetrotting scientist settles down in the town of Paradise Beach, hoping for a little peace and quiet...and along comes a free-spirited heroine who's destined to shake him up...

Avon continues to bring you the very best in romance, so enjoy!

Lucia Macro

Lucia Macro
Senior Editor

AEL 0199

Avon Romances—
the best in exceptional authors and unforgettable novels!

KISS ME GOODNIGHT **by Marlene Suson**
79560-4/ $5.99 US/ $7.99 Can

WHITE EAGLE'S TOUCH **by Karen Kay**
78999-X/ $5.99 US/ $7.99 Can

ONLY IN MY DREAMS **by Eve Byron**
79311-3/ $5.99 US/ $7.99 Can

ARIZONA RENEGADE **by Kit Dee**
79206-0/ $5.99 US/ $7.99 Can

BY LOVE UNDONE **by Suzanne Enoch**
79885-9/ $5.99 US/ $7.99 Can

THE MEN OF PRIDE COUNTY: **by Rosalyn West**
THE OUTSIDER 79580-9/ $5.99 US/ $7.99 Can

WILD CAT CAIT **by Rachelle Morgan**
80039-X/ $5.99 US/ $7.99 Can

HIGHLAND BRIDES: **by Margaret Evans Porter**
HIGHLAND SCOUNDREL 79435-7/ $5.99 US/ $7.99 Can

HER NORMAN CONQUEROR **by Malia Martin**
79896-4/ $5.99 US/ $7.99 Can

THROUGH THE STORM **by Beverly Jenkins**
79864-6/ $5.99 US/ $7.99 Can

Avon Romantic Treasures

*Unforgettable, enthralling love stories,
sparkling with passion and adventure
from Romance's bestselling authors*

❊❊❊❊❊❊❊❊❊❊❊❊❊❊❊❊❊❊❊❊❊❊❊❊❊❊❊❊❊❊❊❊